# LUZ SEES the LIGHT

Kids Can Press acknowledges the financial support of the Government of Ontario, through the Ontario Media Development Corporation's Ontario Book Initiative; the Ontario Arts Council; the Canada Council for the Arts; and the Government of Canada, through the BPIDP, for our publishing activity.

Published in Canada by
Kids Can Press Ltd.
25 Dockside Drive
Toronto, ON  M5A 0B5

Published in the U.S. by
Kids Can Press Ltd.
2250 Military Road
Tonawanda, NY  14150

www.kidscanpress.com

Edited by Karen Li
Designed by Claudia Dávila and Karen Powers

The hardcover edition of this book is smyth sewn casebound.
The paperback edition of this book is limp sewn with a drawn-on cover.
Manufactured in Shen Zhen, Guang Dong, P.R. China, in 3/2011 by Printplus Limited.

CM 11 0 9 8 7 6 5 4 3 2 1
CM PA 11 0 9 8 7 6 5 4 3 2 1

FSC
www.fsc.org
MIX
Paper from
responsible sources
FSC® C018479

**Library and Archives Canada Cataloguing in Publication**

Dávila, Claudia
    Luz sees the light / Claudia Dávila.

ISBN 978-1-55453-581-1 (bound). ISBN 978-1-55453-766-2 (pbk.)

I. Title.

PS8607.A95285L89 2011    jC813'.6    C2011-900083-0

Kids Can Press is a **forus**™ Entertainment company

# LUZ SEES the LIGHT

By
Claudia Dávila

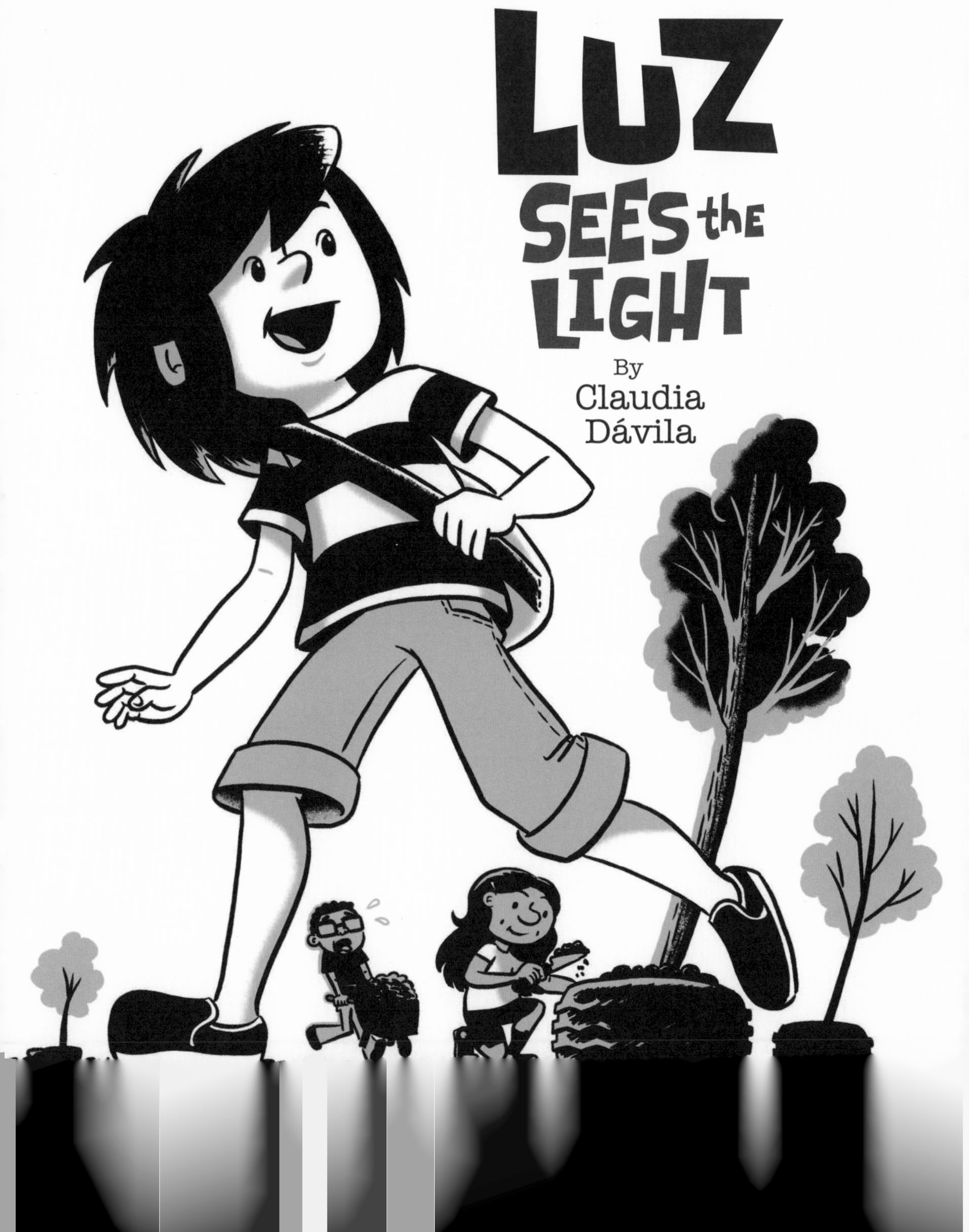

For my husband, Michael,
who makes it all possible.

# Contents

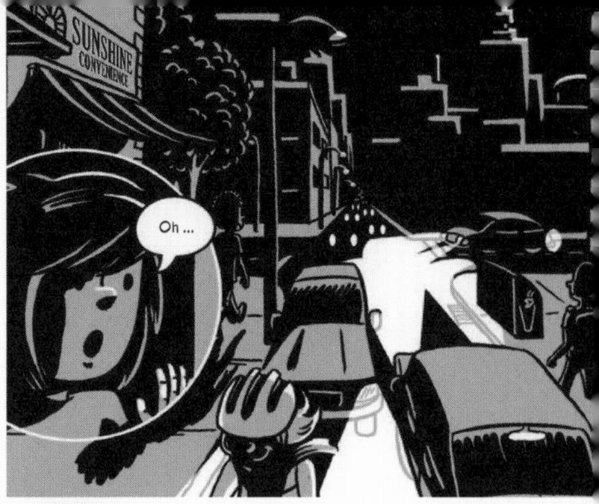
SUNSHINE CONVENIENCE
Oh ...



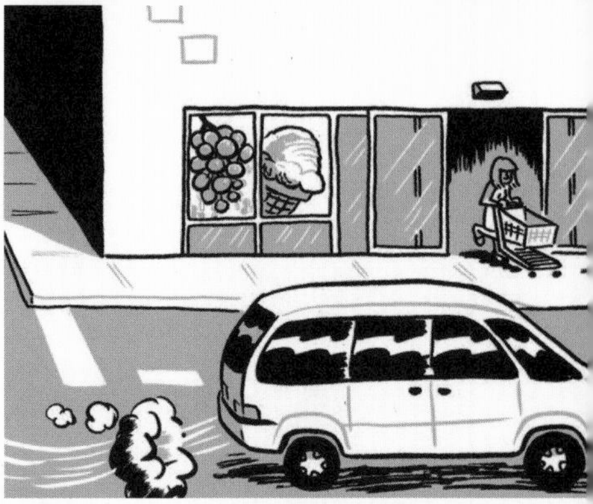



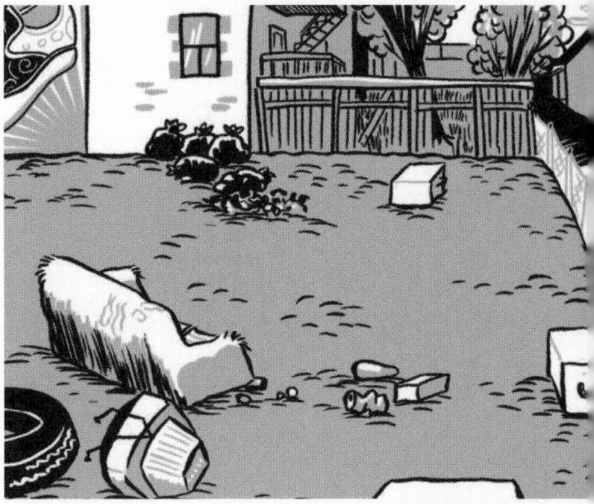



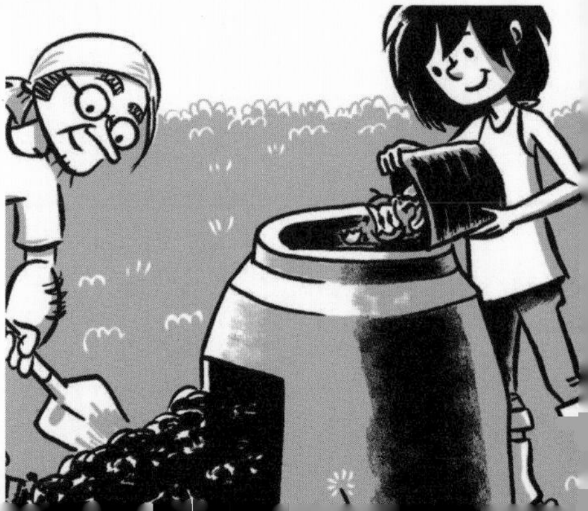

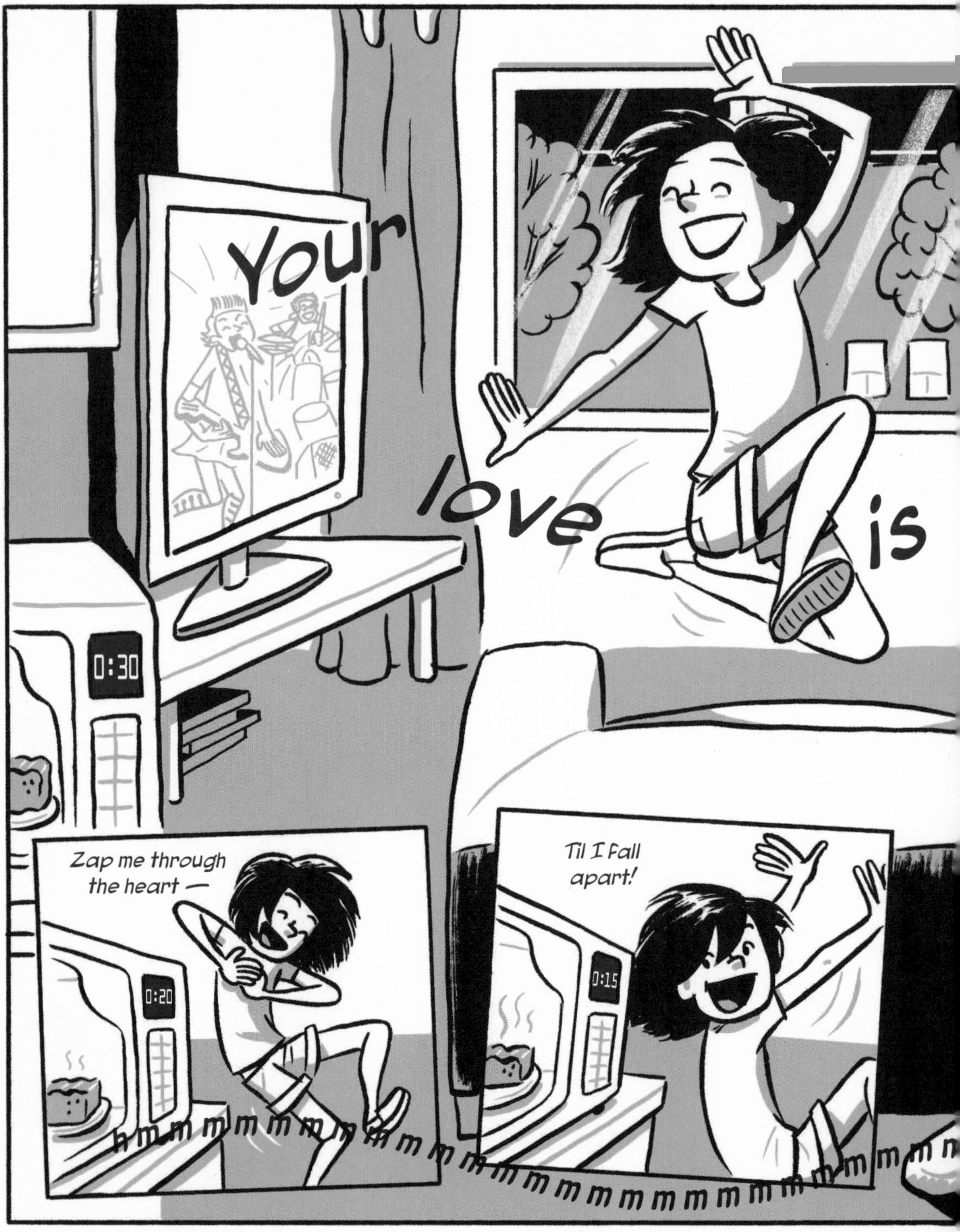

Your
love
is
Zap me through
the heart —
Til I fall
apart!
hmmmmmmmmmmmmmmmmmmmmmmmmmmmmmmmmmmm

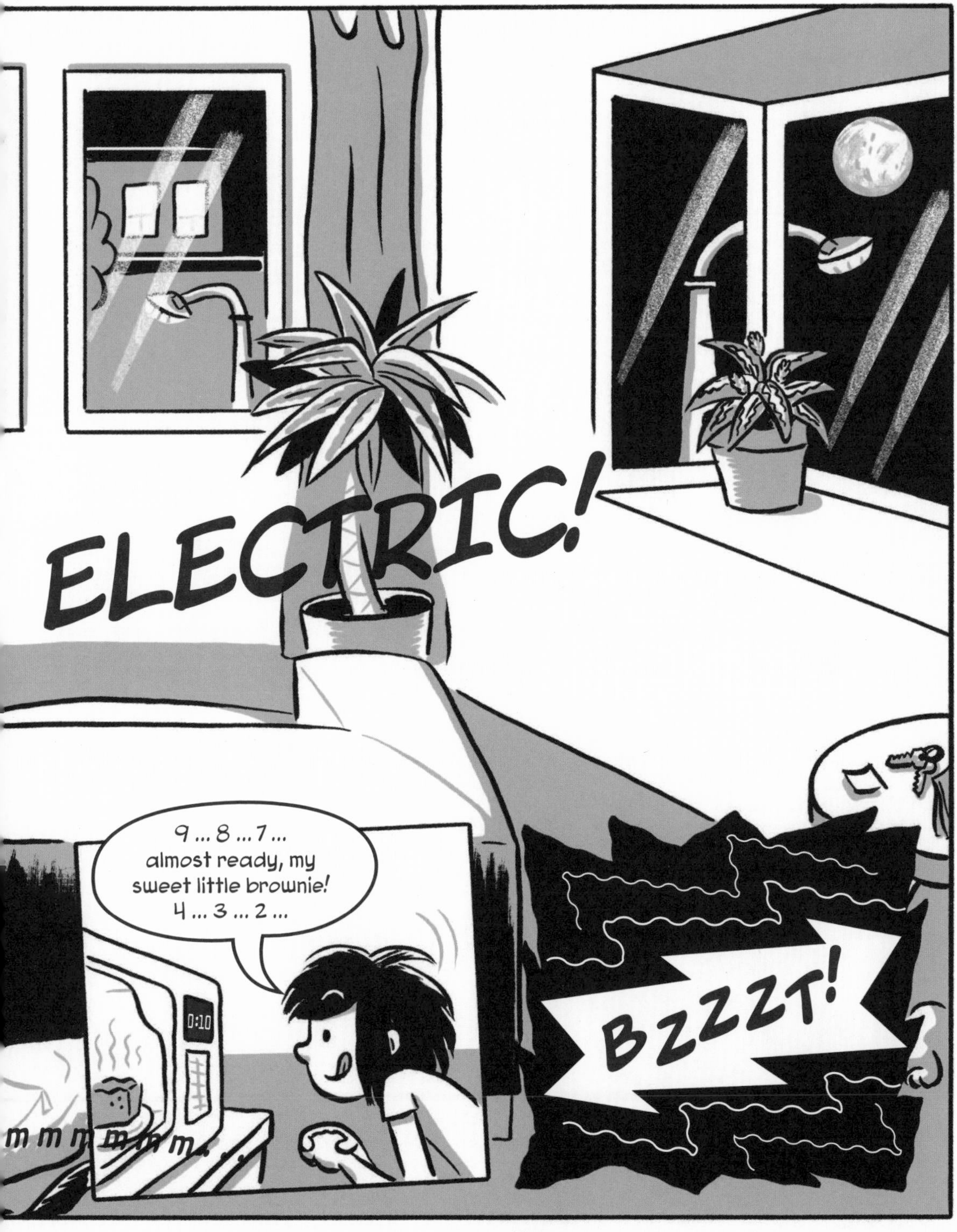
ELECTRIC!
9 ... 8 ... 7 ... almost ready, my sweet little brownie! 4 ... 3 ... 2 ...
mmmmmmm...
BZZZZT!

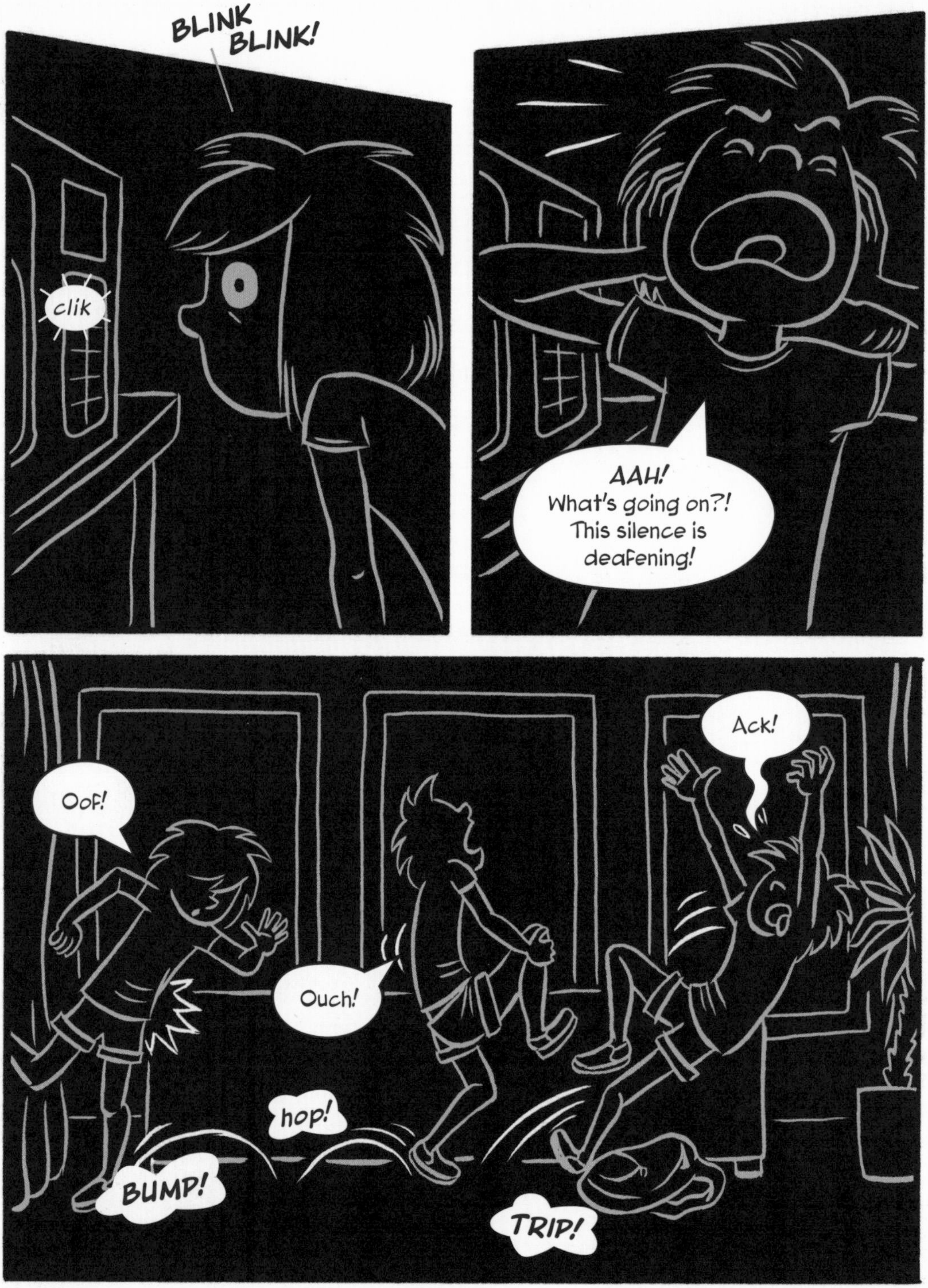
BLINK BLINK!
clik
AAH! What's going on?! This silence is deafening!
Oof!
Ouch!
Ack!
hop!
BUMP!
TRIP!

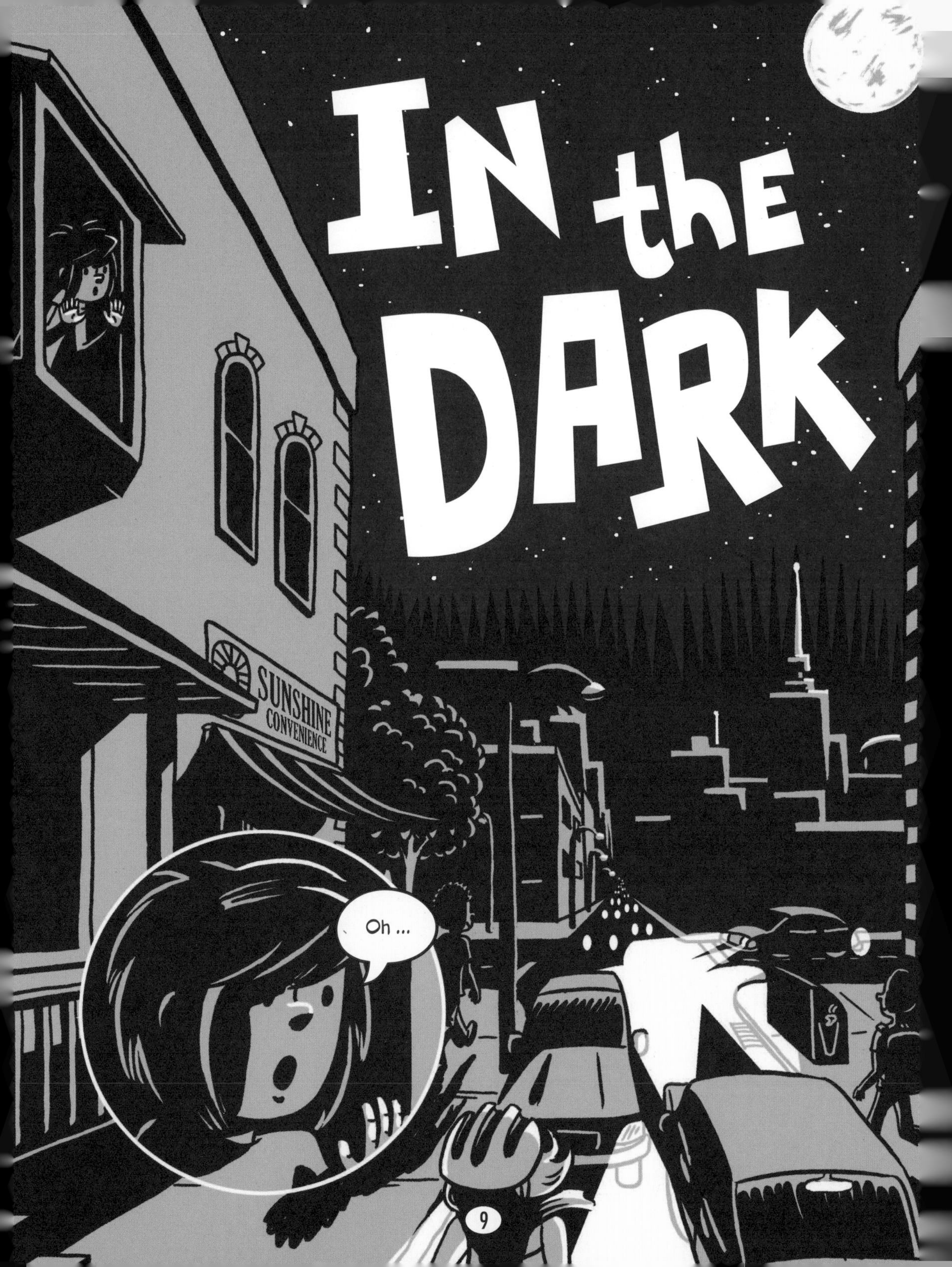
IN the DARK
SUNSHINE
CONVENIENCE
Oh ...

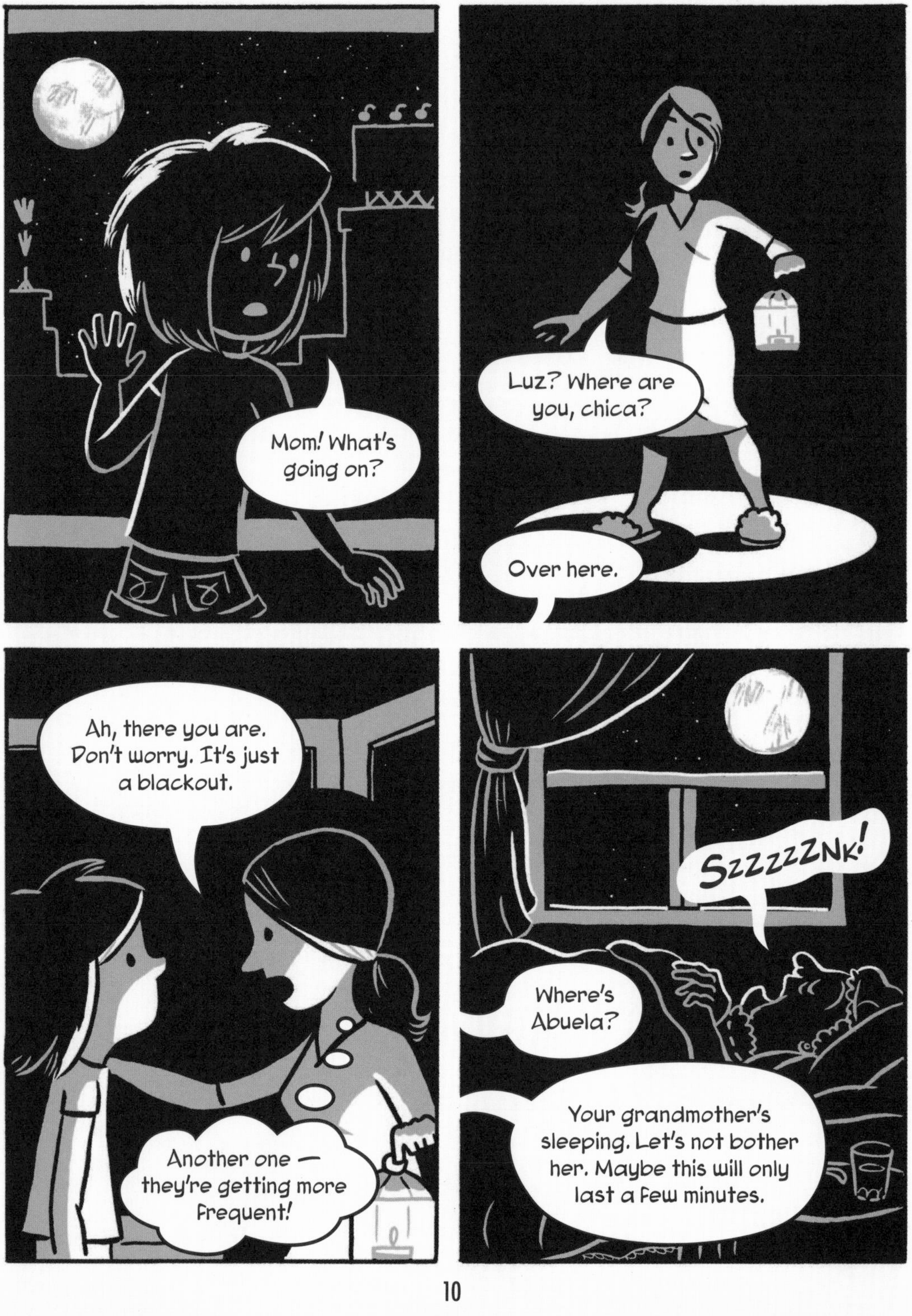
Mom! What's going on?
Luz? Where are you, chica?
Over here.
Ah, there you are. Don't worry. It's just a blackout.
Another one — they're getting more frequent!
SzzzzZNK!
Where's Abuela?
Your grandmother's sleeping. Let's not bother her. Maybe this will only last a few minutes.

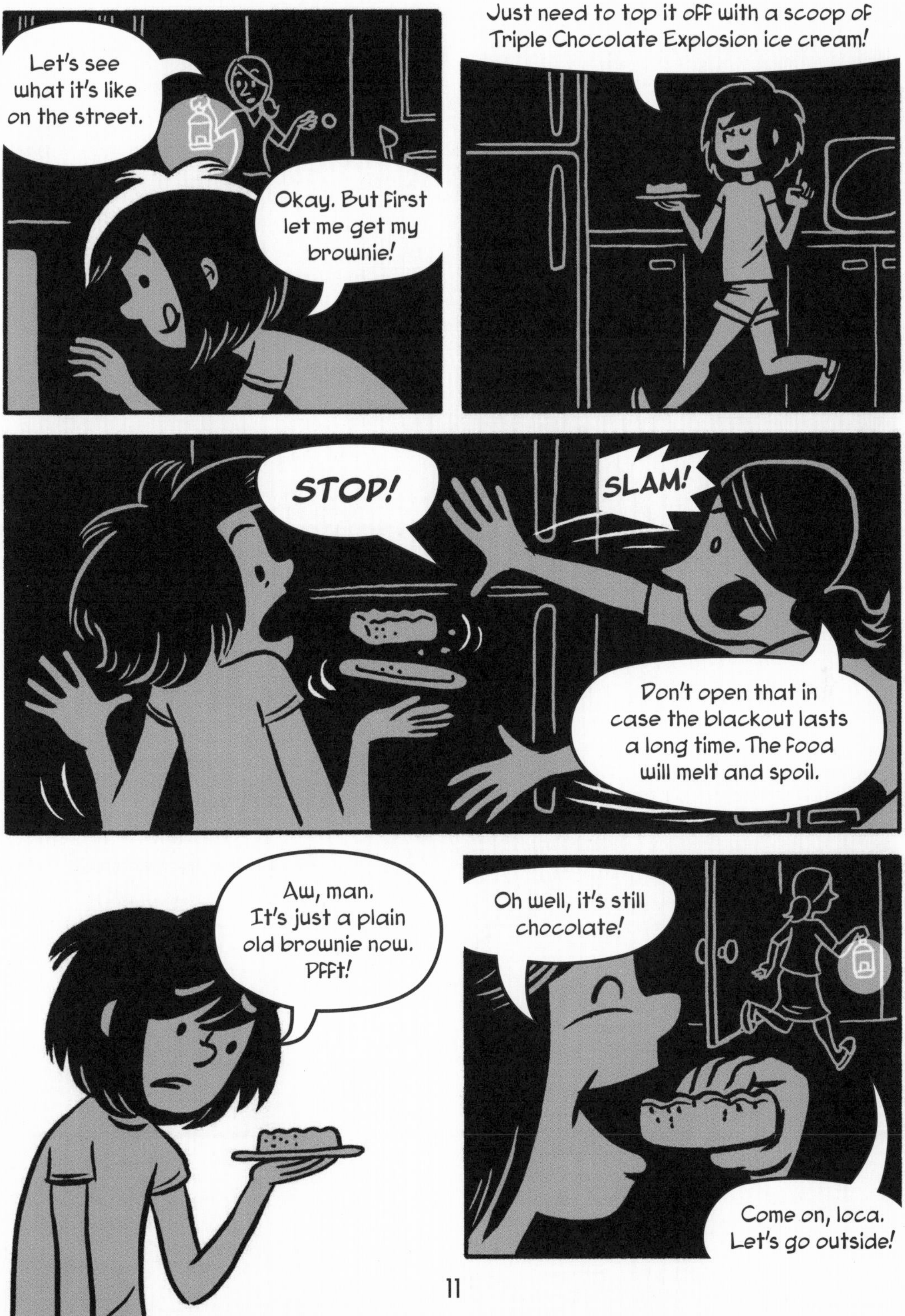
Let's see what it's like on the street.
Okay. But first let me get my brownie!
Just need to top it off with a scoop of Triple Chocolate Explosion ice cream!
STOP!
SLAM!
Don't open that in case the blackout lasts a long time. The food will melt and spoil.
Aw, man. It's just a plain old brownie now. Pfft!
Oh well, it's still chocolate!
Come on, loca. Let's go outside!

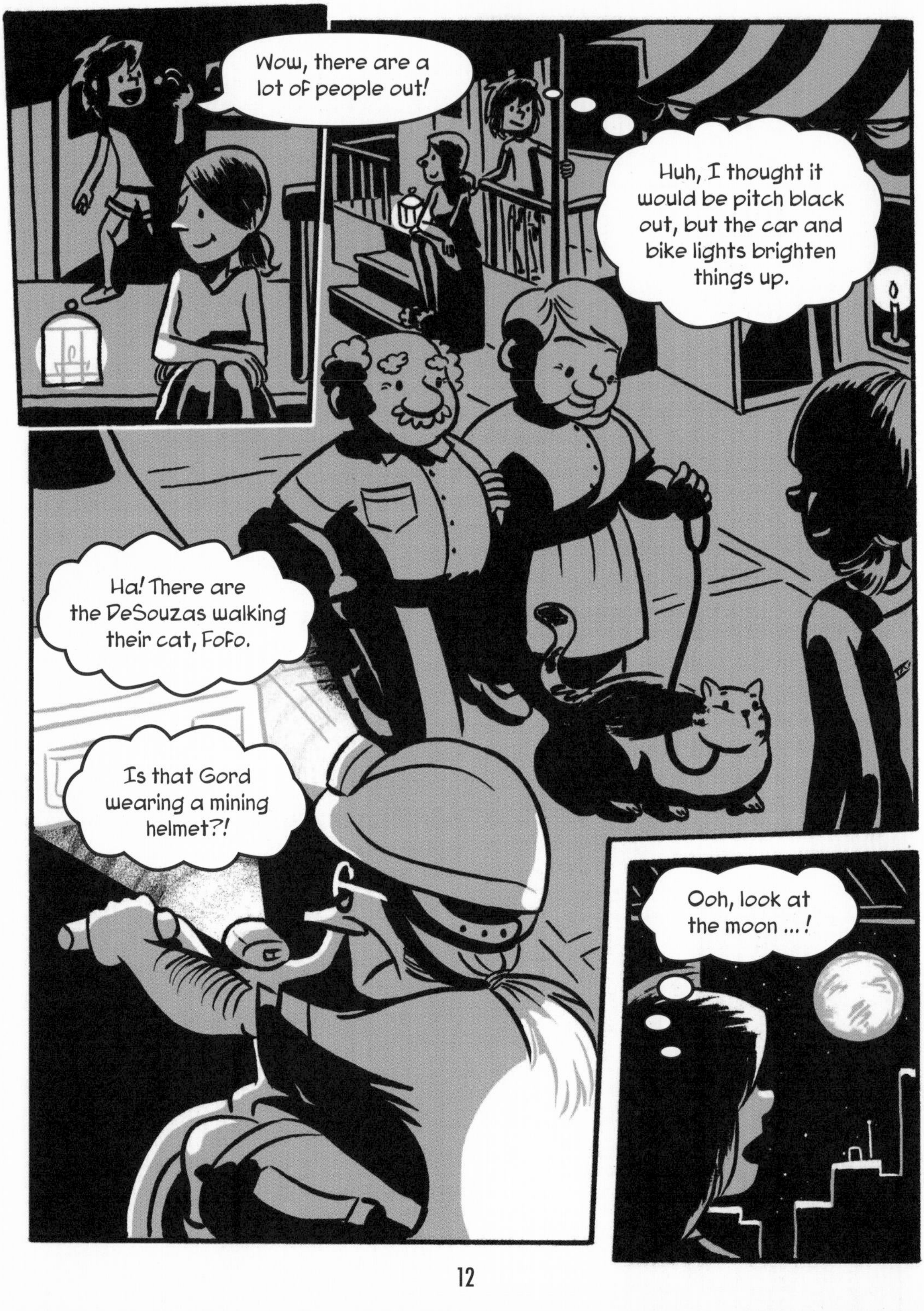
Wow, there are a lot of people out!
Huh, I thought it would be pitch black out, but the car and bike lights brighten things up.
Ha! There are the DeSouzas walking their cat, FoFo.
Is that Gord wearing a mining helmet?!
Ooh, look at the moon ...!

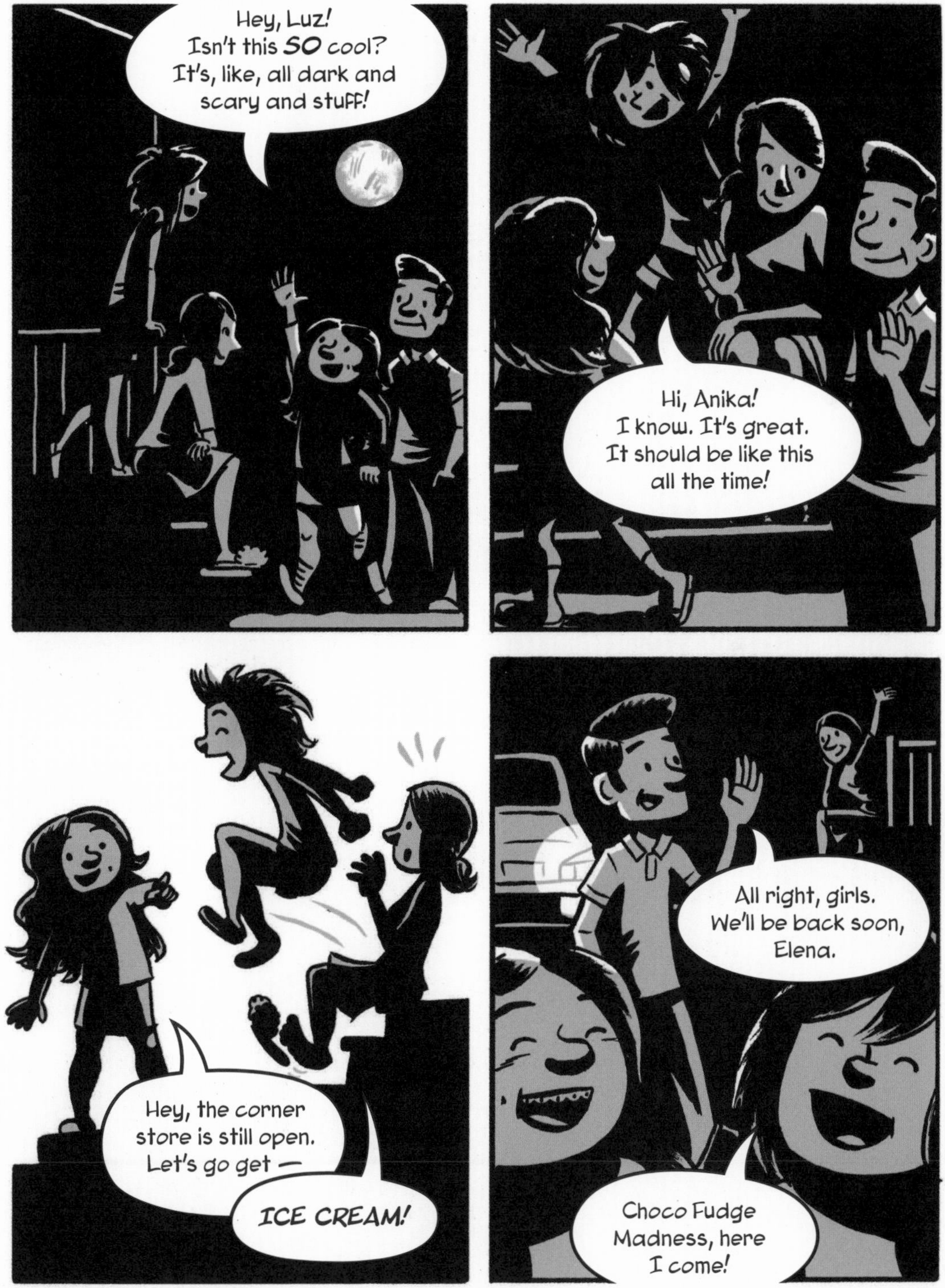
Hey, Luz! Isn't this SO cool? It's, like, all dark and scary and stuff!
Hi, Anika! I know. It's great. It should be like this all the time!
Hey, the corner store is still open. Let's go get —
ICE CREAM!
All right, girls. We'll be back soon, Elena.
Choco Fudge Madness, here I come!

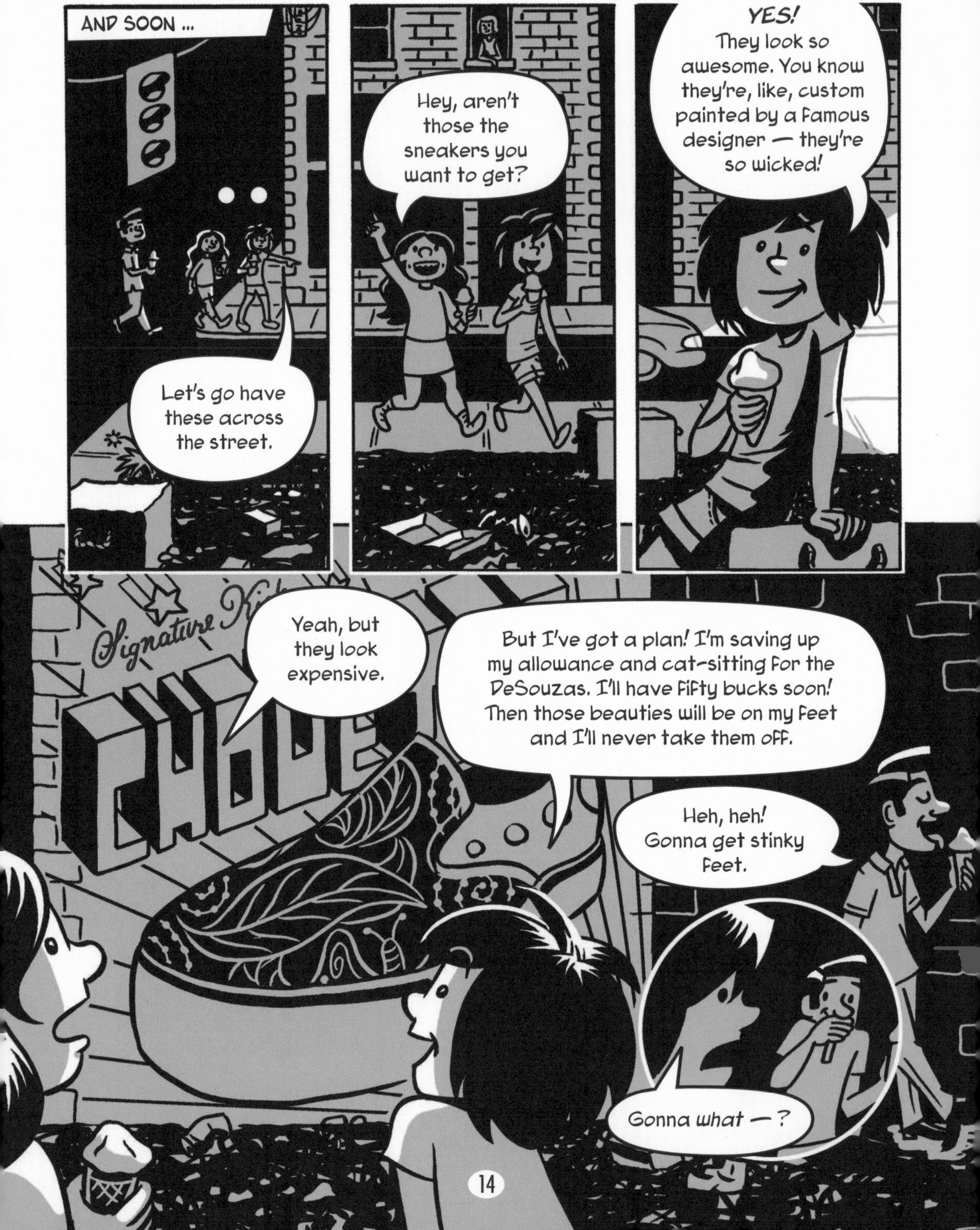
AND SOON ...
Let's go have these across the street.
Hey, aren't those the sneakers you want to get?
YES! They look so awesome. You know they're, like, custom painted by a famous designer — they're so wicked!
Yeah, but they look expensive.
But I've got a plan! I'm saving up my allowance and cat-sitting for the DeSouzas. I'll have fifty bucks soon! Then those beauties will be on my feet and I'll never take them off.
Heh, heh! Gonna get stinky feet.
Gonna what — ?

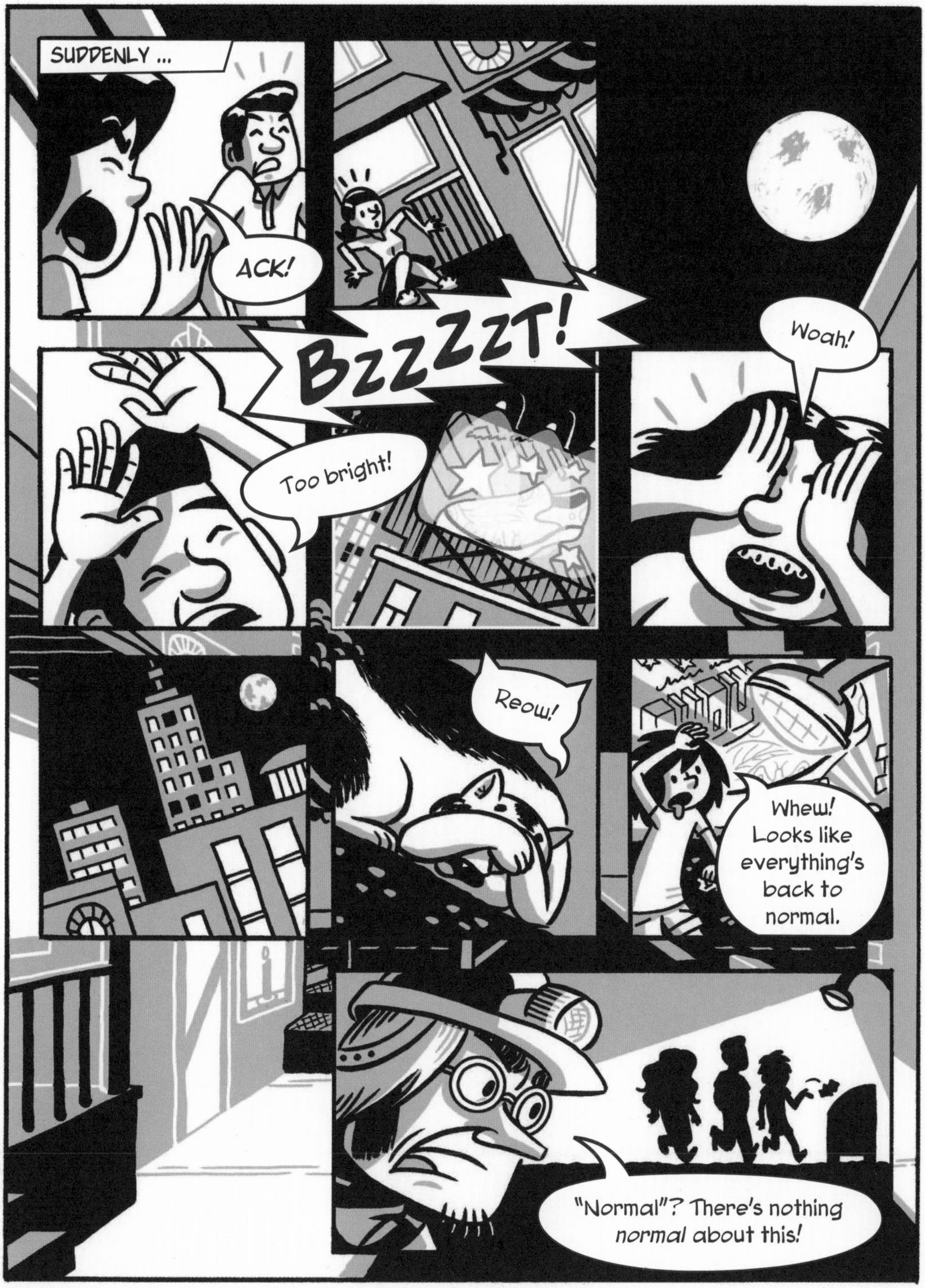
SUDDENLY ...
ACK!
BZZZZZT!
Woah!
Too bright!
Reow!
Whew! Looks like everything's back to normal.
"Normal"? There's nothing *normal* about this!

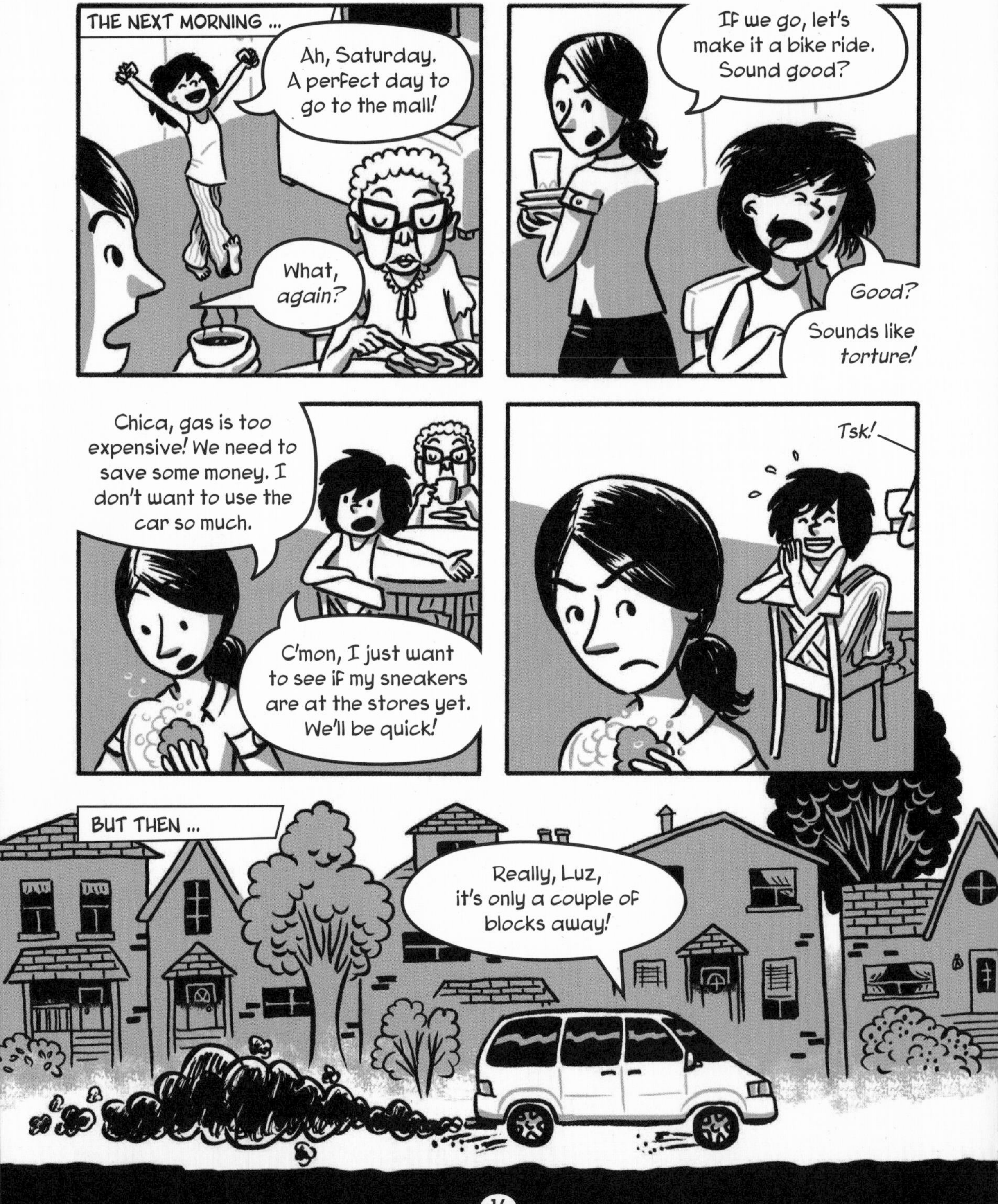
THE NEXT MORNING ...
Ah, Saturday. A perfect day to go to the mall!
What, again?
If we go, let's make it a bike ride. Sound good?
Good?
Sounds like torture!
Chica, gas is too expensive! We need to save some money. I don't want to use the car so much.
C'mon, I just want to see if my sneakers are at the stores yet. We'll be quick!
Tsk!
BUT THEN ...
Really, Luz, it's only a couple of blocks away!

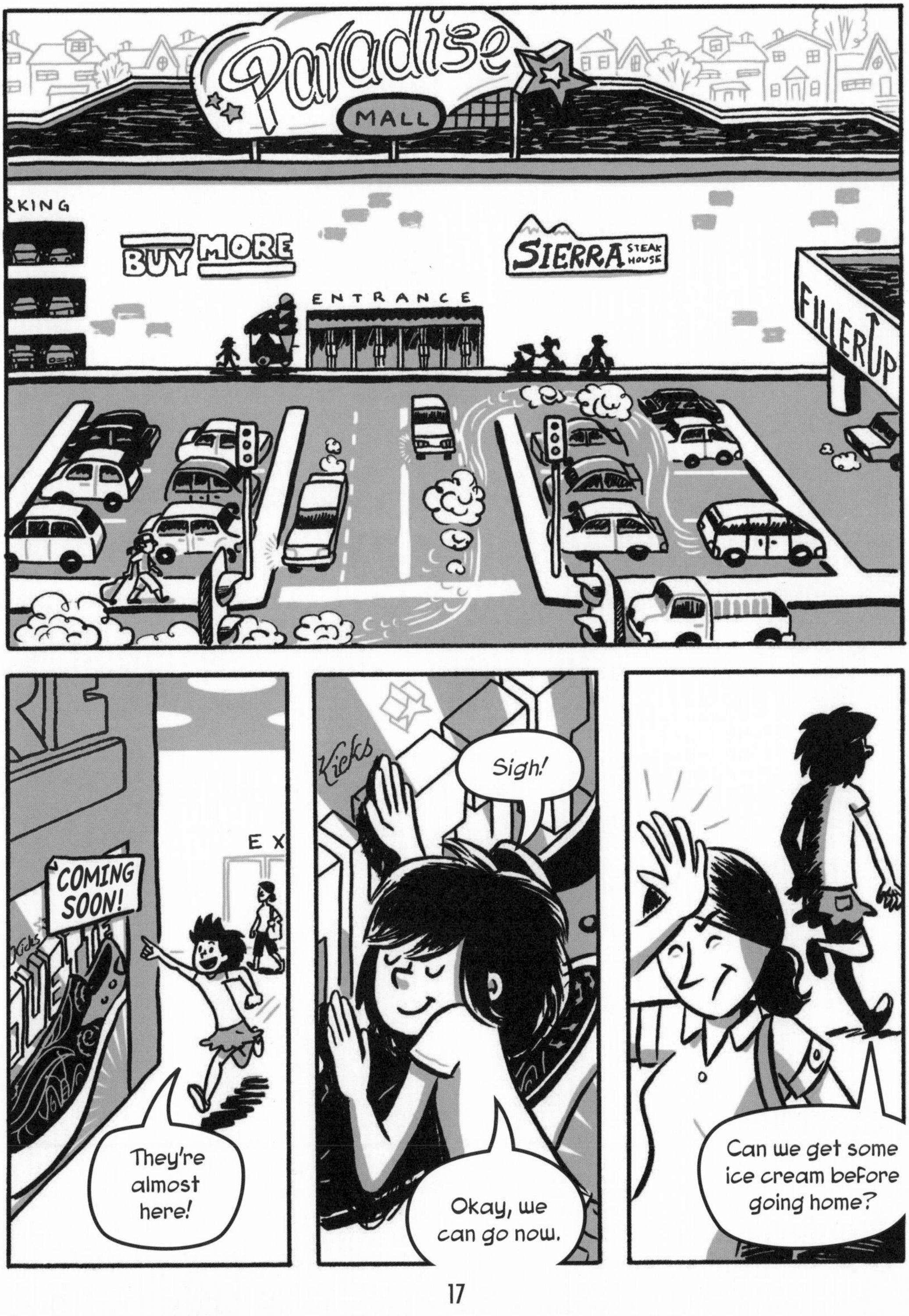
Paradise
MALL
RKING
BUY MORE
SIERRA STEAK HOUSE
ENTRANCE
FILLER UP
COMING SOON!
EX
They're almost here!
Kicks
Sigh!
Okay, we can go now.
Can we get some ice cream before going home?

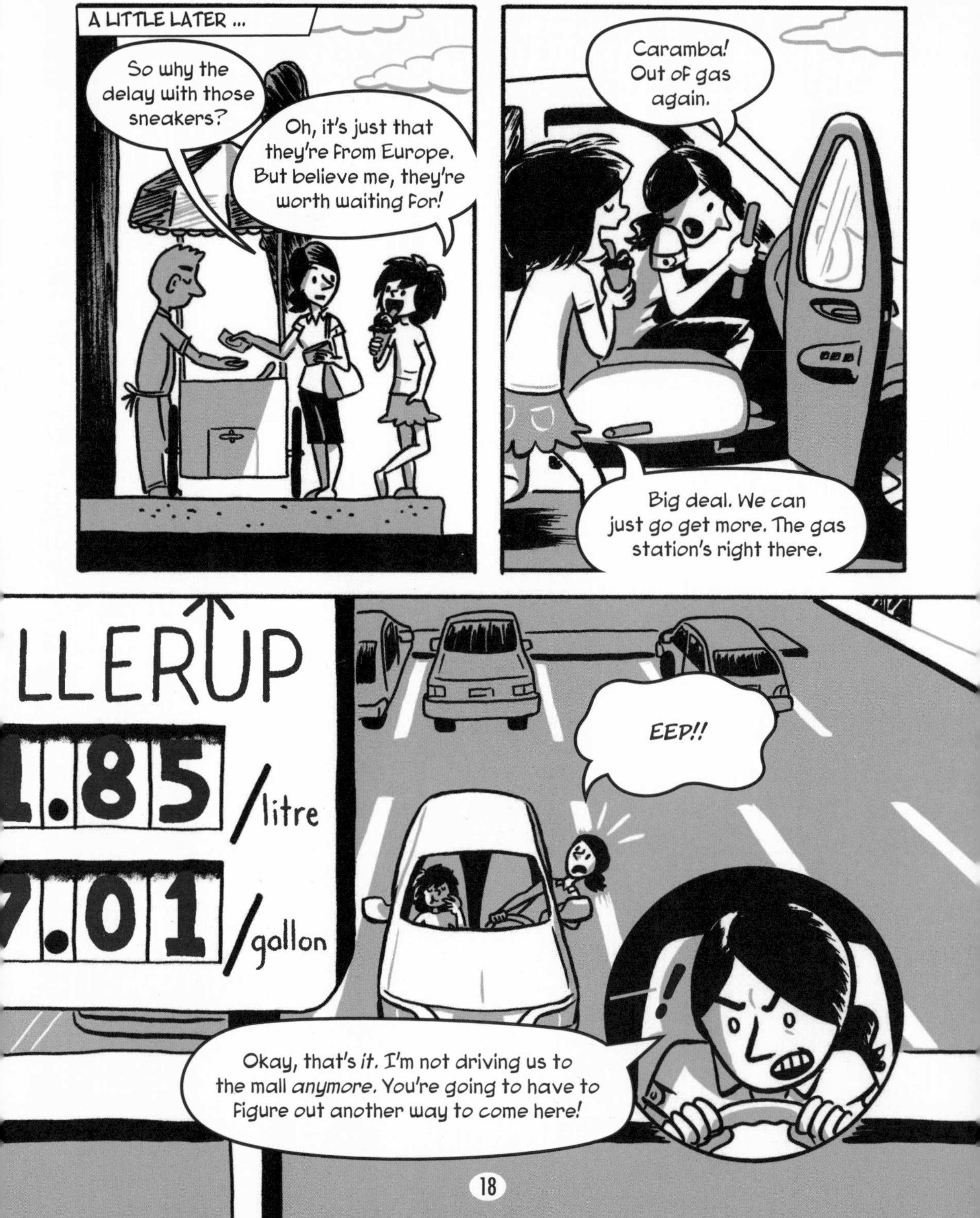
A LITTLE LATER ...
So why the delay with those sneakers?
Oh, it's just that they're from Europe. But believe me, they're worth waiting for!
Caramba! Out of gas again.
Big deal. We can just go get more. The gas station's right there.
LLERUP
1.85 /litre
7.01 /gallon
EEP!!
Okay, that's *it*. I'm not driving us to the mall *anymore*. You're going to have to figure out another way to come here!

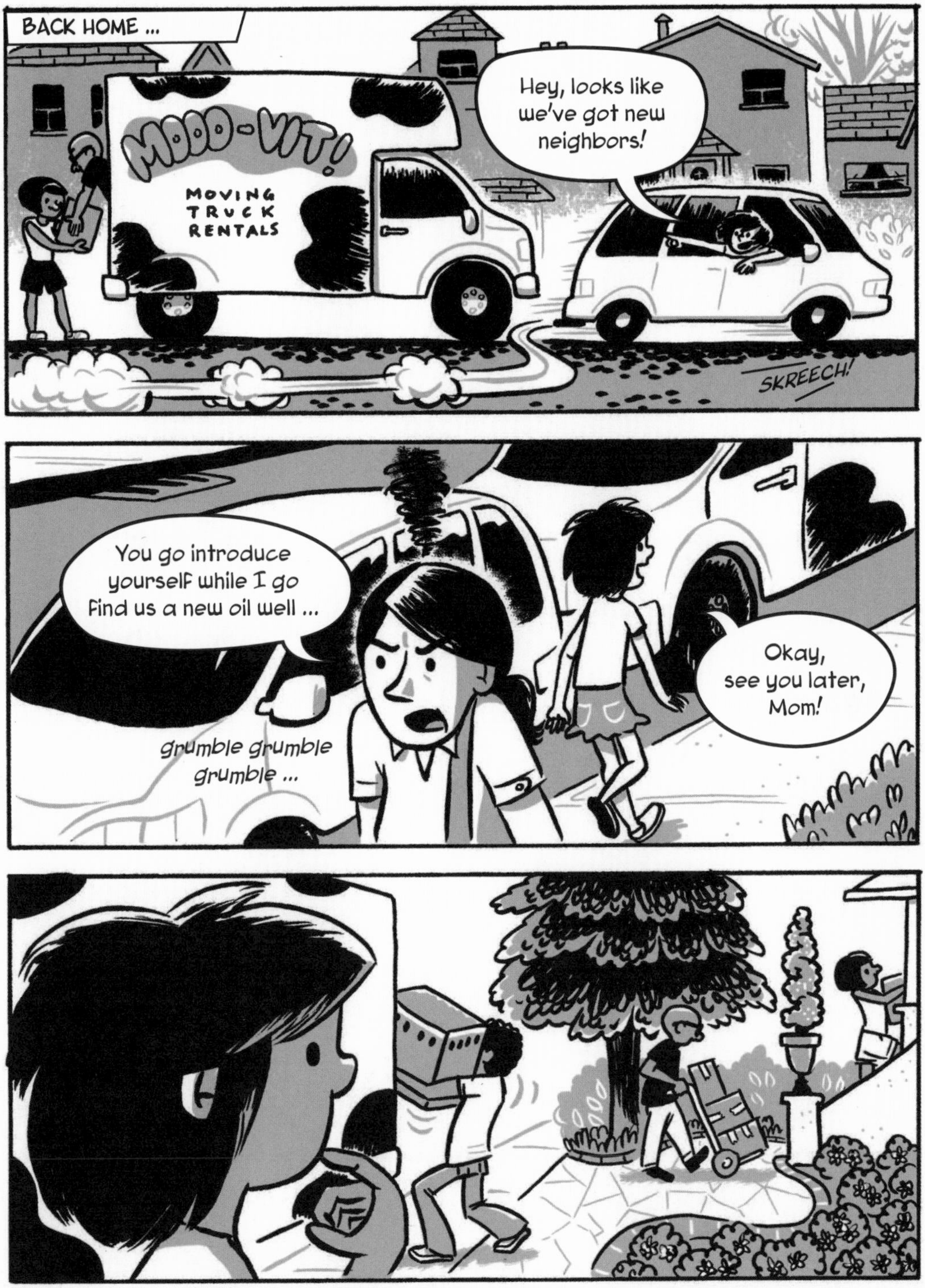
BACK HOME ...
MOOO-VIT!
MOVING TRUCK RENTALS
Hey, looks like we've got new neighbors!
SKREECH!
You go introduce yourself while I go find us a new oil well ...
grumble grumble grumble ...
Okay, see you later, Mom!

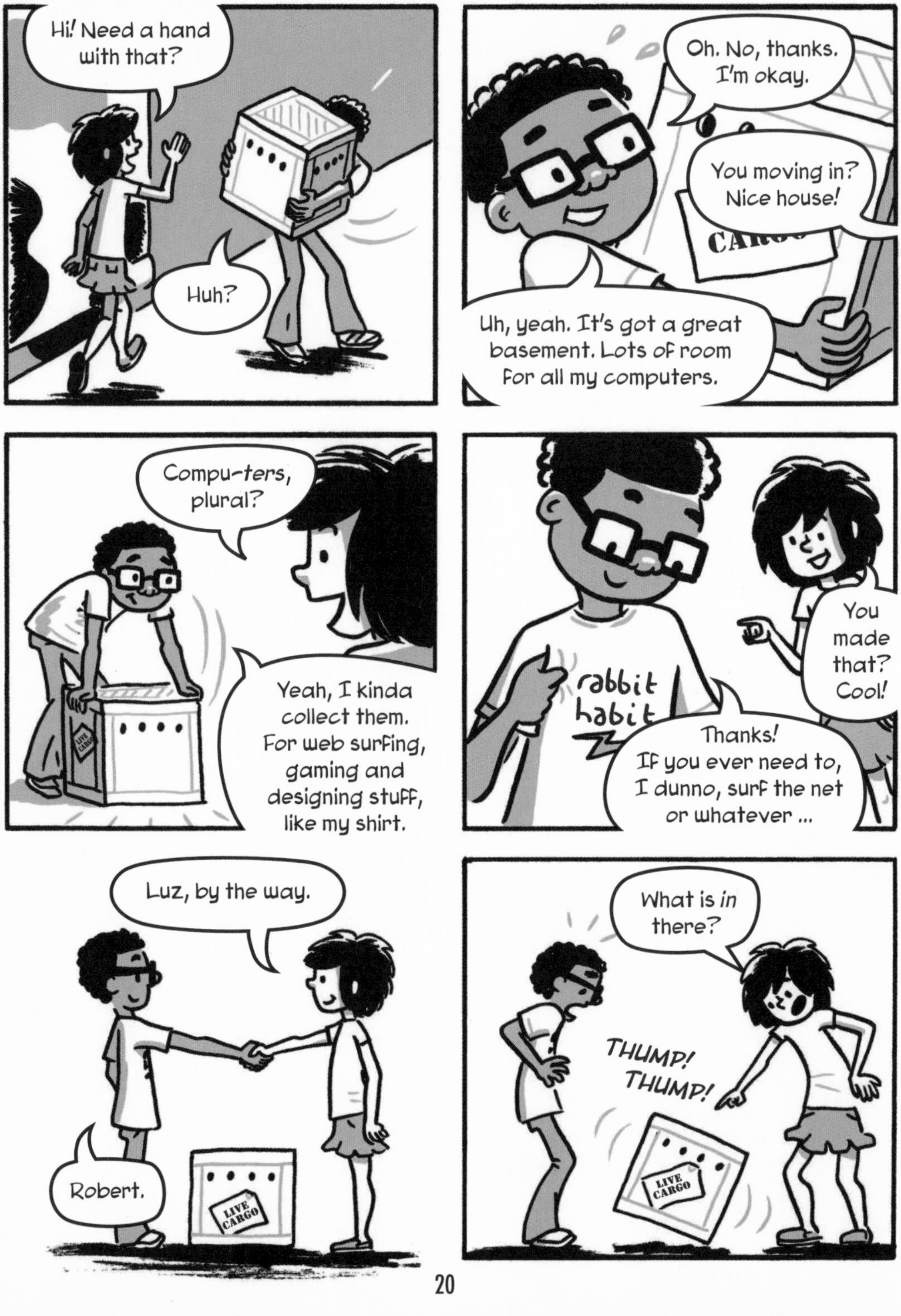

Hi! Need a hand with that?
Huh?
Oh. No, thanks. I'm okay.
You moving in? Nice house!
CARGO
Uh, yeah. It's got a great basement. Lots of room for all my computers.
Compu-*ters*, plural?
Yeah, I kinda collect them. For web surfing, gaming and designing stuff, like my shirt.
LIVE CARGO
rabbit habit
You made that? Cool!
Thanks! If you ever need to, I dunno, surf the net or whatever ...
Luz, by the way.
Robert.
LIVE CARGO
What is *in* there?
THUMP! THUMP!
LIVE CARGO

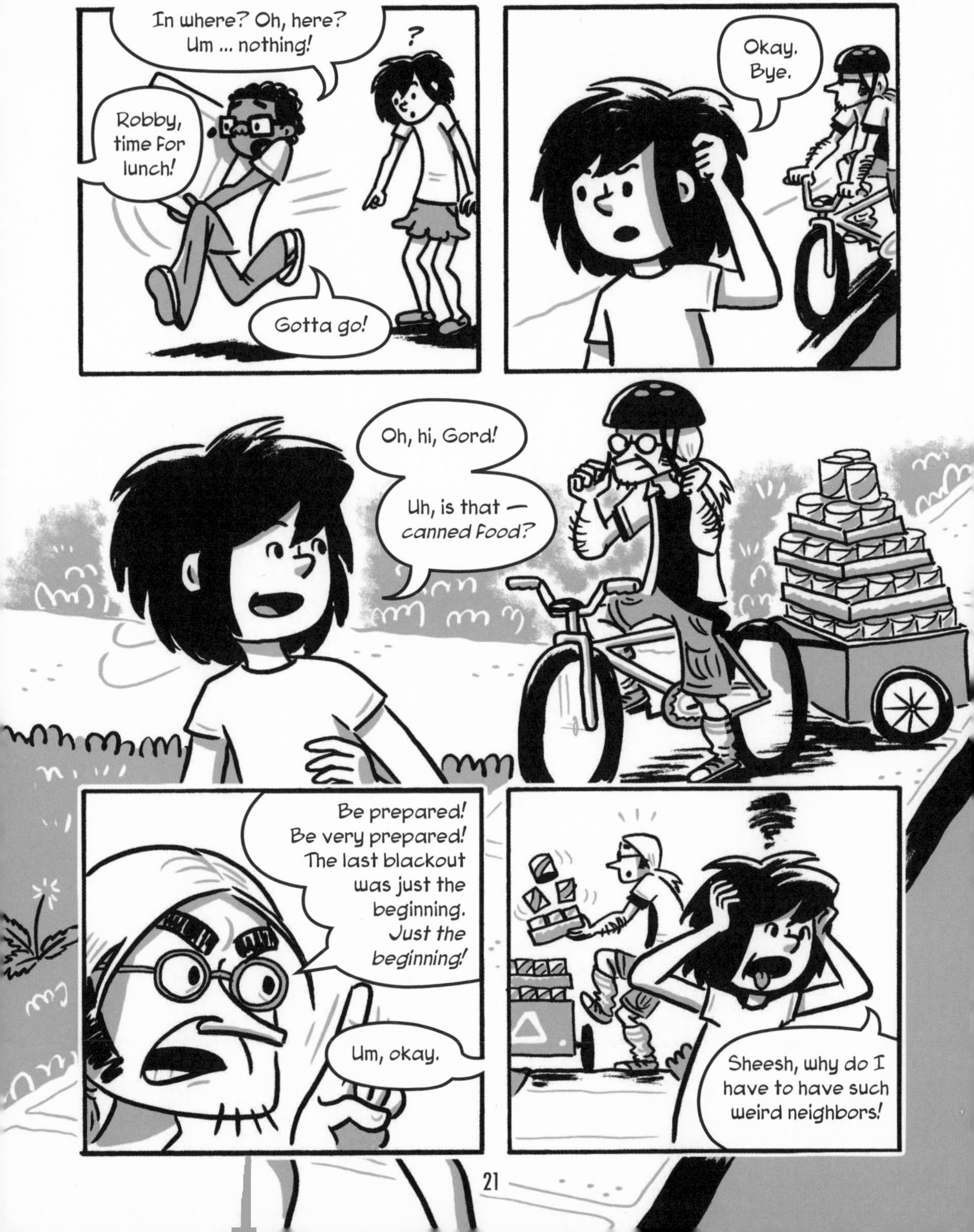
In where? Oh, here? Um ... nothing!
?
Robby, time for lunch!
Gotta go!
Okay. Bye.
Oh, hi, Gord!
Uh, is that — canned food?
Be prepared! Be very prepared! The last blackout was just the beginning. Just the beginning!
Um, okay.
Sheesh, why do I have to have such weird neighbors!

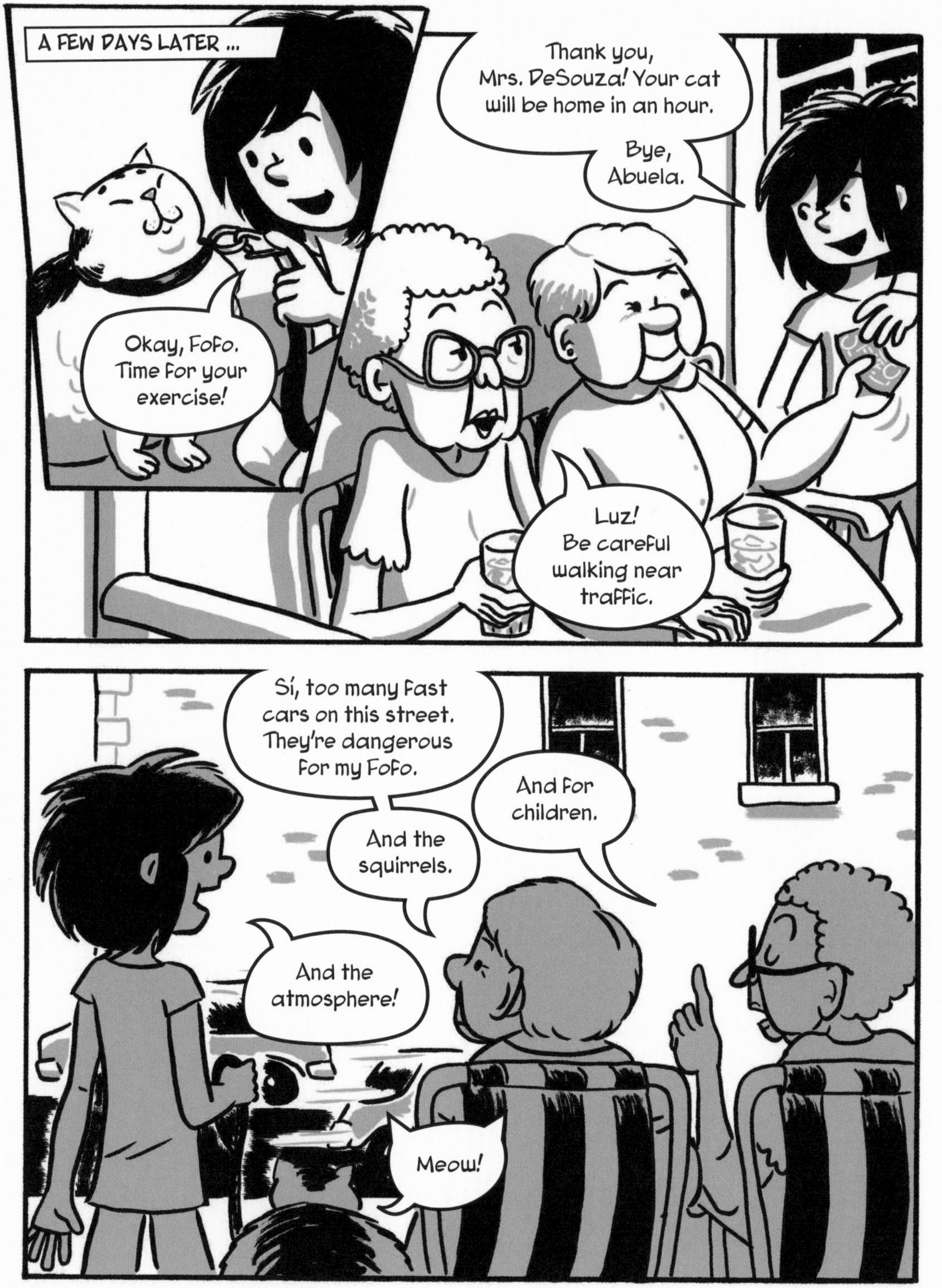
A FEW DAYS LATER ...
Okay, FoFo. Time for your exercise!
Thank you, Mrs. DeSouza! Your cat will be home in an hour.
Bye, Abuela.
Luz! Be careful walking near traffic.
Sí, too many fast cars on this street. They're dangerous for my FoFo.
And for children.
And the squirrels.
And the atmosphere!
Meow!

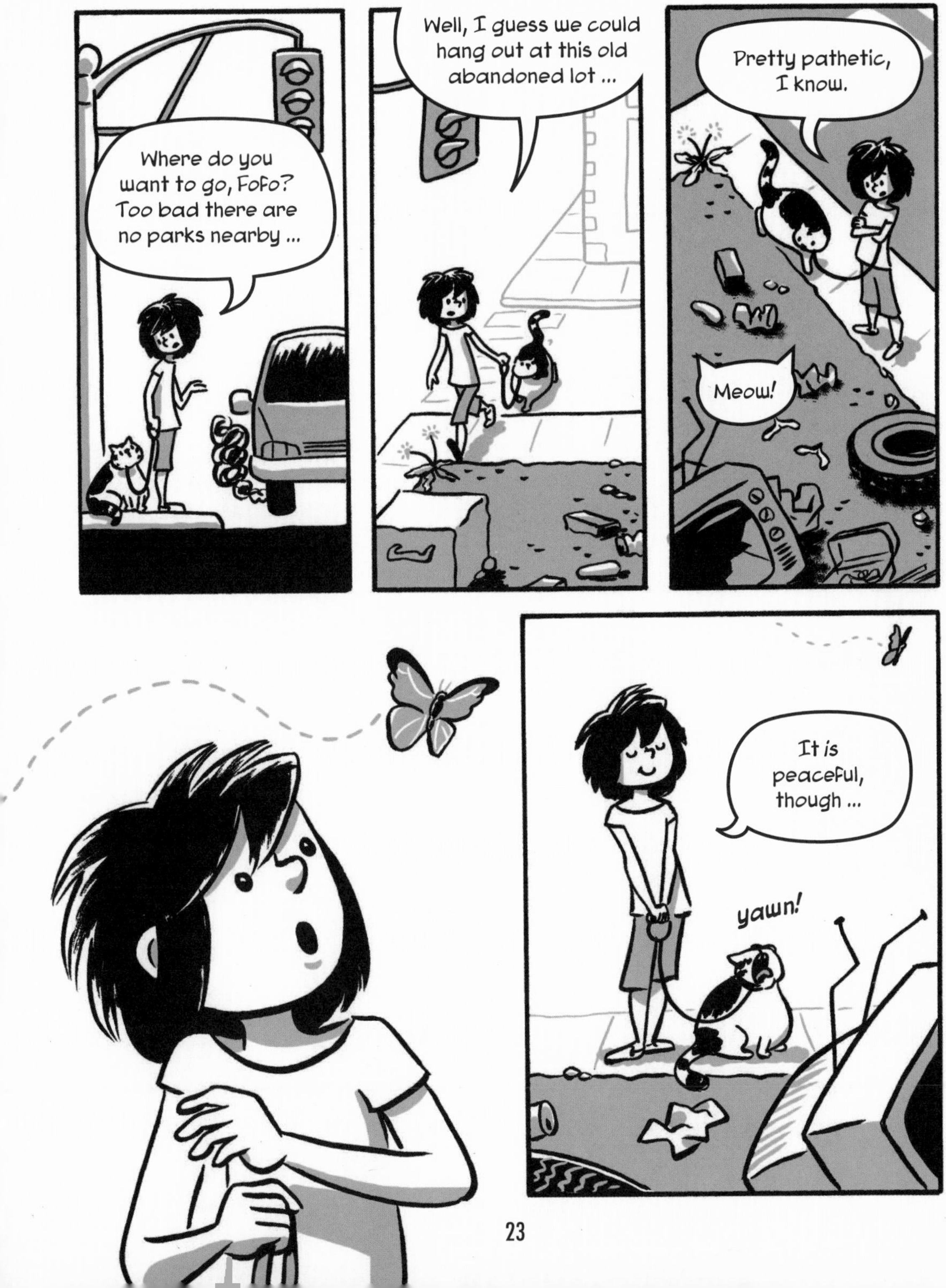
Where do you want to go, Fofo? Too bad there are no parks nearby ...
Well, I guess we could hang out at this old abandoned lot ...
Pretty pathetic, I know.
Meow!
It *is* peaceful, though ...
yawn!

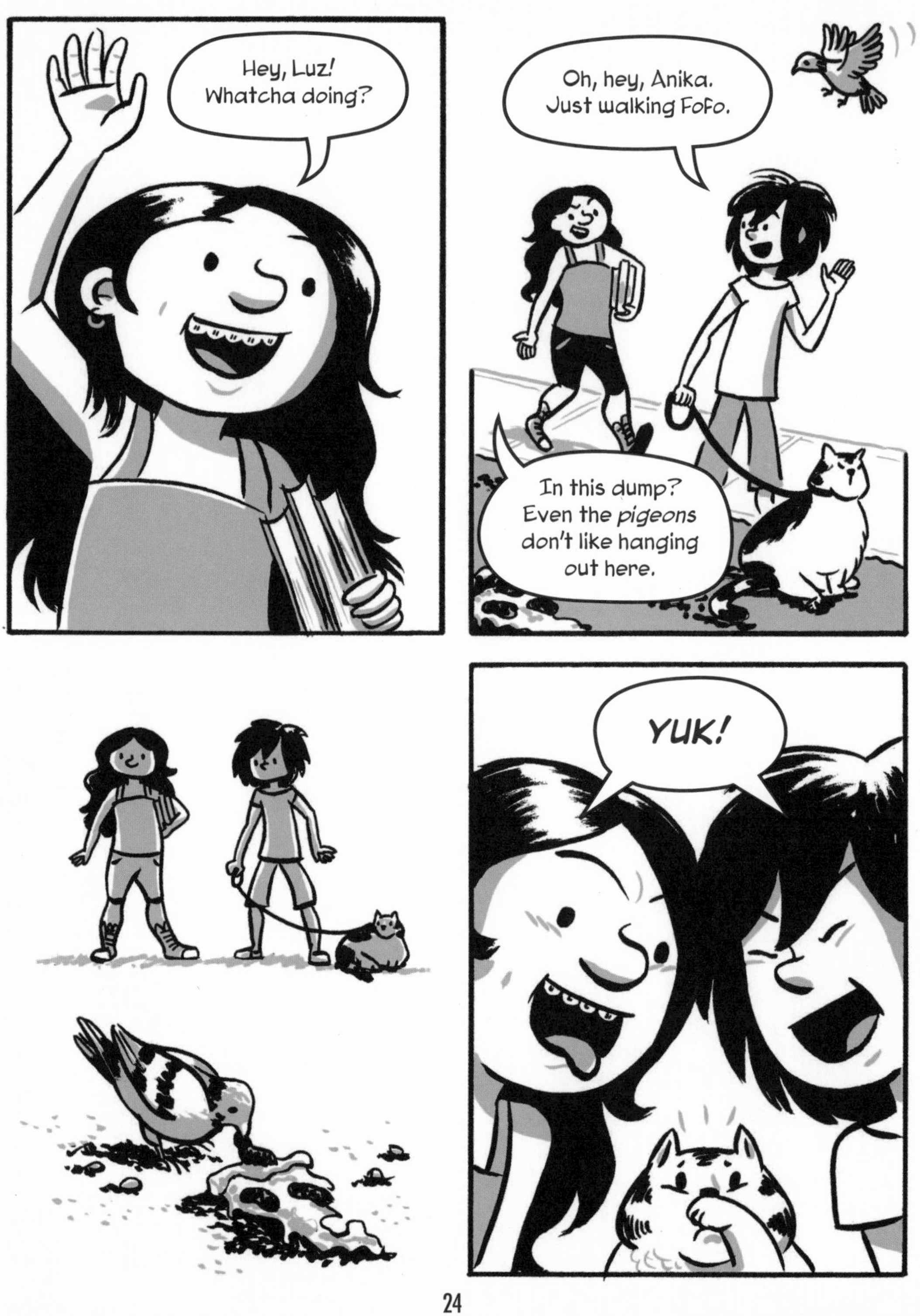
Hey, Luz!
Whatcha doing?
Oh, hey, Anika.
Just walking Fofo.
In this dump? Even the *pigeons* don't like hanging out here.
YUK!

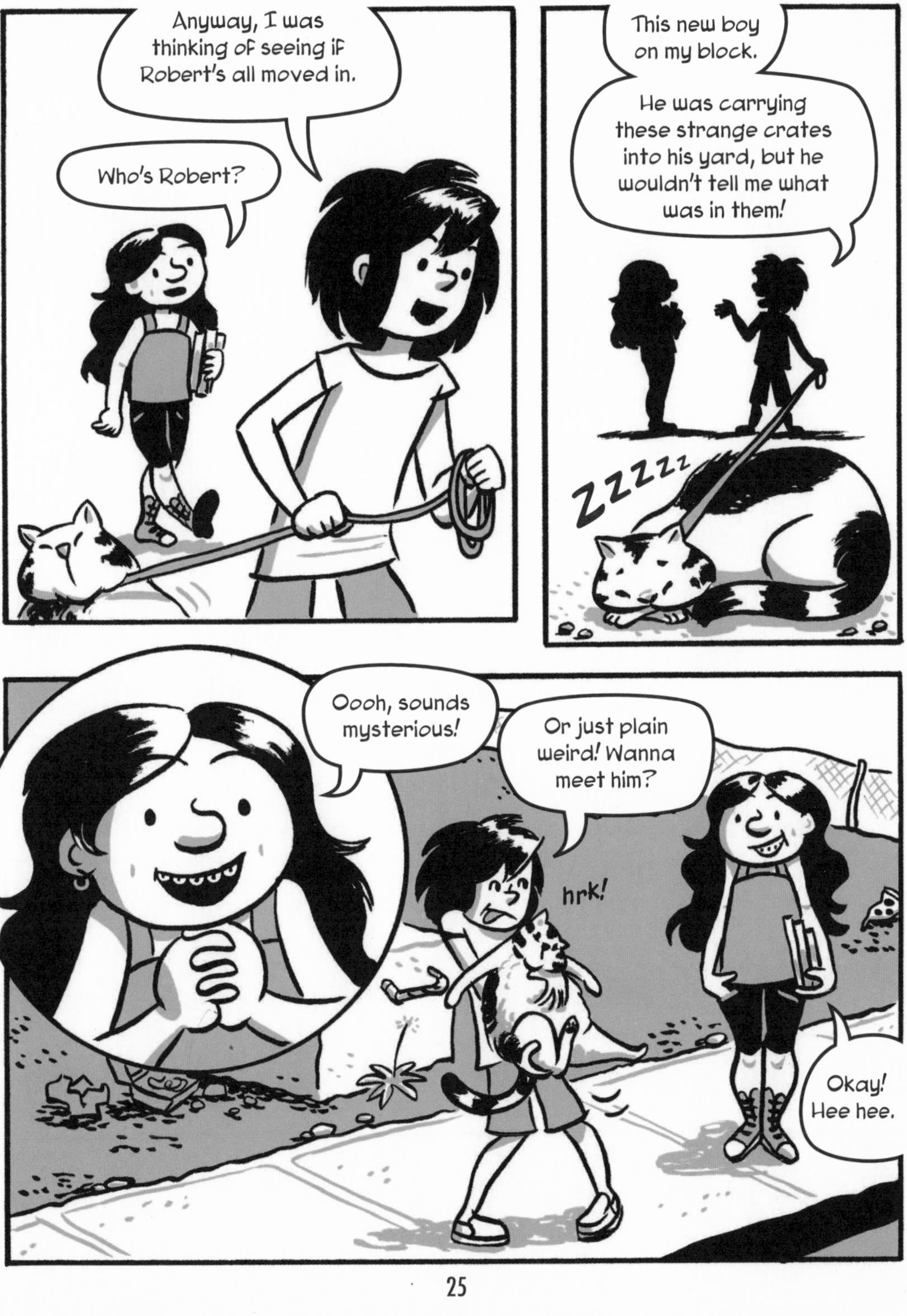

Anyway, I was thinking of seeing if Robert's all moved in.
Who's Robert?
This new boy on my block.
He was carrying these strange crates into his yard, but he wouldn't tell me what was in them!
ZZZZZz
Oooh, sounds mysterious!
Or just plain weird! Wanna meet him?
hrk!
Okay! Hee hee.

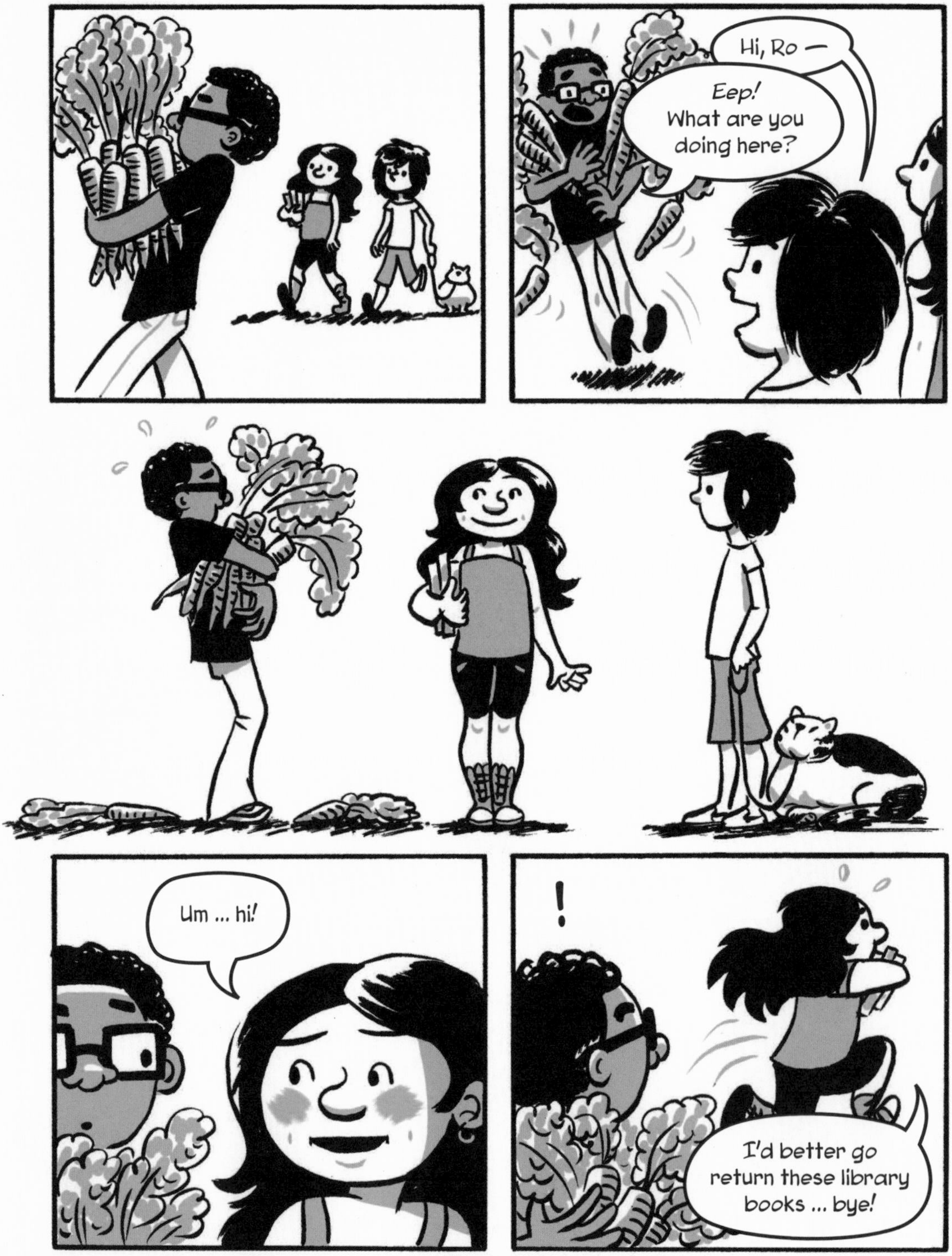
Hi, Ro —
Eep! What are you doing here?
Um ... hi!
!
I'd better go return these library books ... bye!

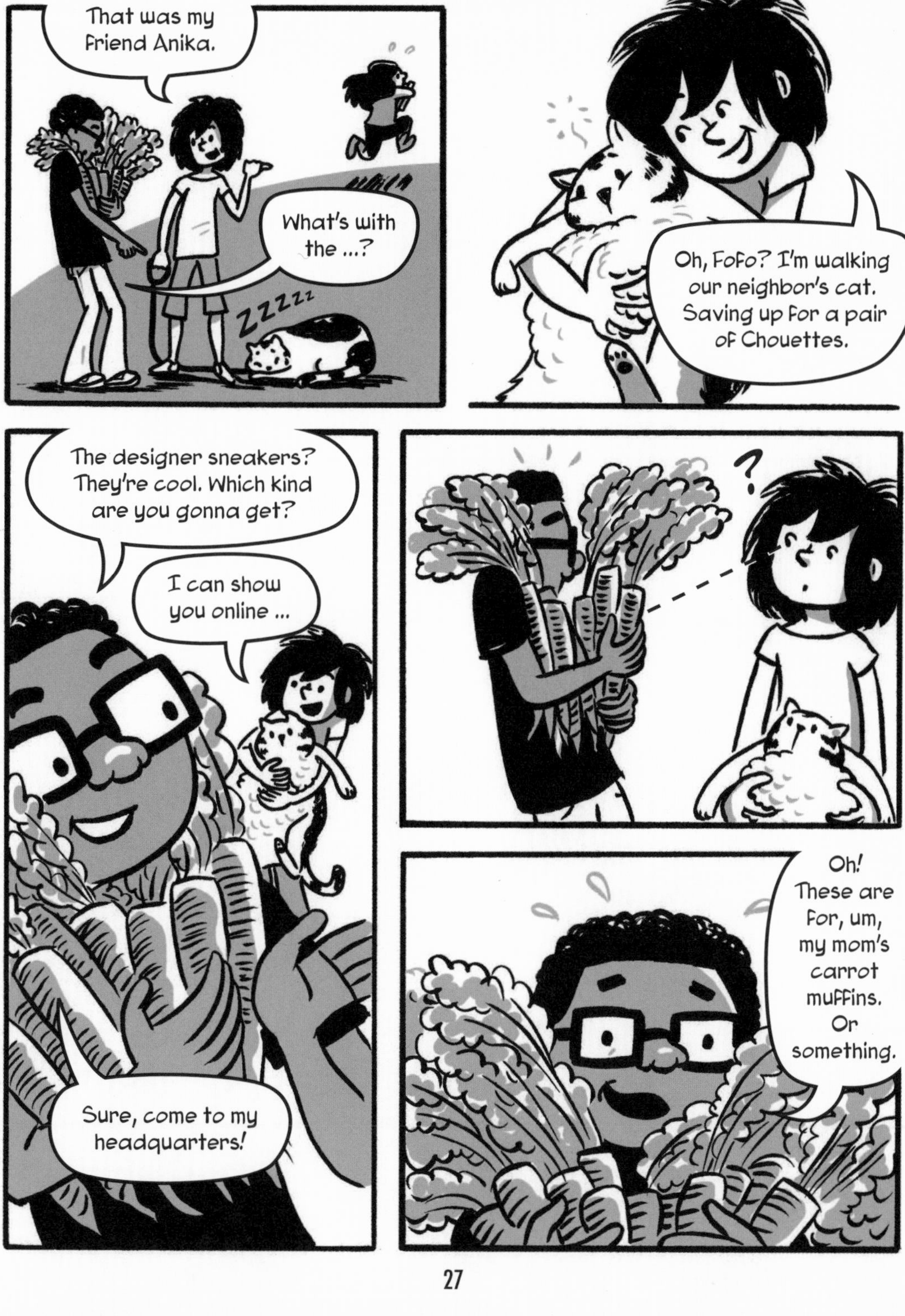
That was my friend Anika.
What's with the ...?
ZZZZz
Oh, Fofo? I'm walking our neighbor's cat. Saving up for a pair of Chouettes.
The designer sneakers? They're cool. Which kind are you gonna get?
I can show you online ...
Sure, come to my headquarters!
?
Oh! These are for, um, my mom's carrot muffins. Or something.

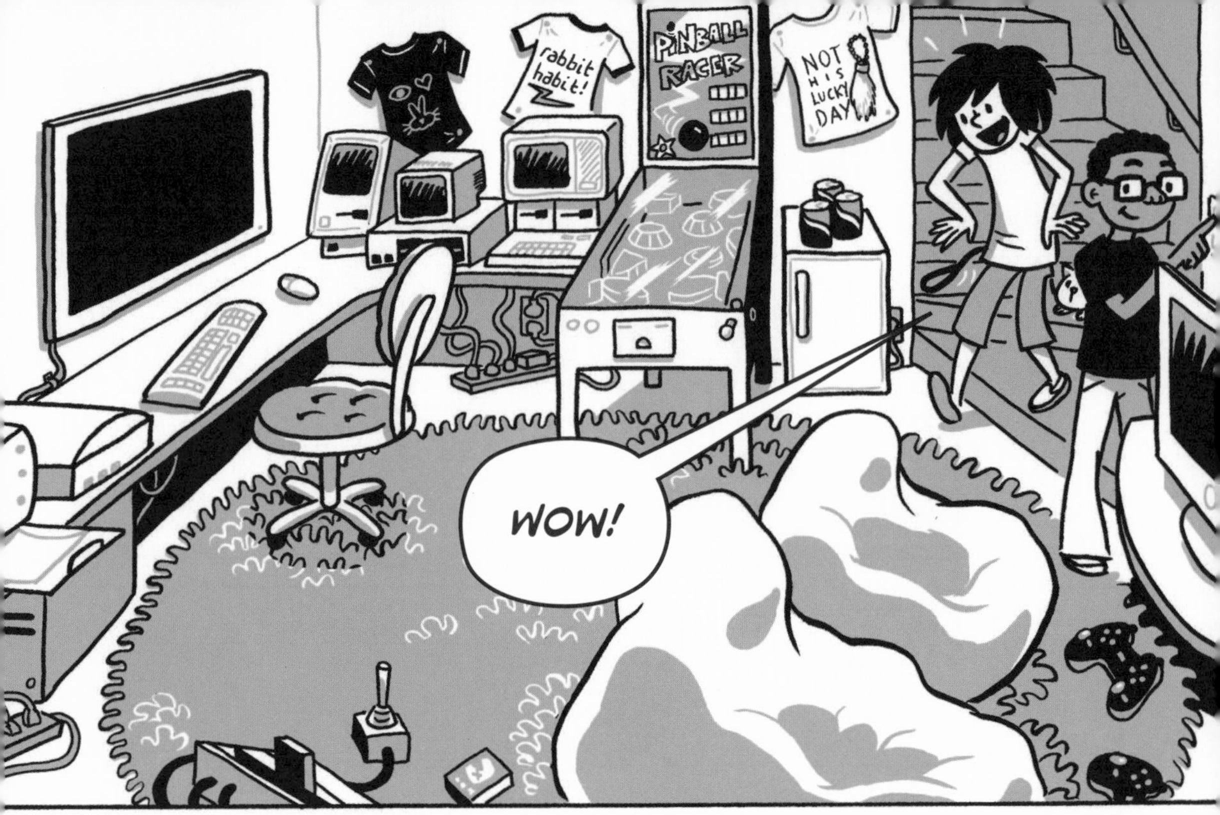
rabbit habit!
PINBALL RACER
NOT HIS LUCKY DAY
WOW!

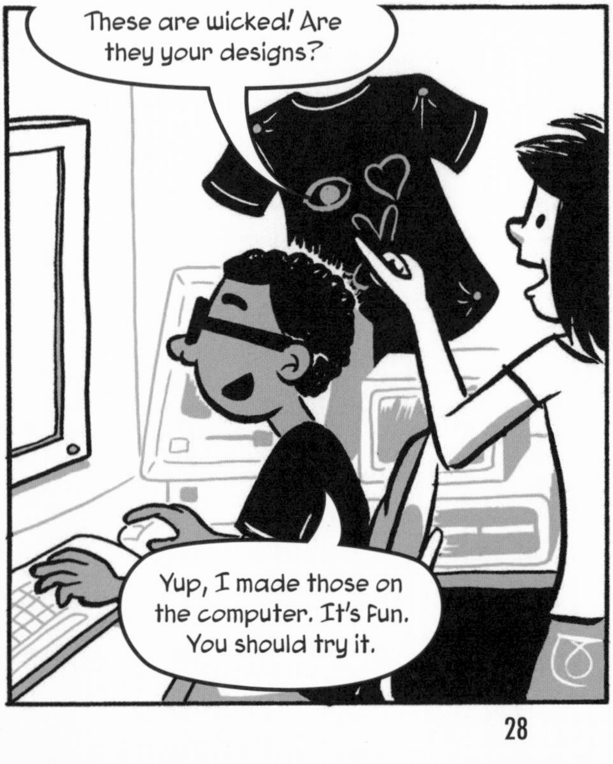
These are wicked! Are they your designs?
Yup, I made those on the computer. It's fun. You should try it.

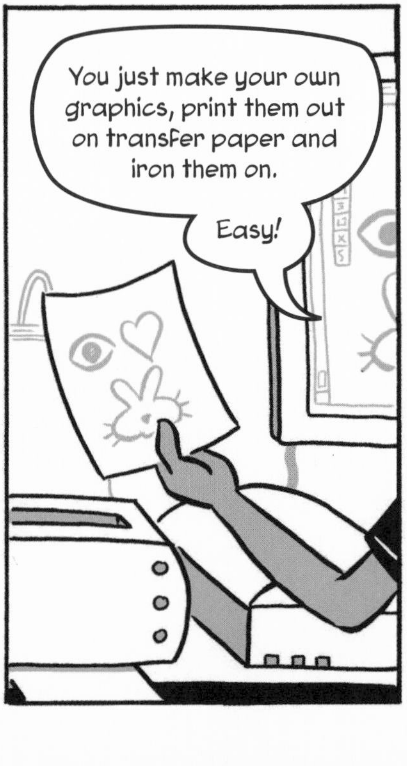
You just make your own graphics, print them out on transfer paper and iron them on.
Easy!

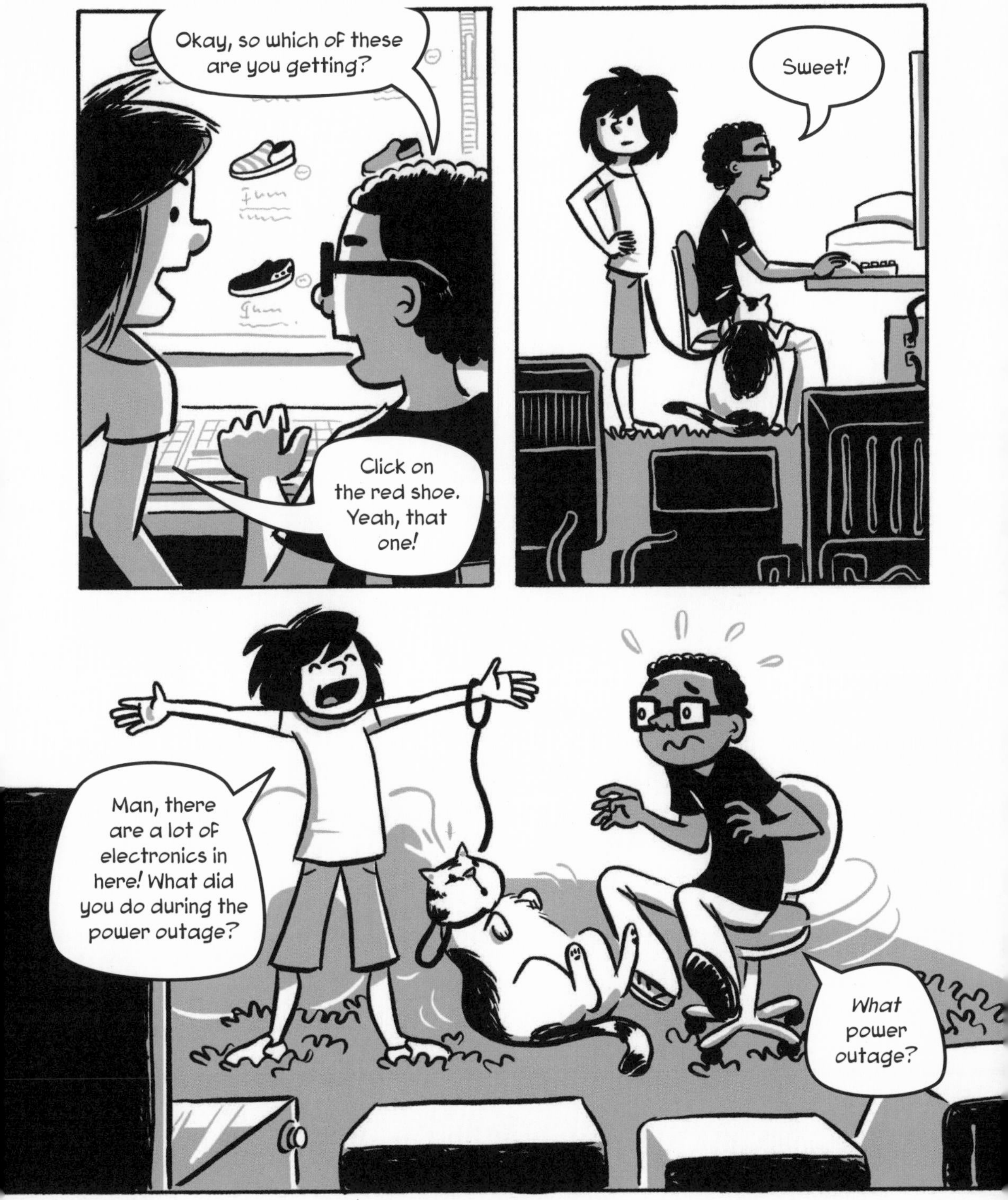
Okay, so which of these are you getting?
Click on the red shoe. Yeah, that one!
Sweet!
Man, there are a lot of electronics in here! What did you do during the power outage?
What power outage?

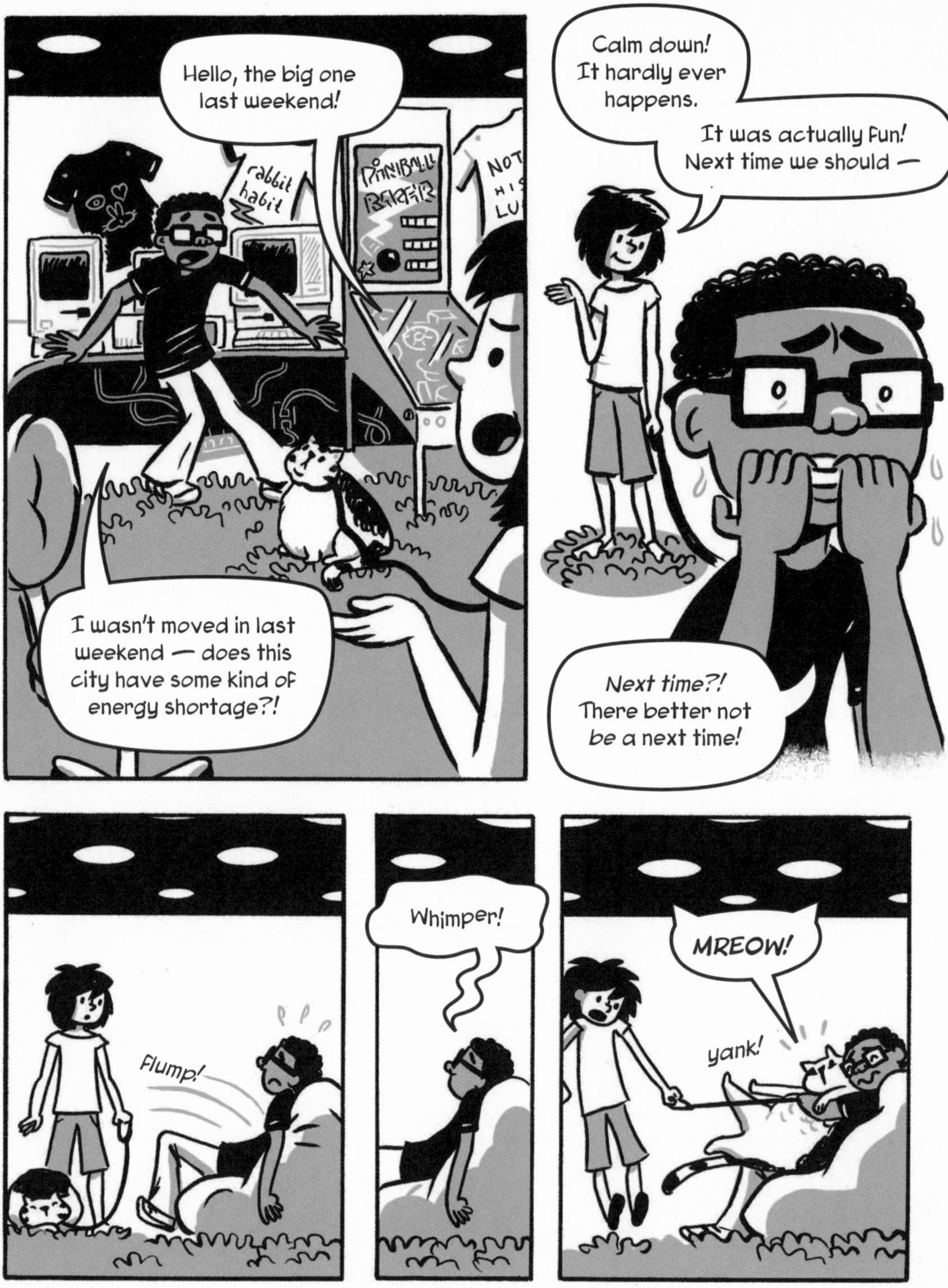
Hello, the big one last weekend!
I wasn't moved in last weekend — does this city have some kind of energy shortage?!
Calm down! It hardly ever happens.
It was actually fun! Next time we should —
Next time?! There better not be a next time!
Flump!
Whimper!
MREOW!
yank!

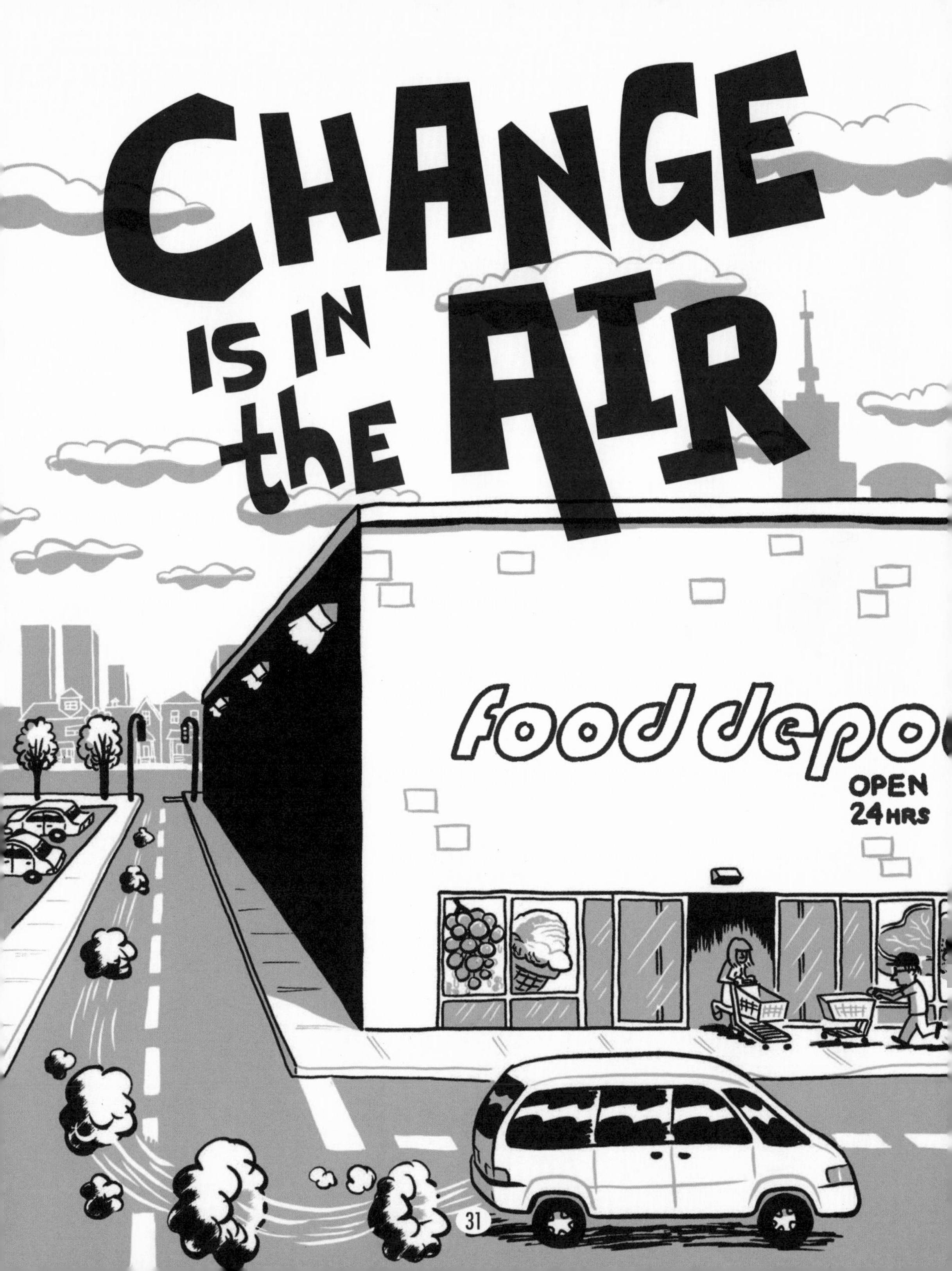
CHANGE IS IN the AIR
food depo
OPEN 24HRS

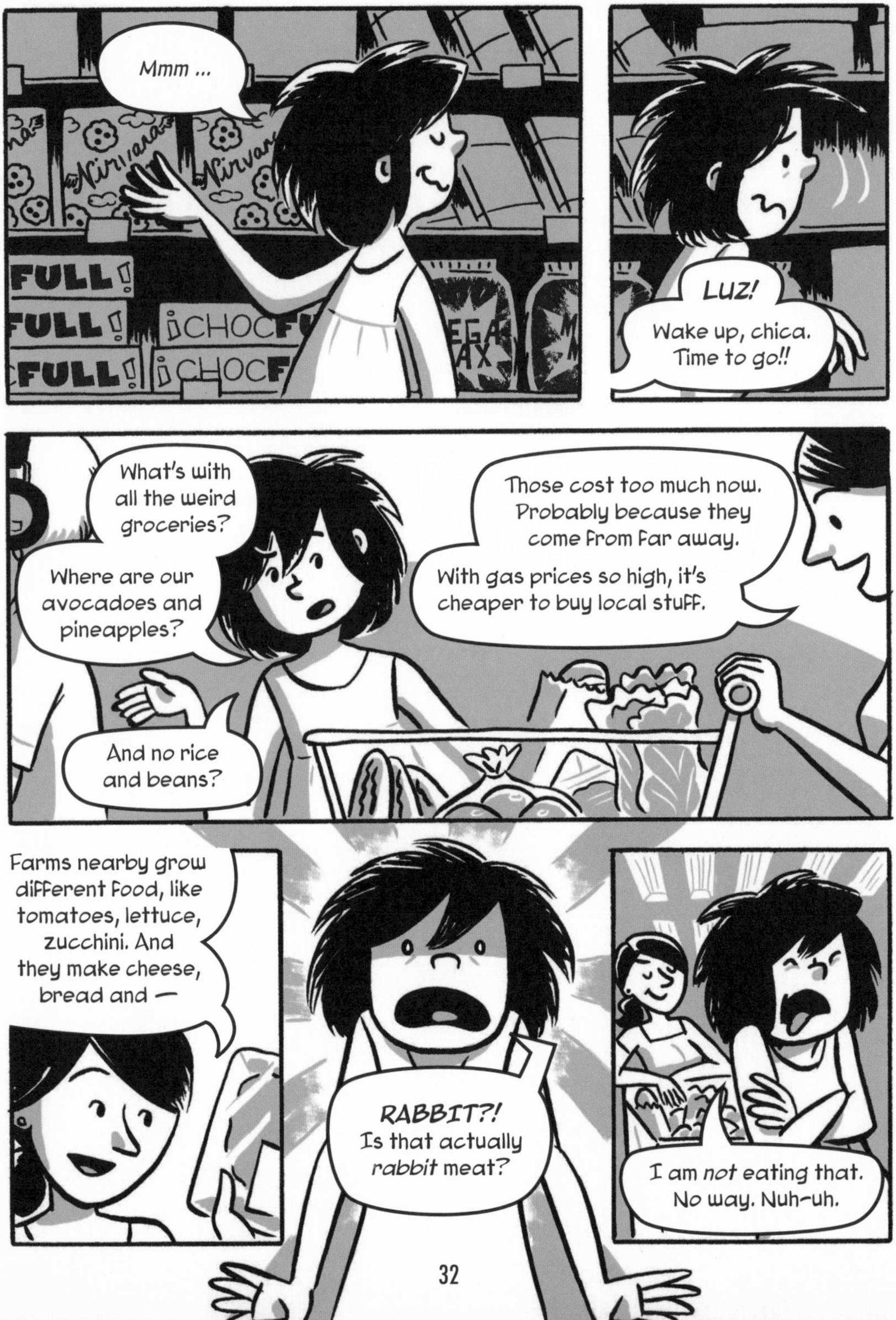

Mmm ...
Nirvana
FULL!
¡CHOC
MEGA MAX
LUZ! Wake up, chica. Time to go!!
What's with all the weird groceries?
Where are our avocadoes and pineapples?
Those cost too much now. Probably because they come from far away.
With gas prices so high, it's cheaper to buy local stuff.
And no rice and beans?
Farms nearby grow different food, like tomatoes, lettuce, zucchini. And they make cheese, bread and —
RABBIT?! Is that actually *rabbit* meat?
I am *not* eating that. No way. Nuh-uh.

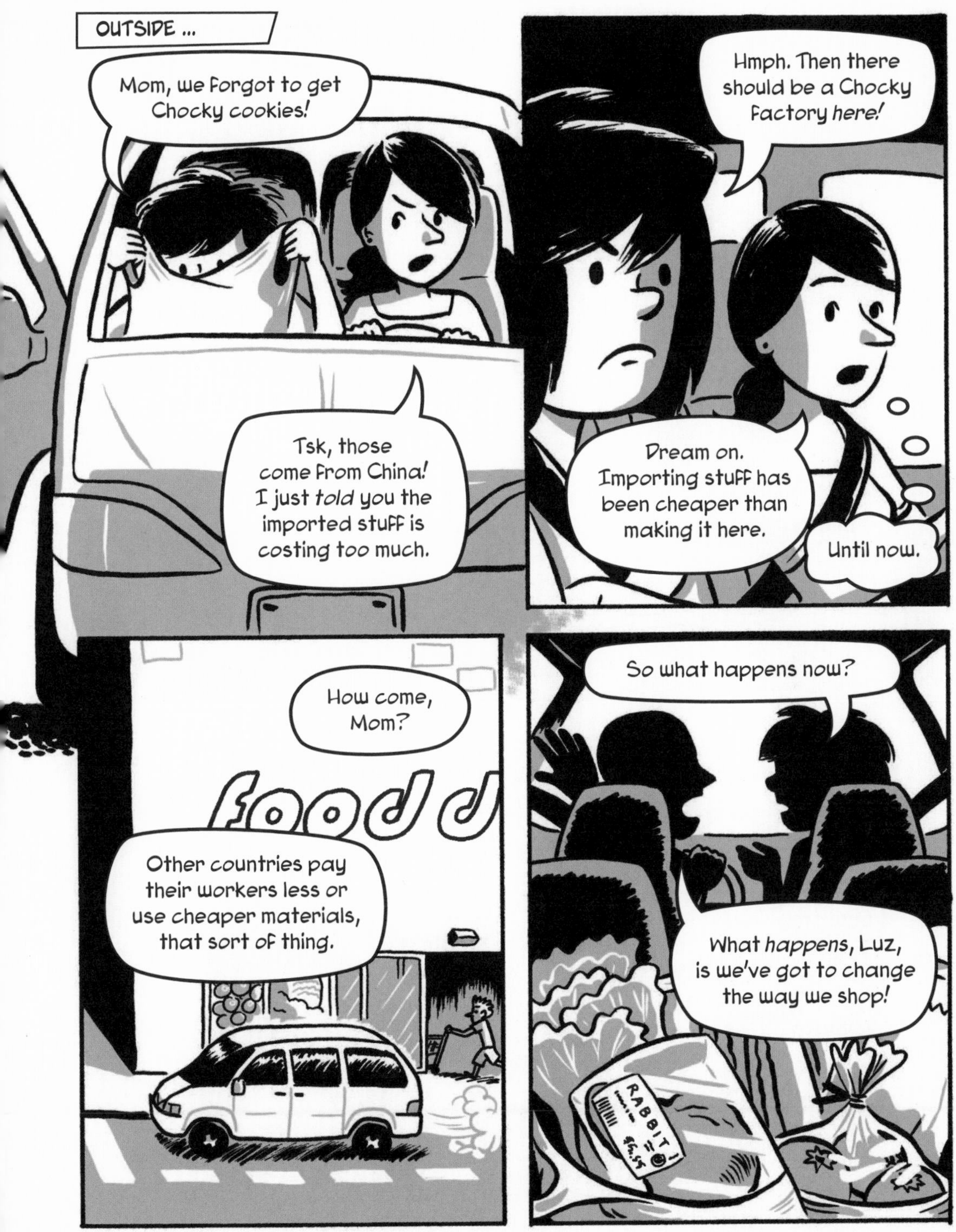

OUTSIDE ...
Mom, we forgot to get Chocky cookies!
Tsk, those come from China! I just *told* you the imported stuff is costing too much.
Hmph. Then there should be a Chocky Factory *here!*
Dream on. Importing stuff has been cheaper than making it here.
Until now.
How come, Mom?
food
Other countries pay their workers less or use cheaper materials, that sort of thing.
So what happens now?
What *happens*, Luz, is we've got to change the way we shop!
RABBIT

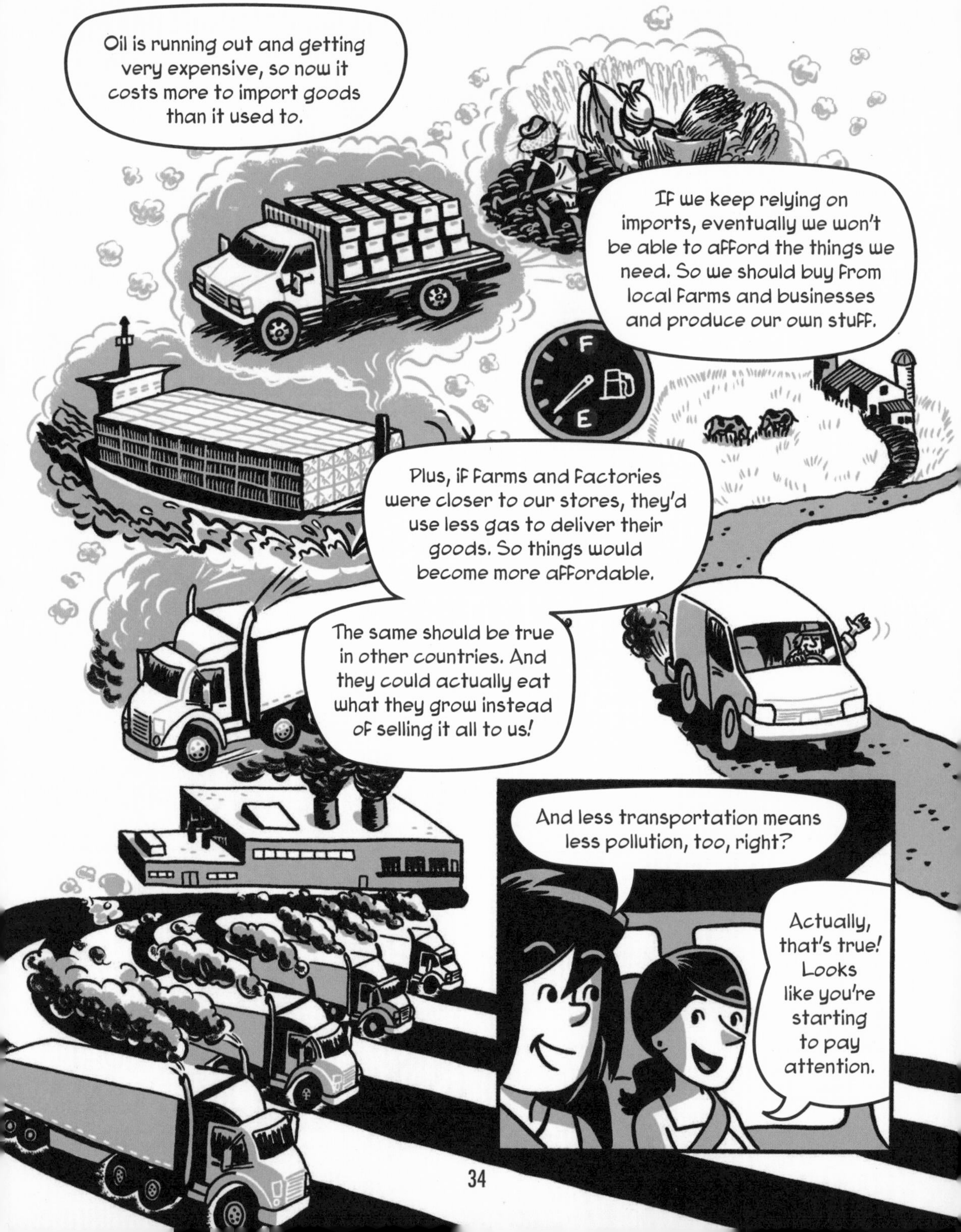
Oil is running out and getting very expensive, so now it costs more to import goods than it used to.
If we keep relying on imports, eventually we won't be able to afford the things we need. So we should buy from local farms and businesses and produce our own stuff.
F
E
Plus, if farms and factories were closer to our stores, they'd use less gas to deliver their goods. So things would become more affordable.
The same should be true in other countries. And they could actually eat what they grow instead of selling it all to us!
And less transportation means less pollution, too, right?
Actually, that's true! Looks like you're starting to pay attention.

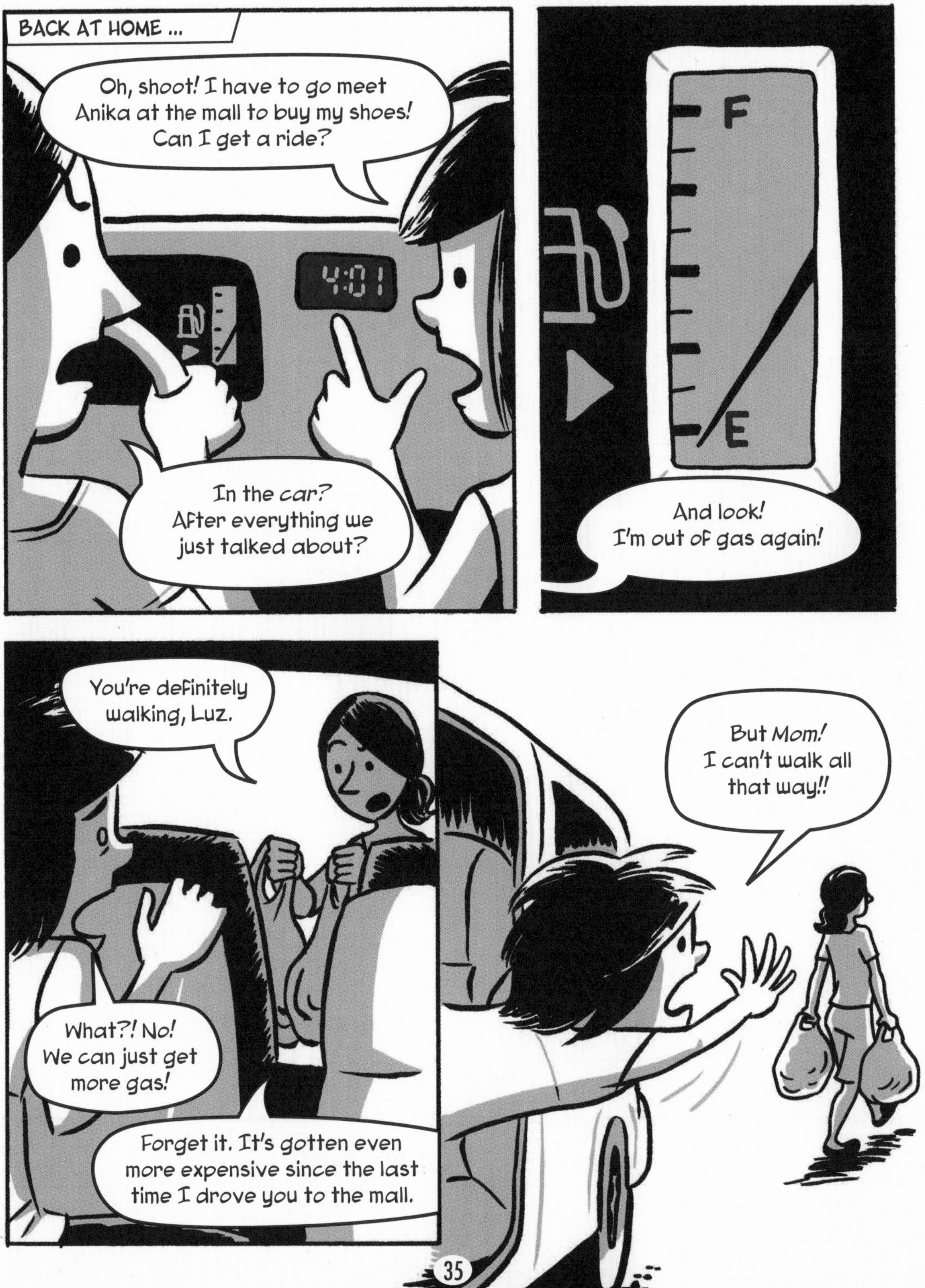
BACK AT HOME ...
Oh, shoot! I have to go meet Anika at the mall to buy my shoes! Can I get a ride?
4:01
In the *car*? After everything we just talked about?
F
E
And look! I'm out of gas again!
You're definitely walking, Luz.
What?! No! We can just get more gas!
Forget it. It's gotten even more expensive since the last time I drove you to the mall.
But *Mom!* I can't walk all that way!!

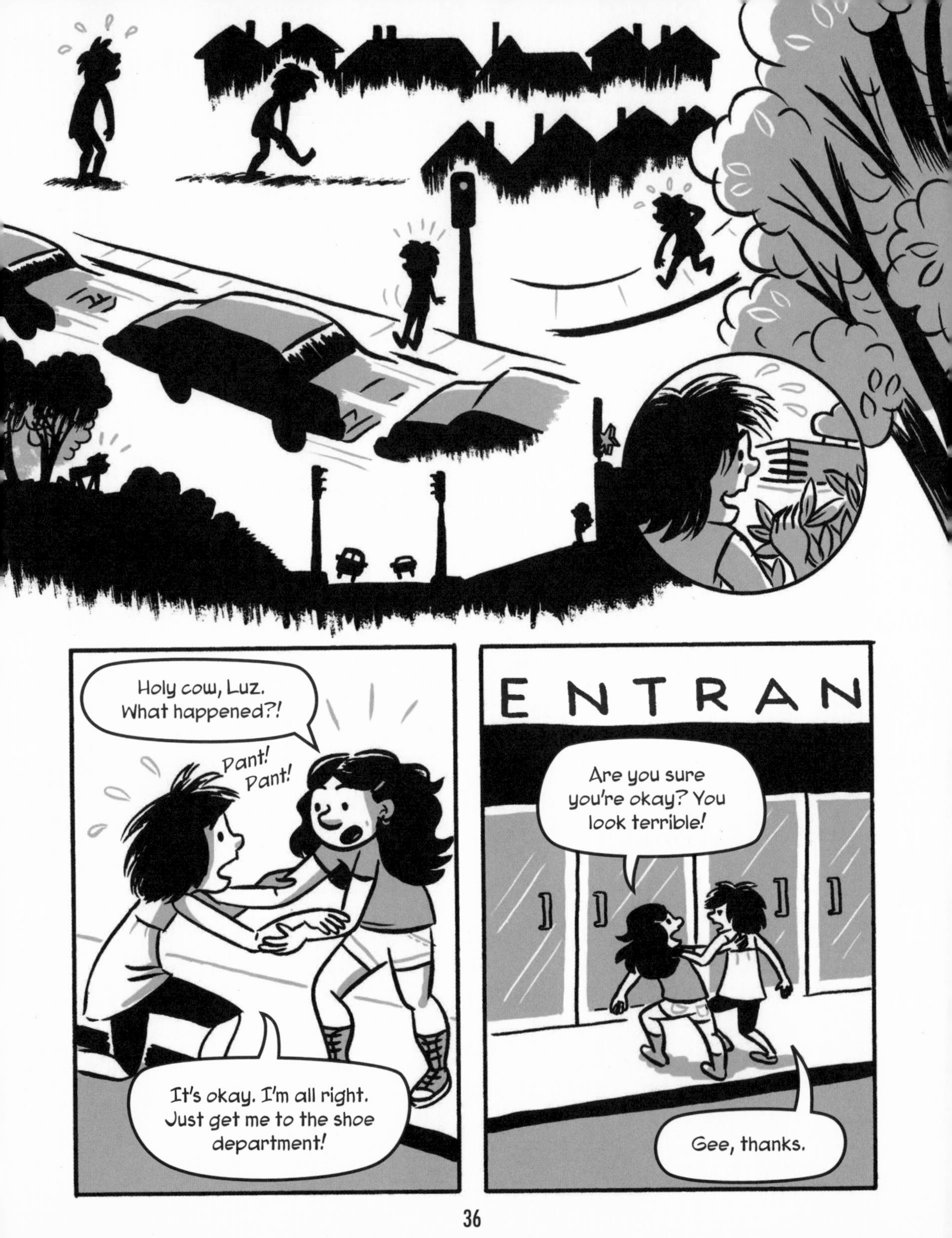
Holy cow, Luz. What happened?!
Pant! Pant!
It's okay. I'm all right. Just get me to the shoe department!
ENTRAN
Are you sure you're okay? You look terrible!
Gee, thanks.

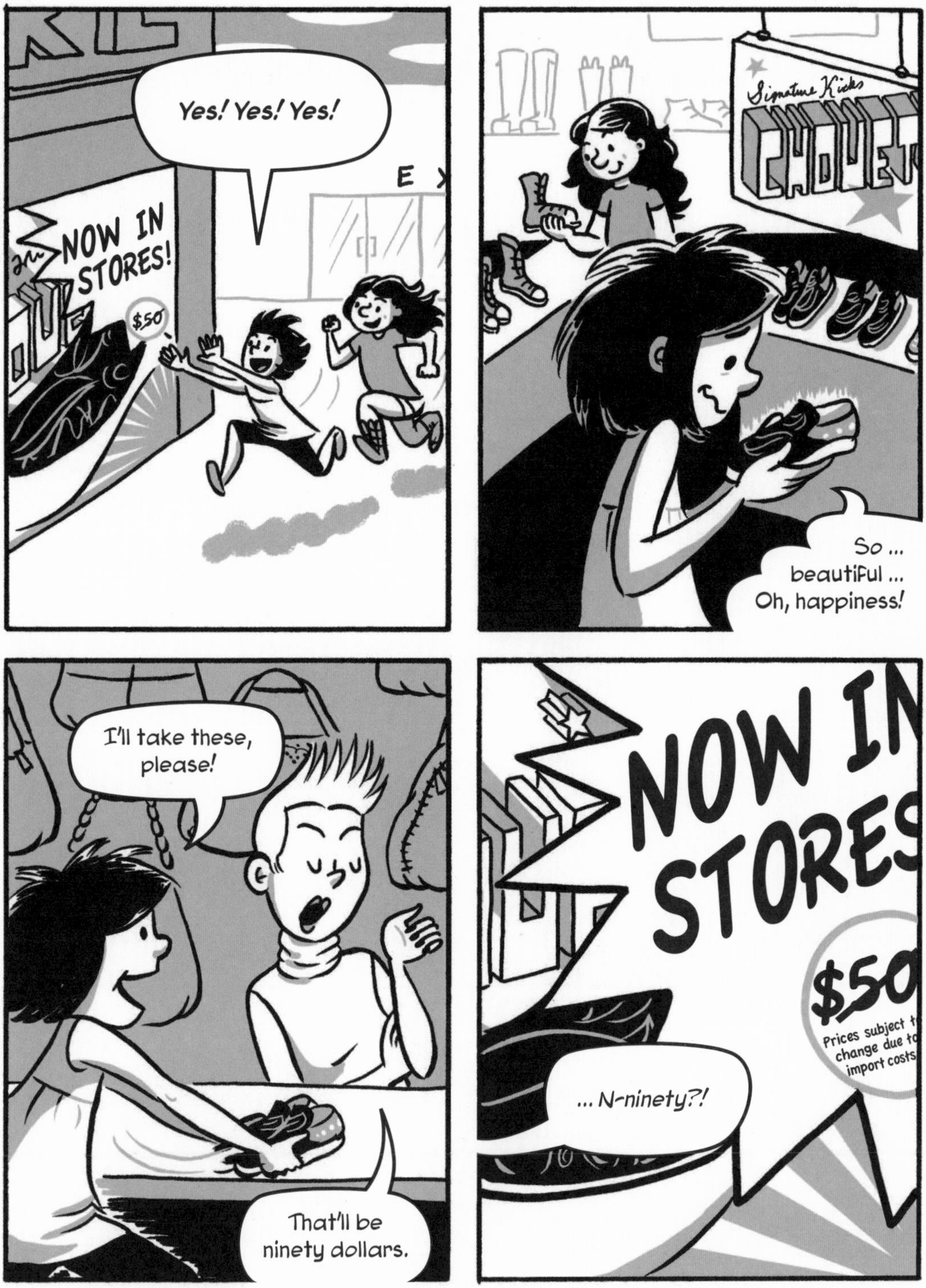
Yes! Yes! Yes!
NOW IN STORES!
$50
Signature Kicks
So ... beautiful ... Oh, happiness!
I'll take these, please!
That'll be ninety dollars.
NOW IN STORES
$50
... N-ninety?!

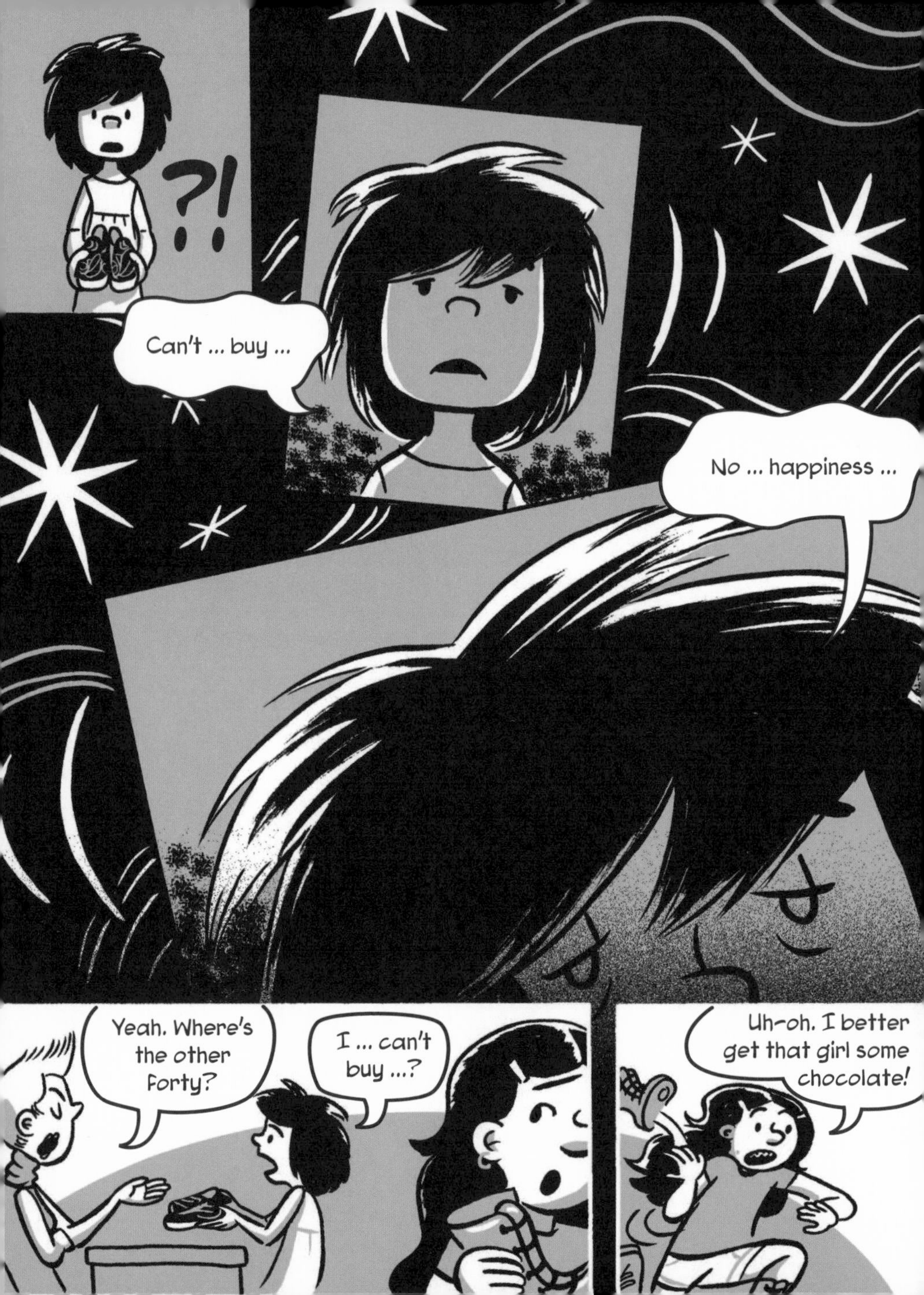
?!
Can't ... buy ...
No ... happiness ...
Yeah. Where's the other forty?
I ... can't buy ...?
Uh-oh. I better get that girl some chocolate!

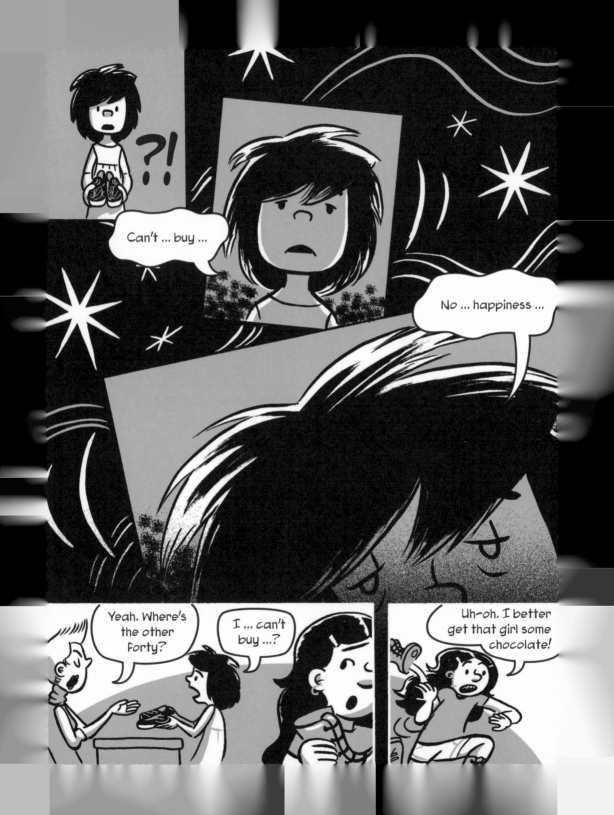

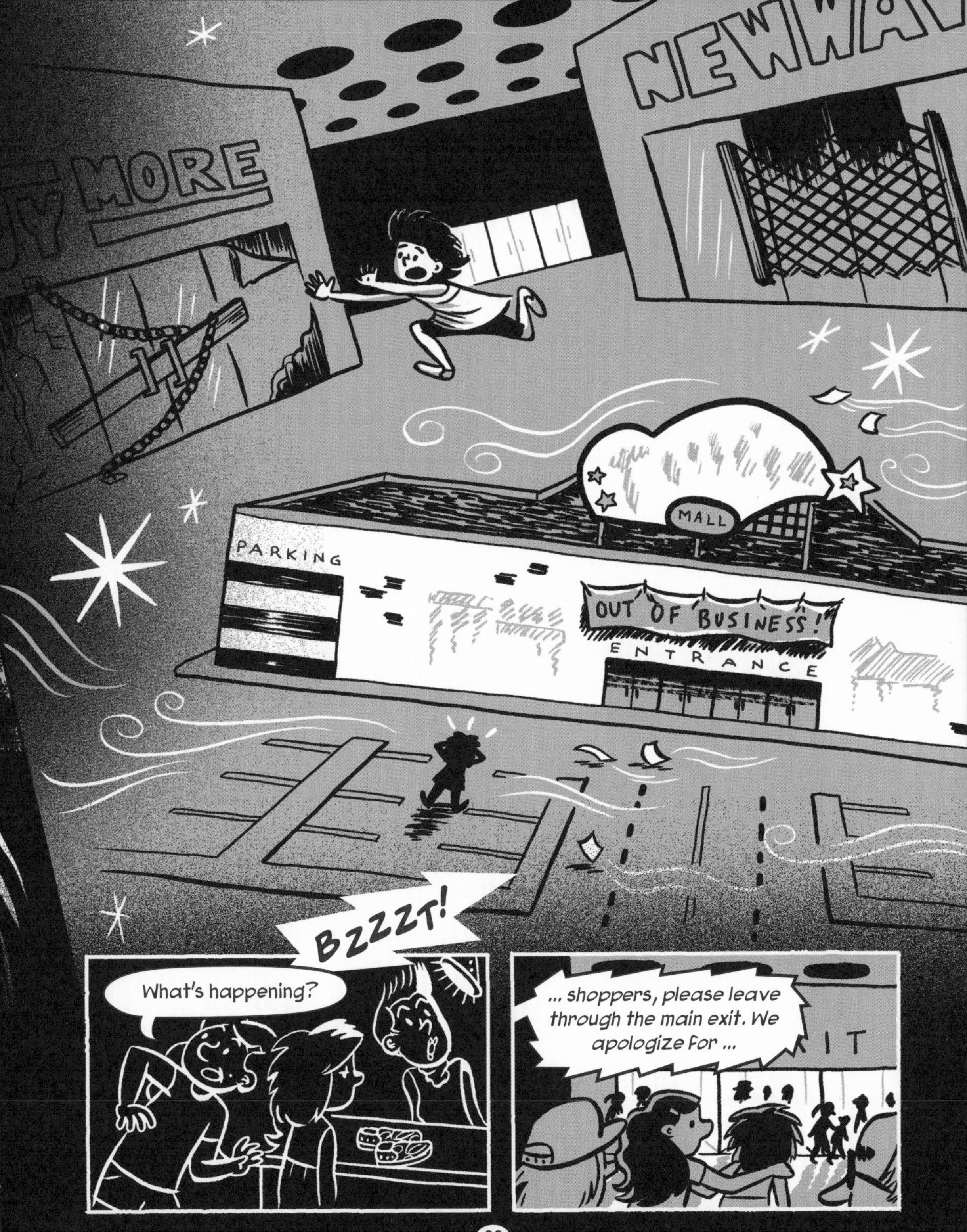
MORE
MALL
PARKING
OUT OF BUSINESS!
ENTRANCE
BZZZT!
What's happening?
... shoppers, please leave through the main exit. We apologize for ...

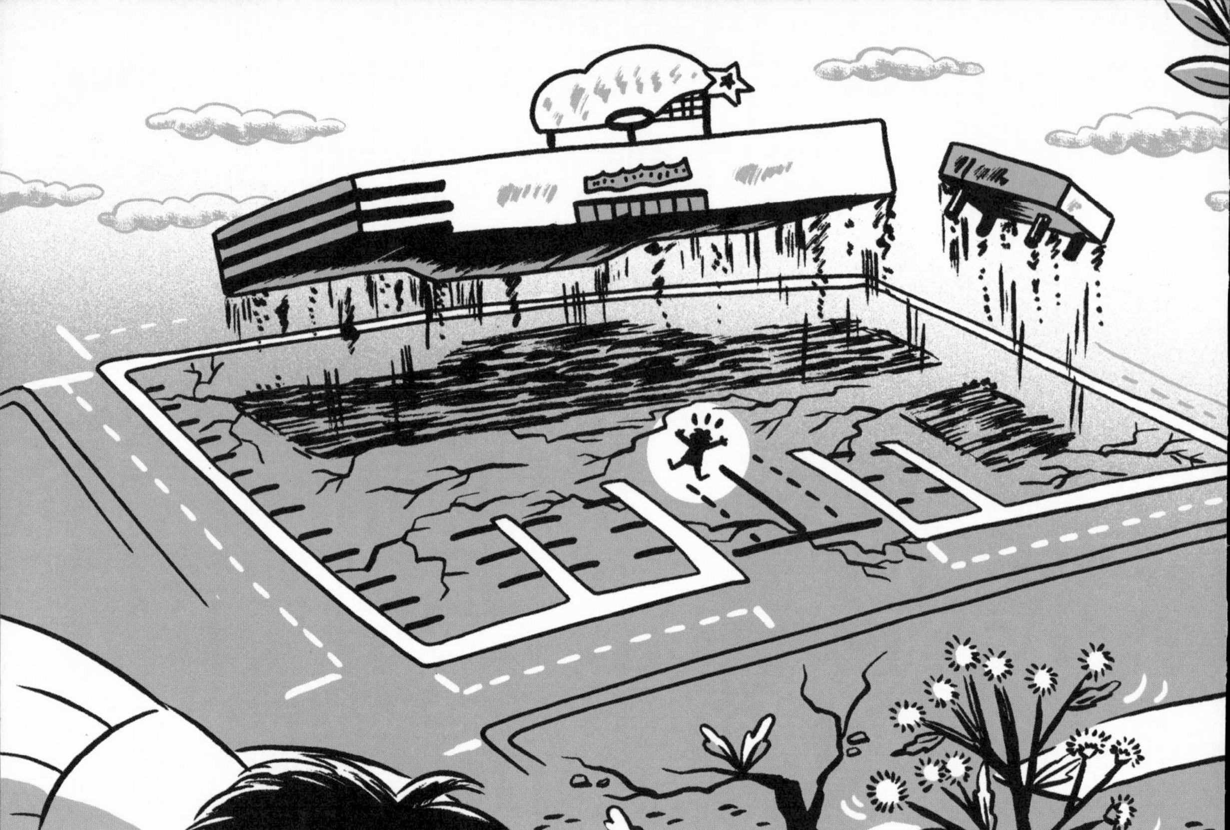

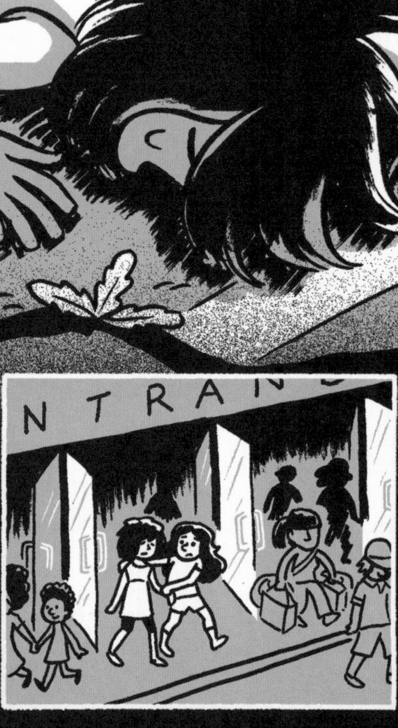
N T R A N

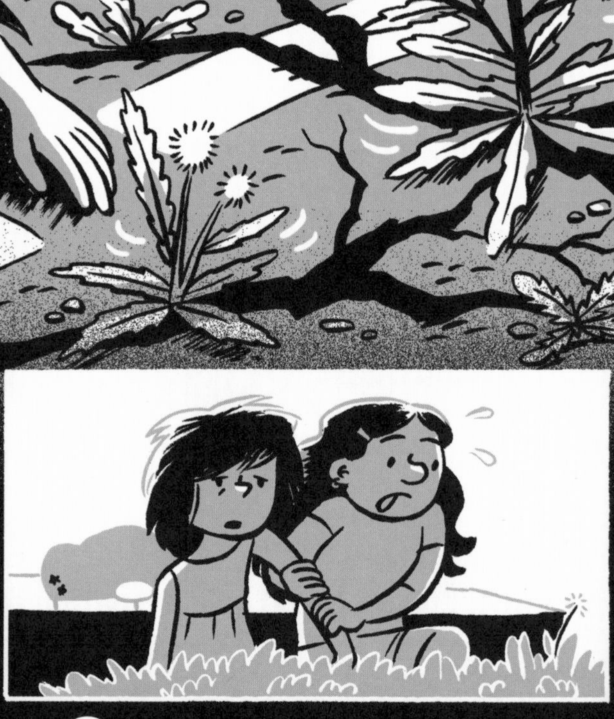

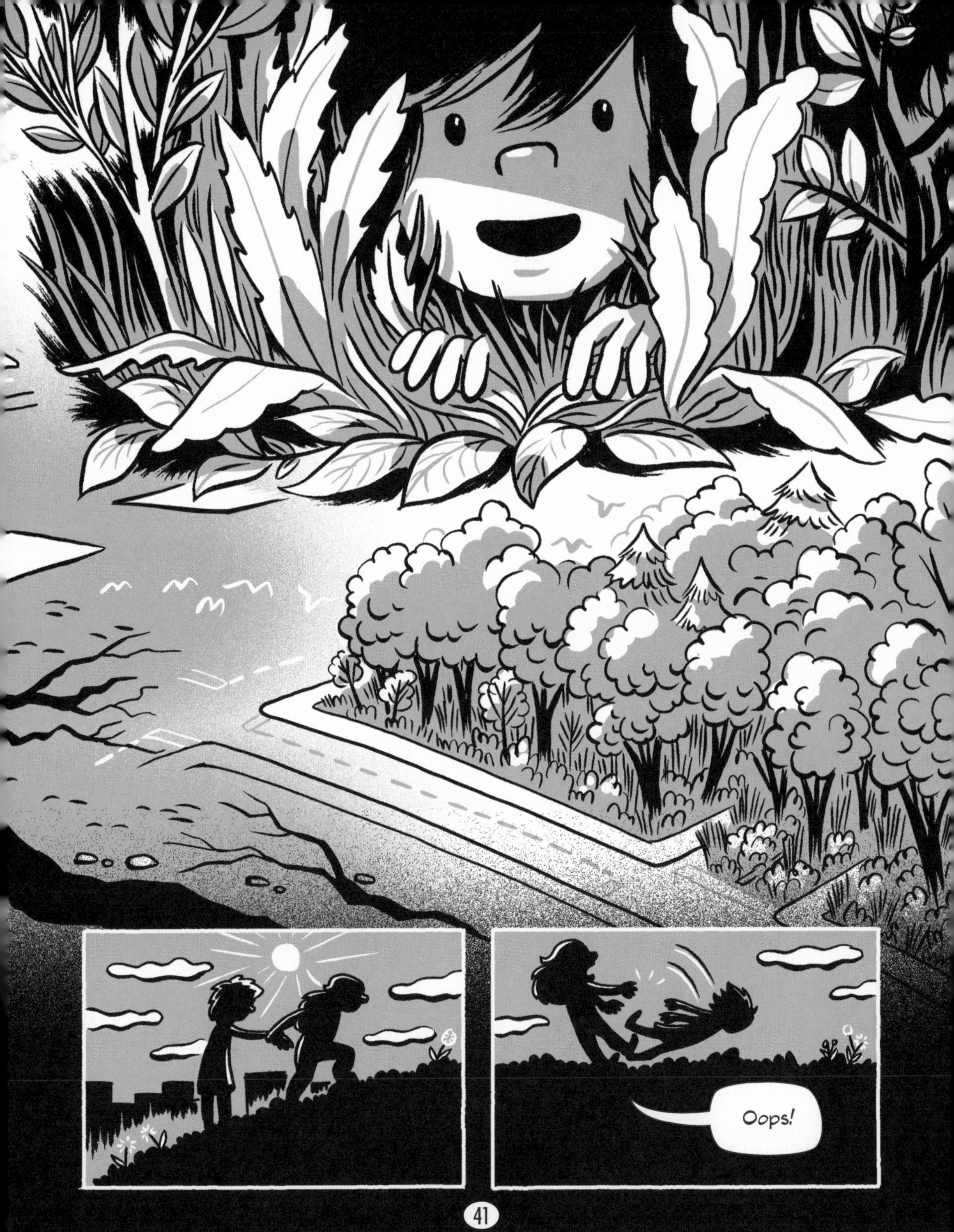
Oops!

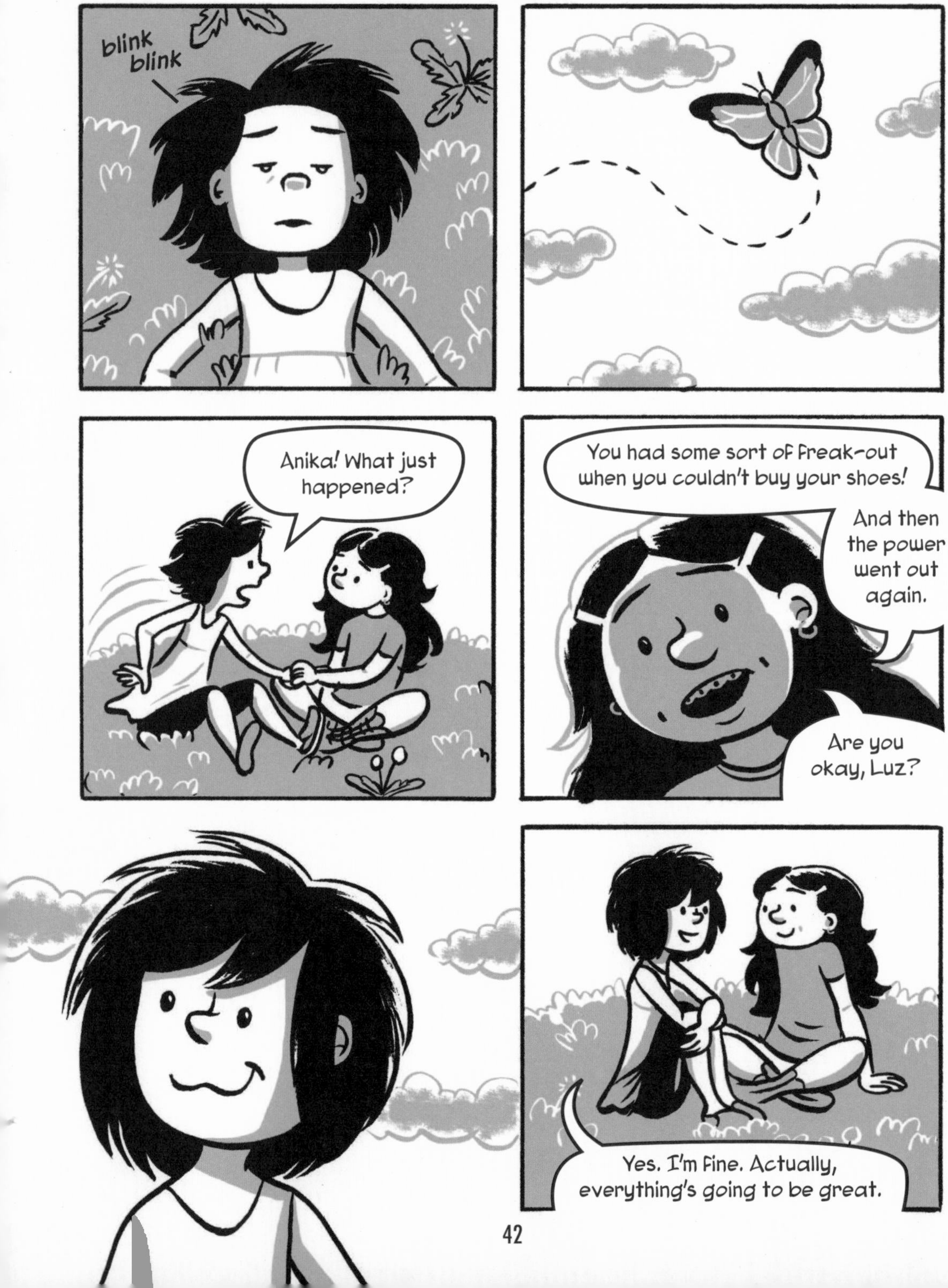
blink blink
Anika! What just happened?
You had some sort of freak-out when you couldn't buy your shoes!
And then the power went out again.
Are you okay, Luz?
Yes. I'm fine. Actually, everything's going to be great.

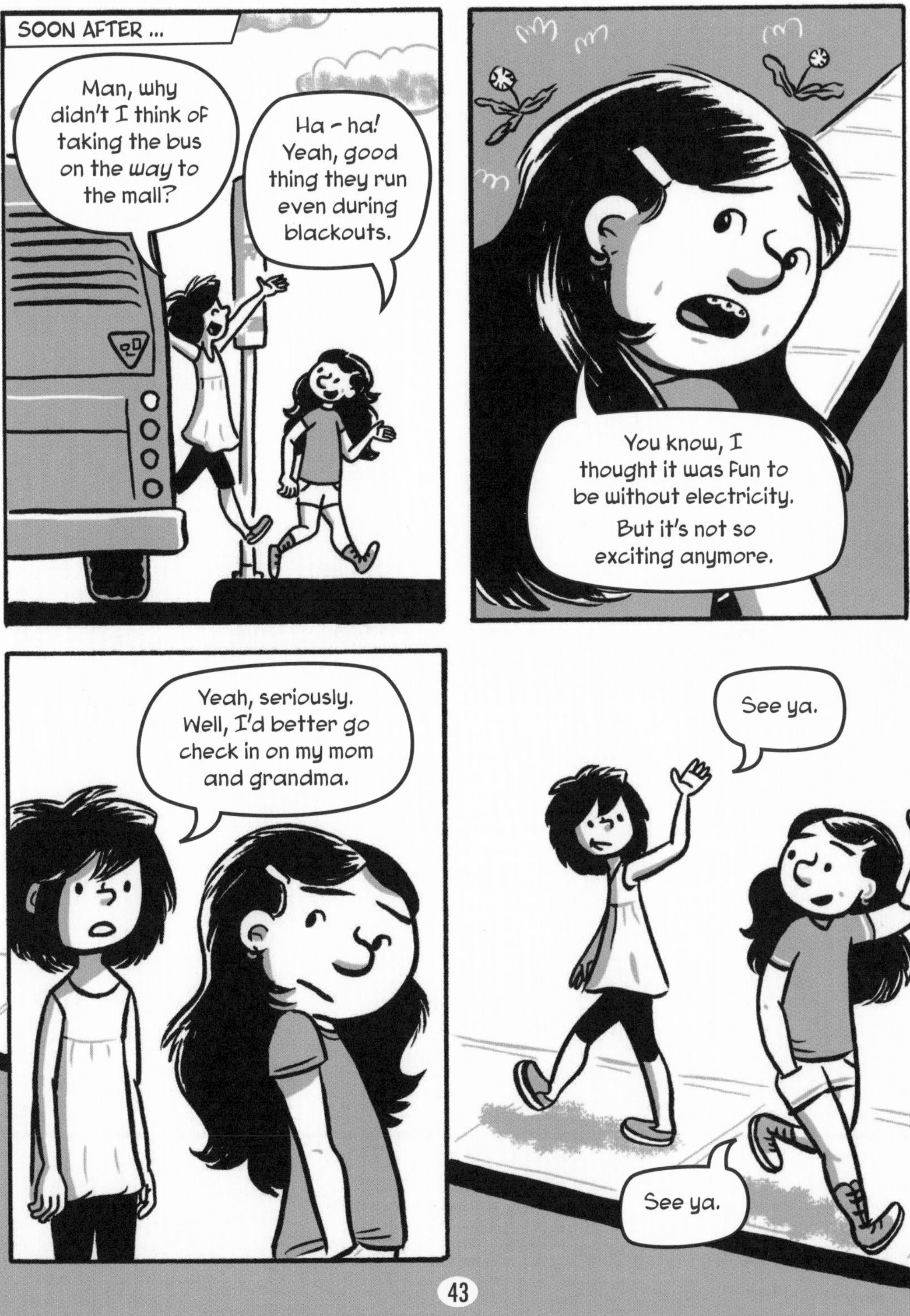
SOON AFTER ...
Man, why didn't I think of taking the bus on the way to the mall?
Ha - ha! Yeah, good thing they run even during blackouts.
You know, I thought it was fun to be without electricity. But it's not so exciting anymore.
Yeah, seriously. Well, I'd better go check in on my mom and grandma.
See ya.
See ya.

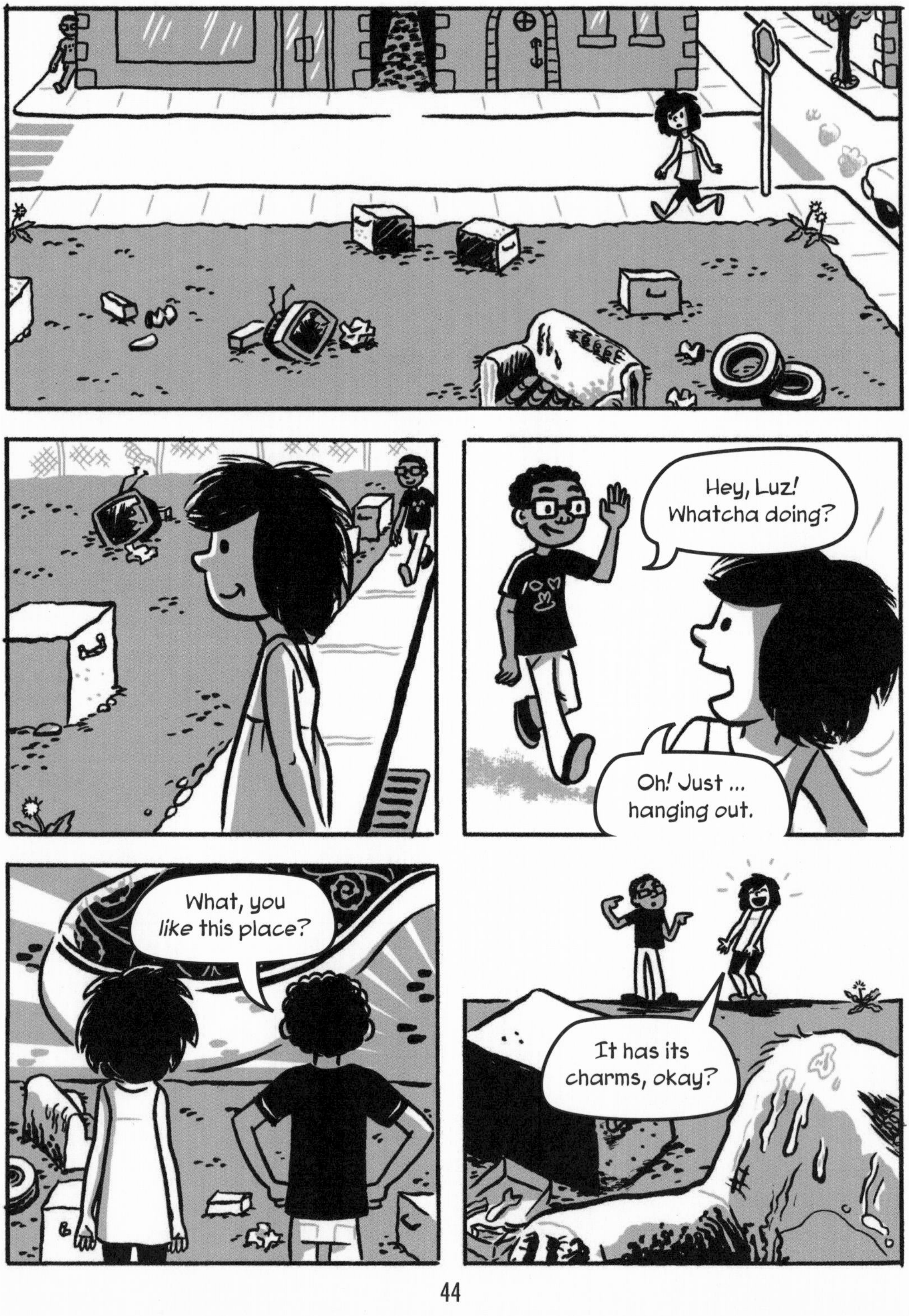
Hey, Luz! Whatcha doing?
Oh! Just ... hanging out.
What, you like this place?
It has its charms, okay?

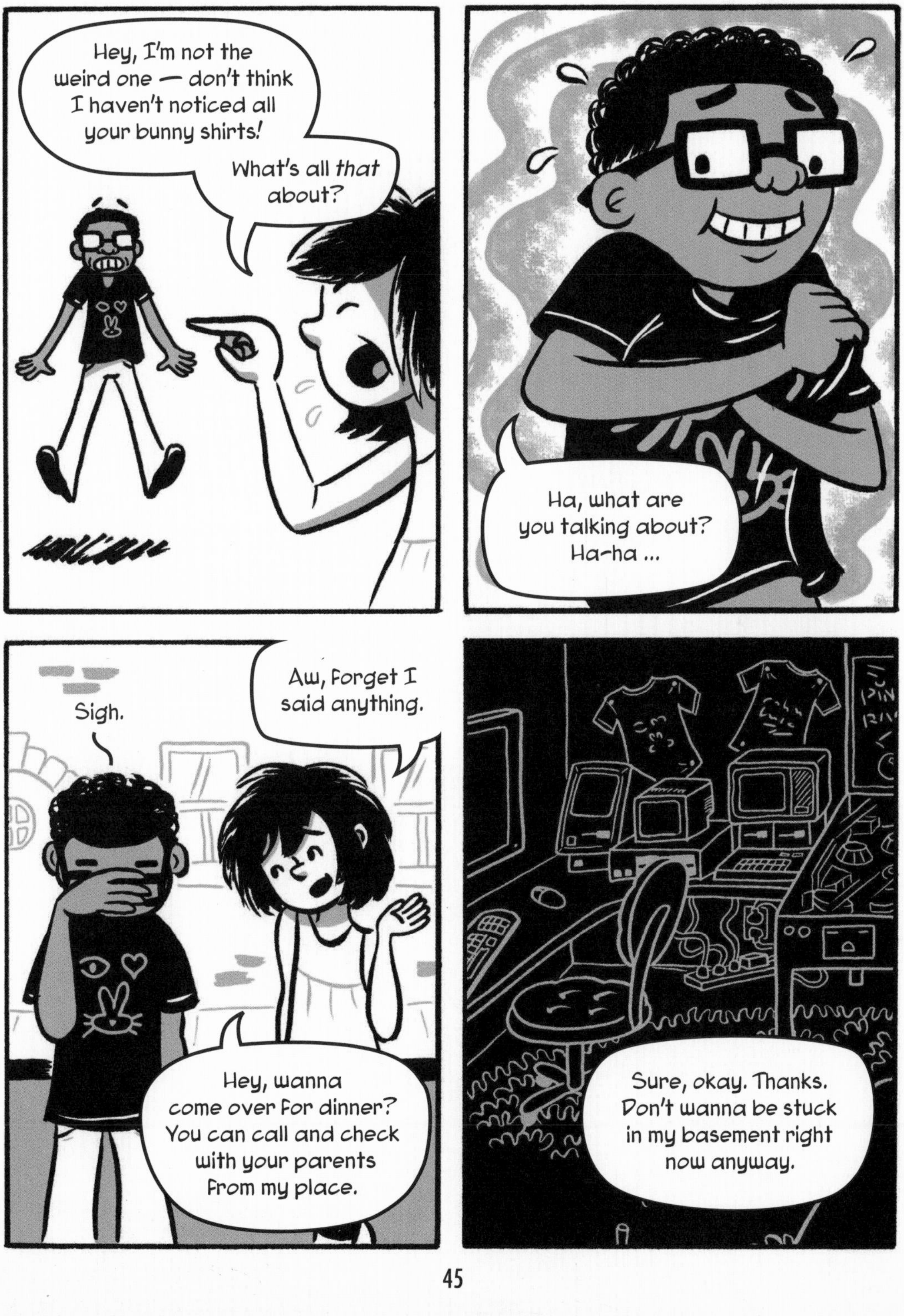

Hey, I'm not the weird one — don't think I haven't noticed all your bunny shirts!
What's all *that* about?
Ha, what are you talking about? Ha-ha ...
Aw, forget I said anything.
Sigh.
Hey, wanna come over for dinner? You can call and check with your parents from my place.
Sure, okay. Thanks. Don't wanna be stuck in my basement right now anyway.

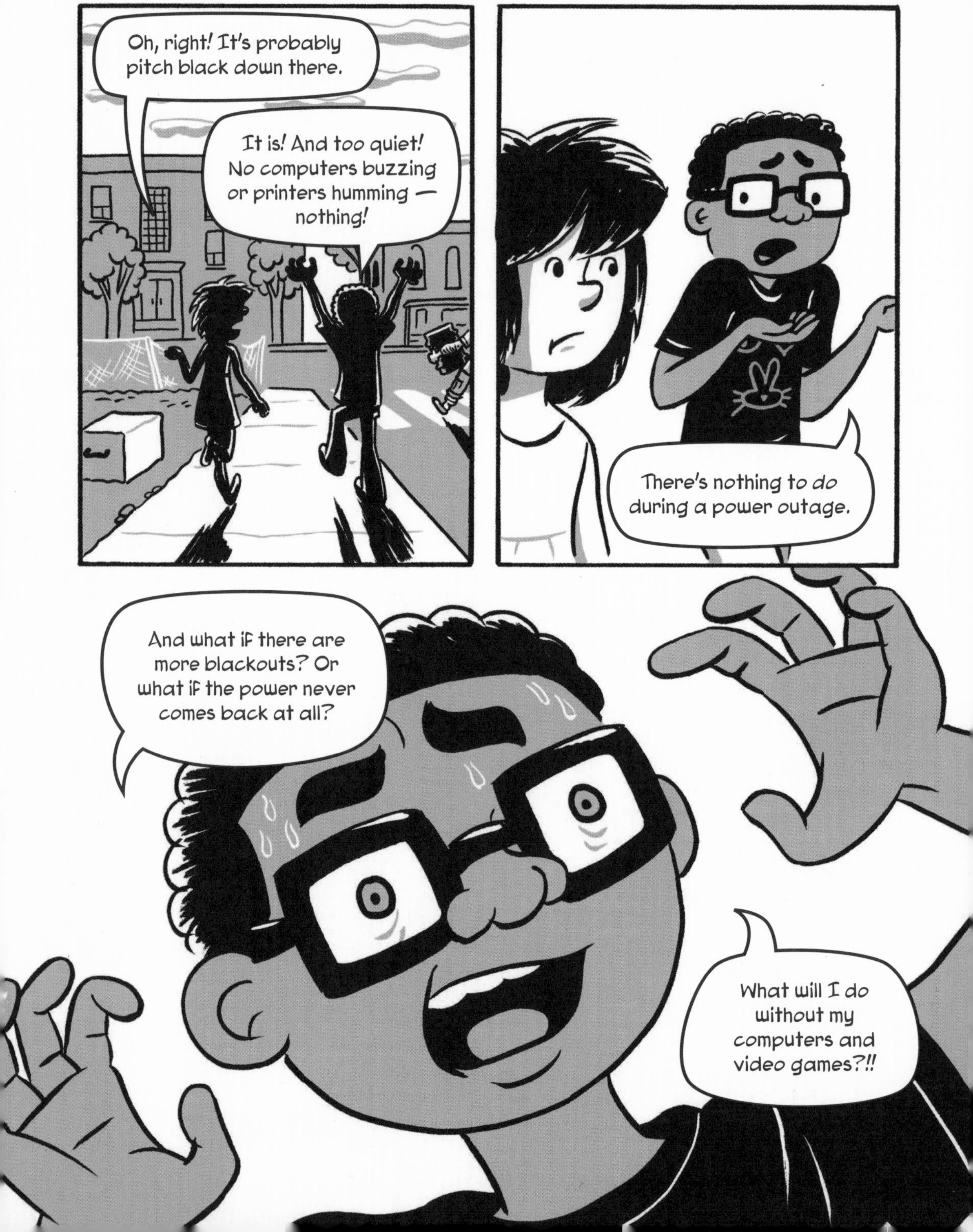
Oh, right! It's probably pitch black down there.
It is! And too quiet! No computers buzzing or printers humming — nothing!
There's nothing to do during a power outage.
And what if there are more blackouts? Or what if the power never comes back at all?
What will I do without my computers and video games?!!

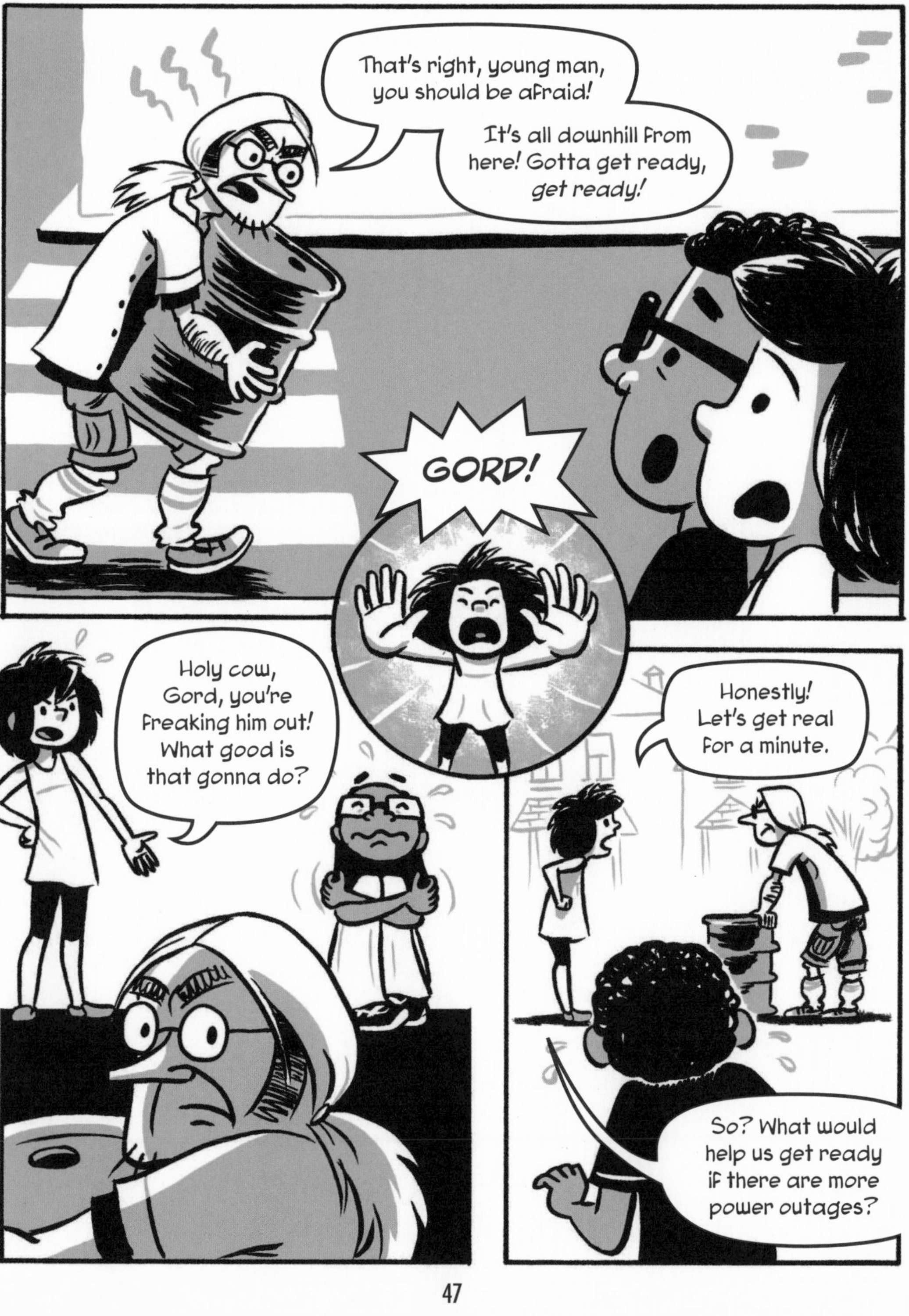
That's right, young man, you should be afraid!
It's all downhill from here! Gotta get ready, get ready!
GORD!
Holy cow, Gord, you're freaking him out! What good is that gonna do?
Honestly! Let's get real for a minute.
So? What would help us get ready if there are more power outages?

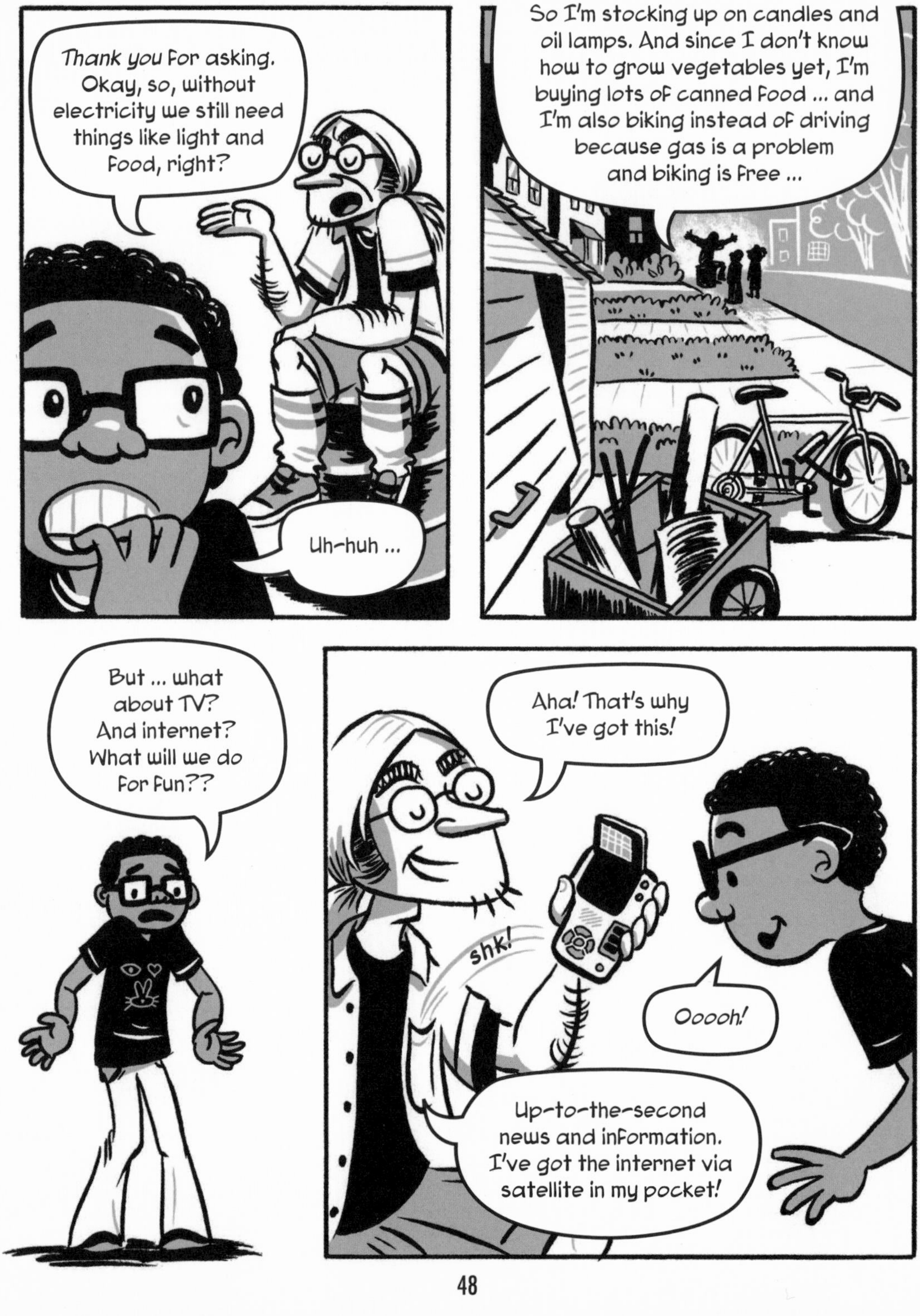

Thank you for asking. Okay, so, without electricity we still need things like light and food, right?
Uh-huh ...
So I'm stocking up on candles and oil lamps. And since I don't know how to grow vegetables yet, I'm buying lots of canned food ... and I'm also biking instead of driving because gas is a problem and biking is free ...
But ... what about TV? And internet? What will we do for fun??
Aha! That's why I've got this!
shk!
Ooooh!
Up-to-the-second news and information. I've got the internet via satellite in my pocket!

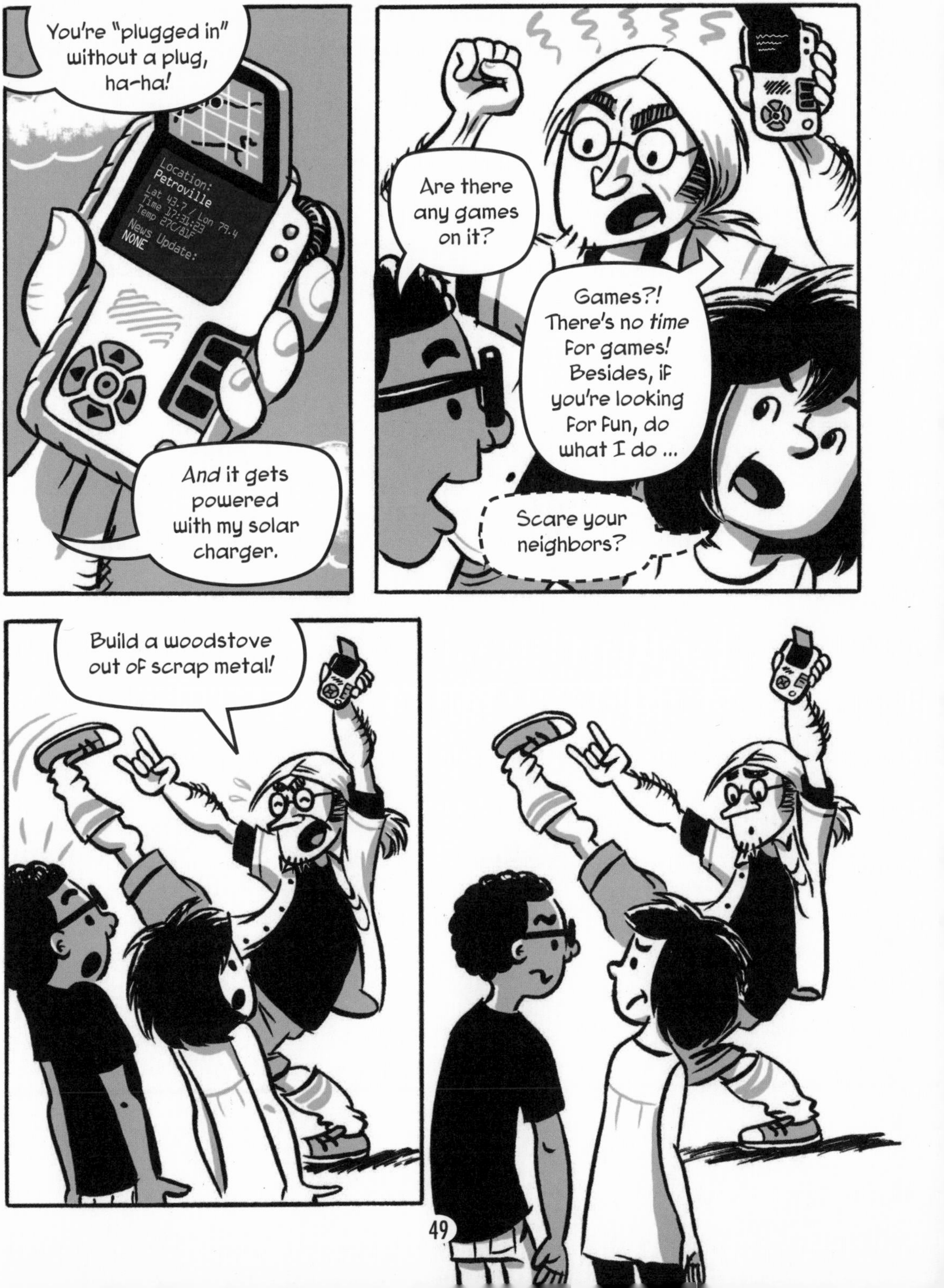
You're "plugged in" without a plug, ha-ha!
Location: Petroville
Lat 43.7 / Lon 79.4
Time 17:31:23
Temp 27C/81F
News Update:
NONE
And it gets powered with my solar charger.
Are there any games on it?
Games?! There's no *time* for games! Besides, if you're looking for fun, do what I do ...
Scare your neighbors?
Build a woodstove out of scrap metal!

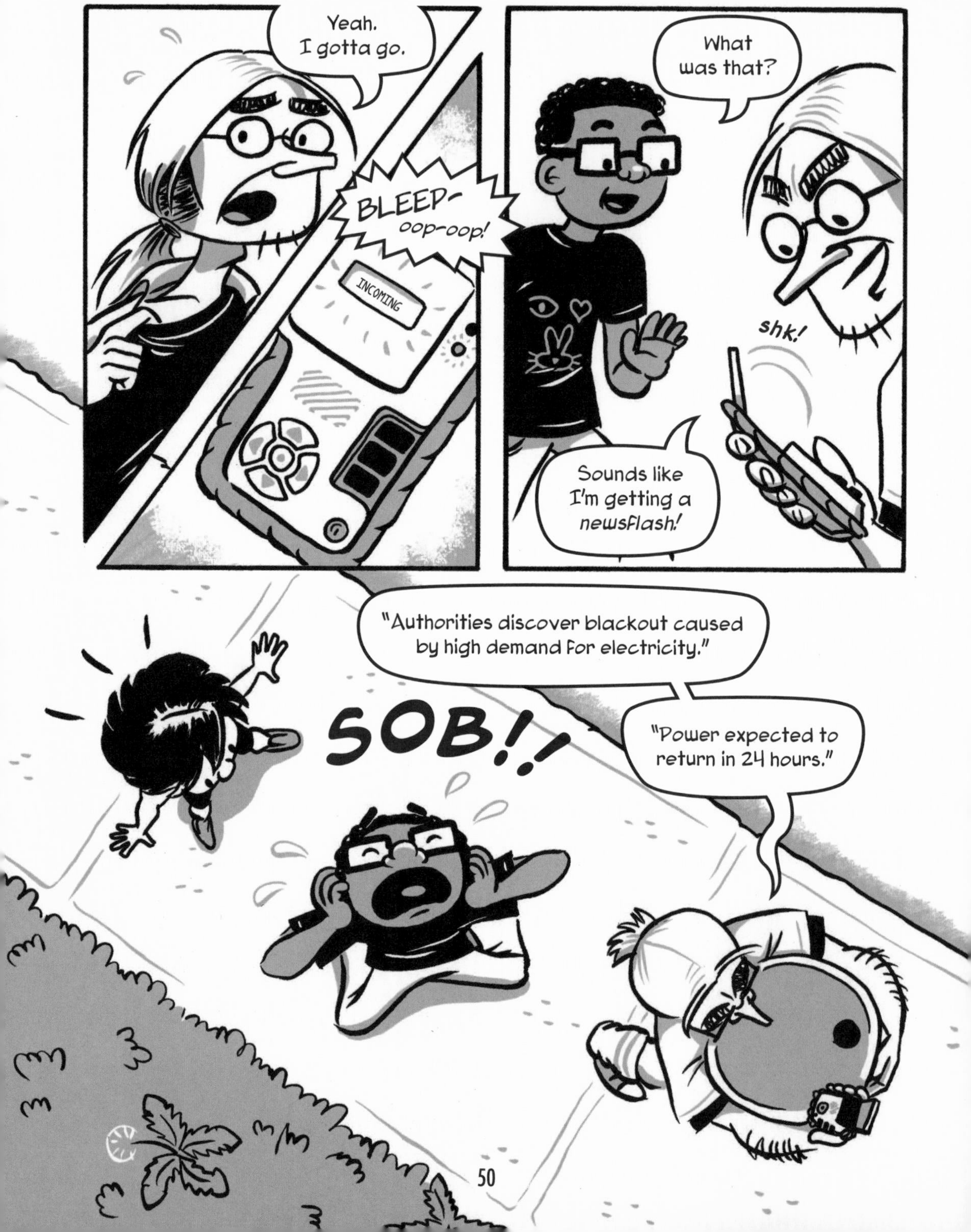
Yeah. I gotta go.
BLEEP-oop-oop!
INCOMING
What was that?
shk!
Sounds like I'm getting a *newsflash!*
"Authorities discover blackout caused by high demand for electricity."
SOB!!
"Power expected to return in 24 hours."

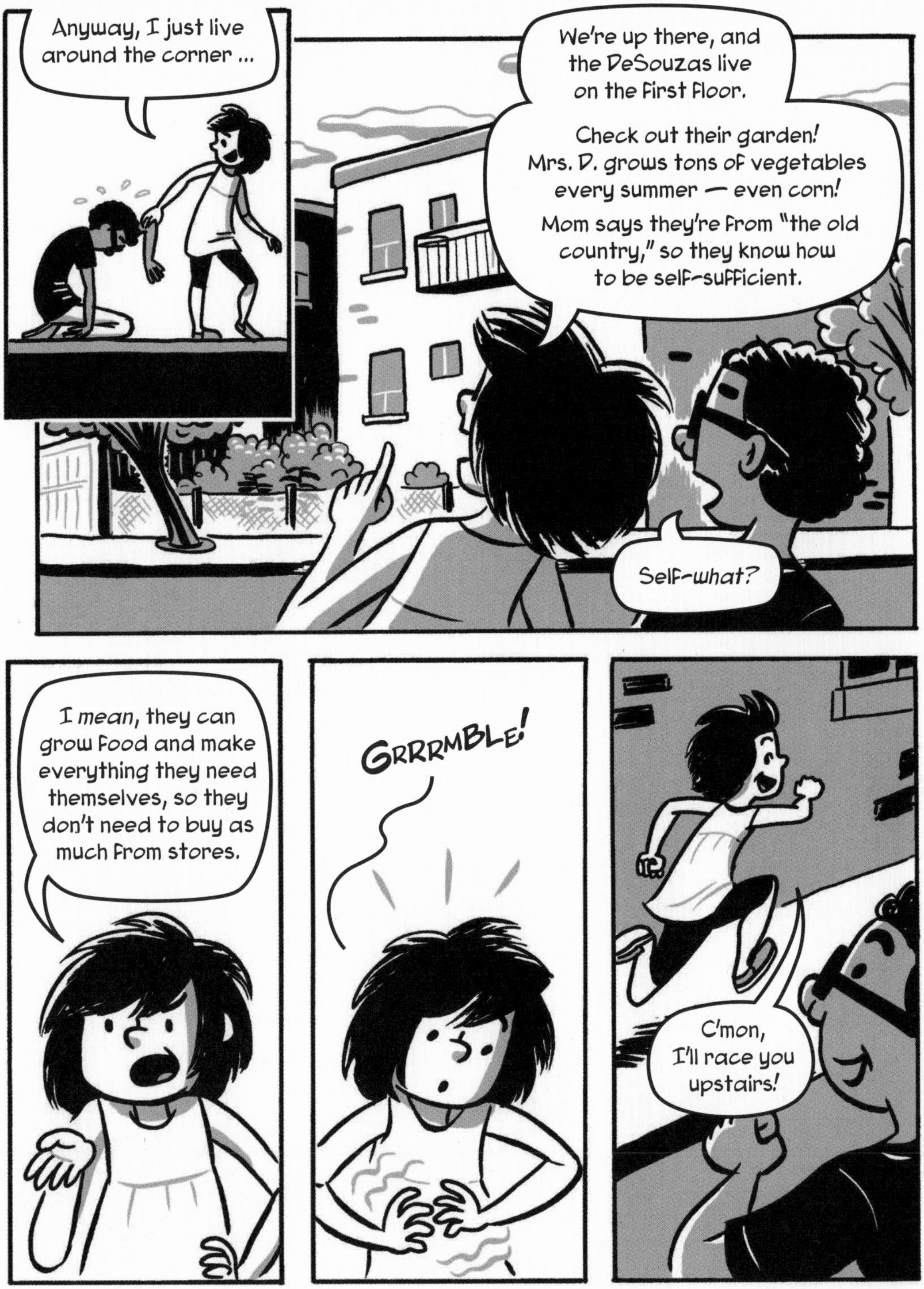

Anyway, I just live around the corner ...
We're up there, and the DeSouzas live on the first floor.
Check out their garden! Mrs. D. grows tons of vegetables every summer — even corn!
Mom says they're from "the old country," so they know how to be self-sufficient.
Self-what?
I *mean*, they can grow food and make everything they need themselves, so they don't need to buy as much from stores.
GRRRMBLE!
C'mon, I'll race you upstairs!

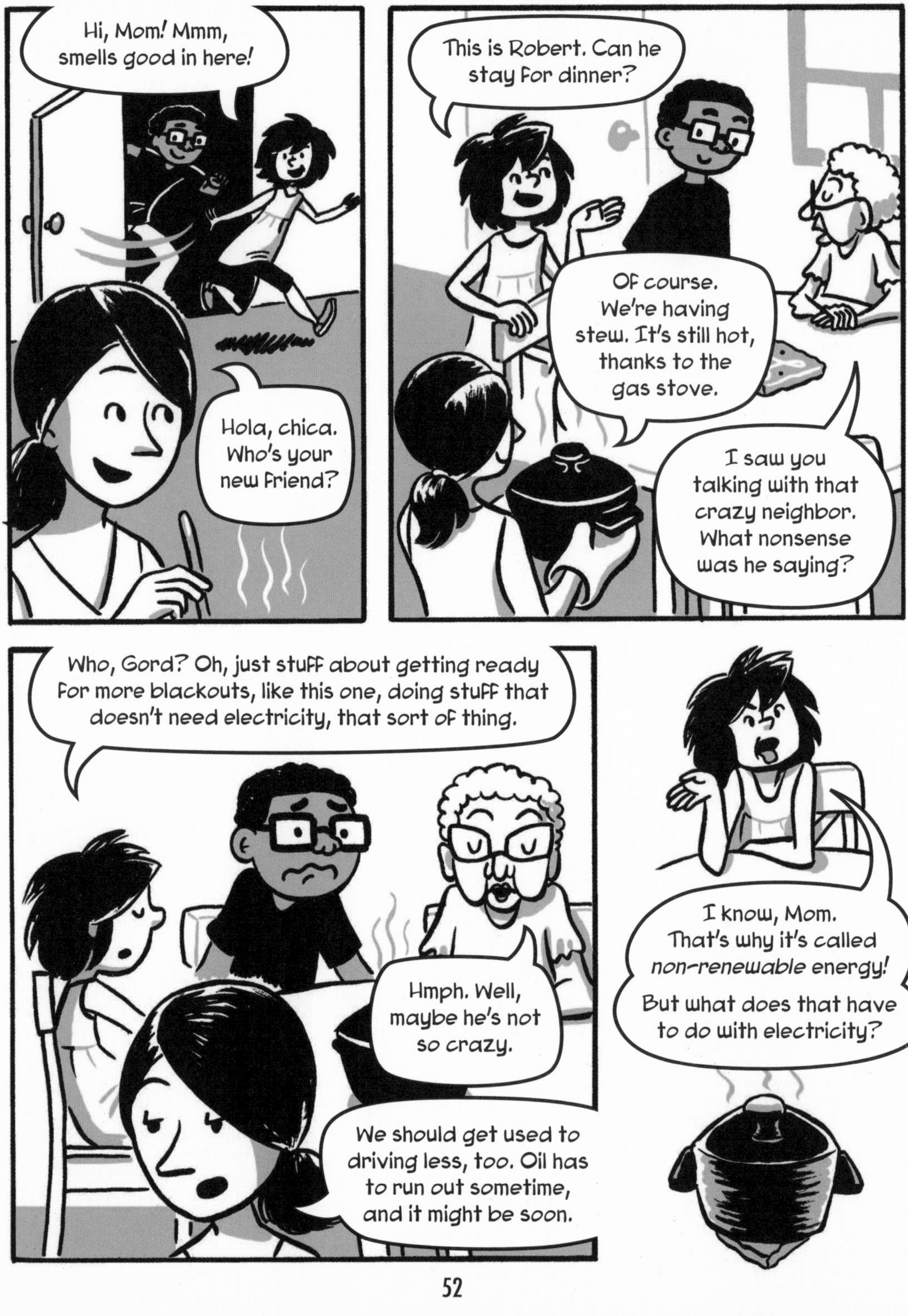
Hi, Mom! Mmm, smells good in here!
Hola, chica. Who's your new friend?
This is Robert. Can he stay for dinner?
Of course. We're having stew. It's still hot, thanks to the gas stove.
I saw you talking with that crazy neighbor. What nonsense was he saying?
Who, Gord? Oh, just stuff about getting ready for more blackouts, like this one, doing stuff that doesn't need electricity, that sort of thing.
Hmph. Well, maybe he's not so crazy.
We should get used to driving less, too. Oil has to run out sometime, and it might be soon.
I know, Mom. That's why it's called *non-renewable* energy!
But what does that have to do with electricity?

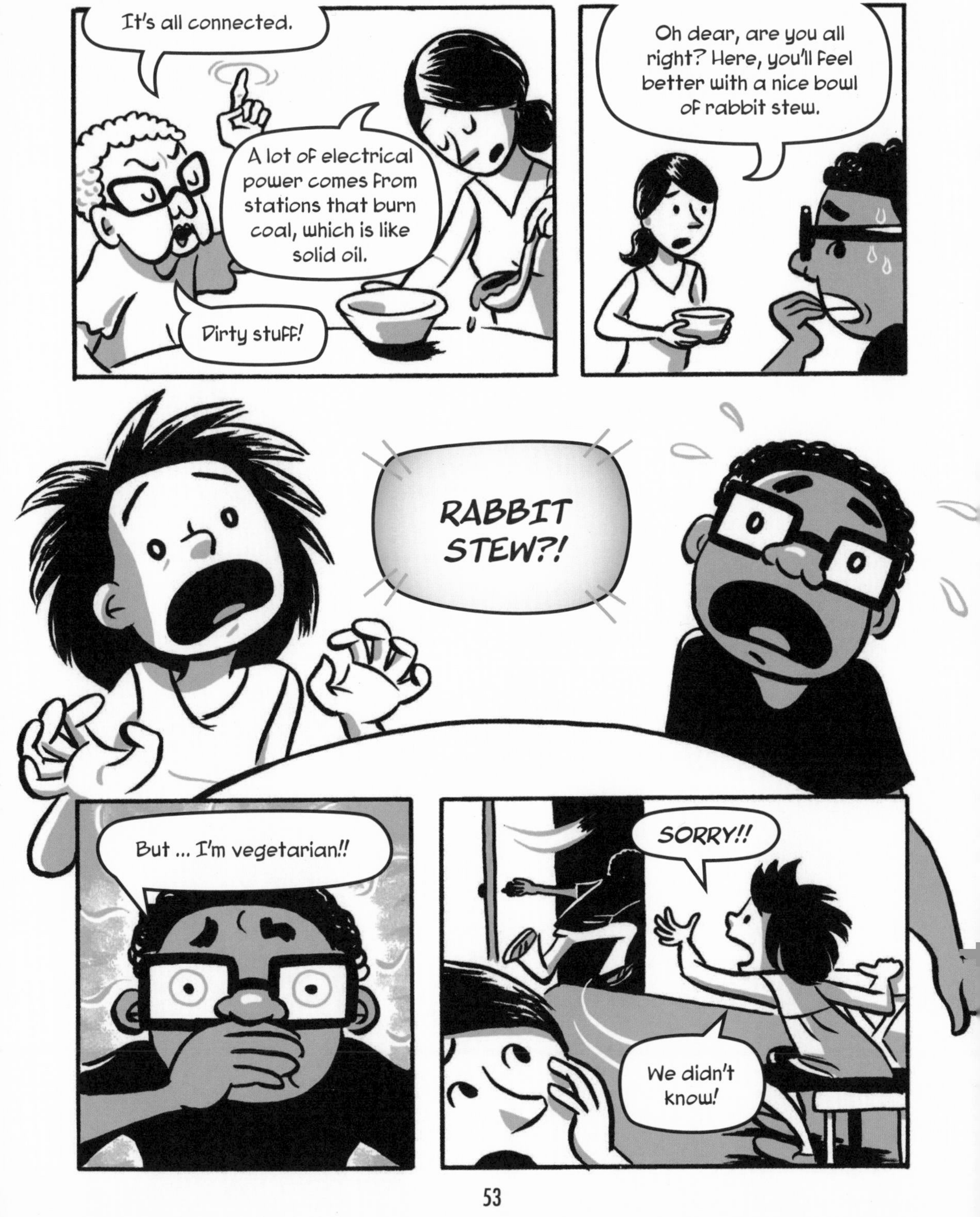
It's all connected.
A lot of electrical power comes from stations that burn coal, which is like solid oil.
Dirty stuff!
Oh dear, are you all right? Here, you'll feel better with a nice bowl of rabbit stew.
RABBIT STEW?!
But ... I'm vegetarian!!
SORRY!!
We didn't know!

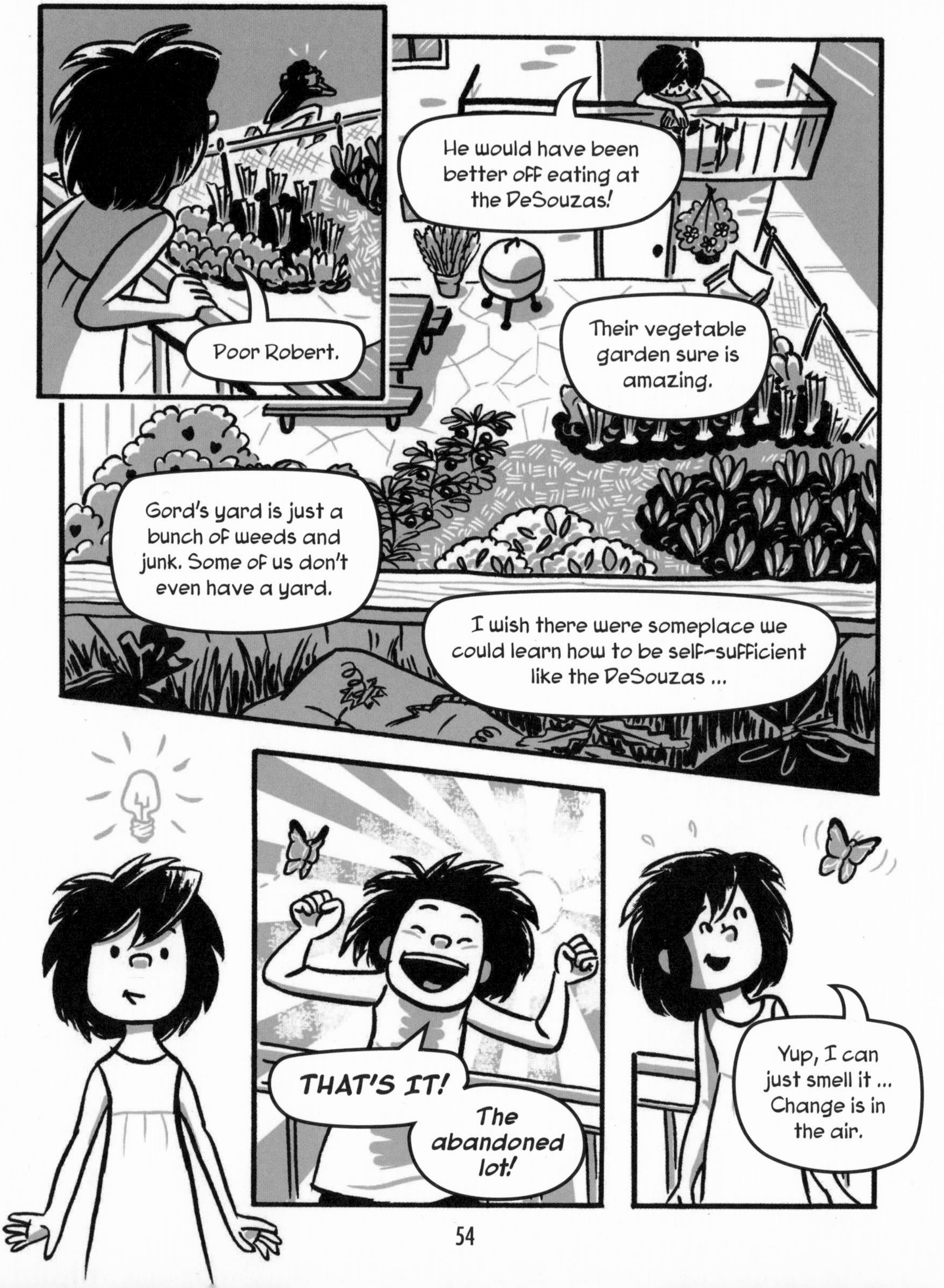
Poor Robert.
He would have been better off eating at the DeSouzas!
Their vegetable garden sure is amazing.
Gord's yard is just a bunch of weeds and junk. Some of us don't even have a yard.
I wish there were someplace we could learn how to be self-sufficient like the DeSouzas ...
THAT'S IT!
The abandoned lot!
Yup, I can just smell it ... Change is in the air.

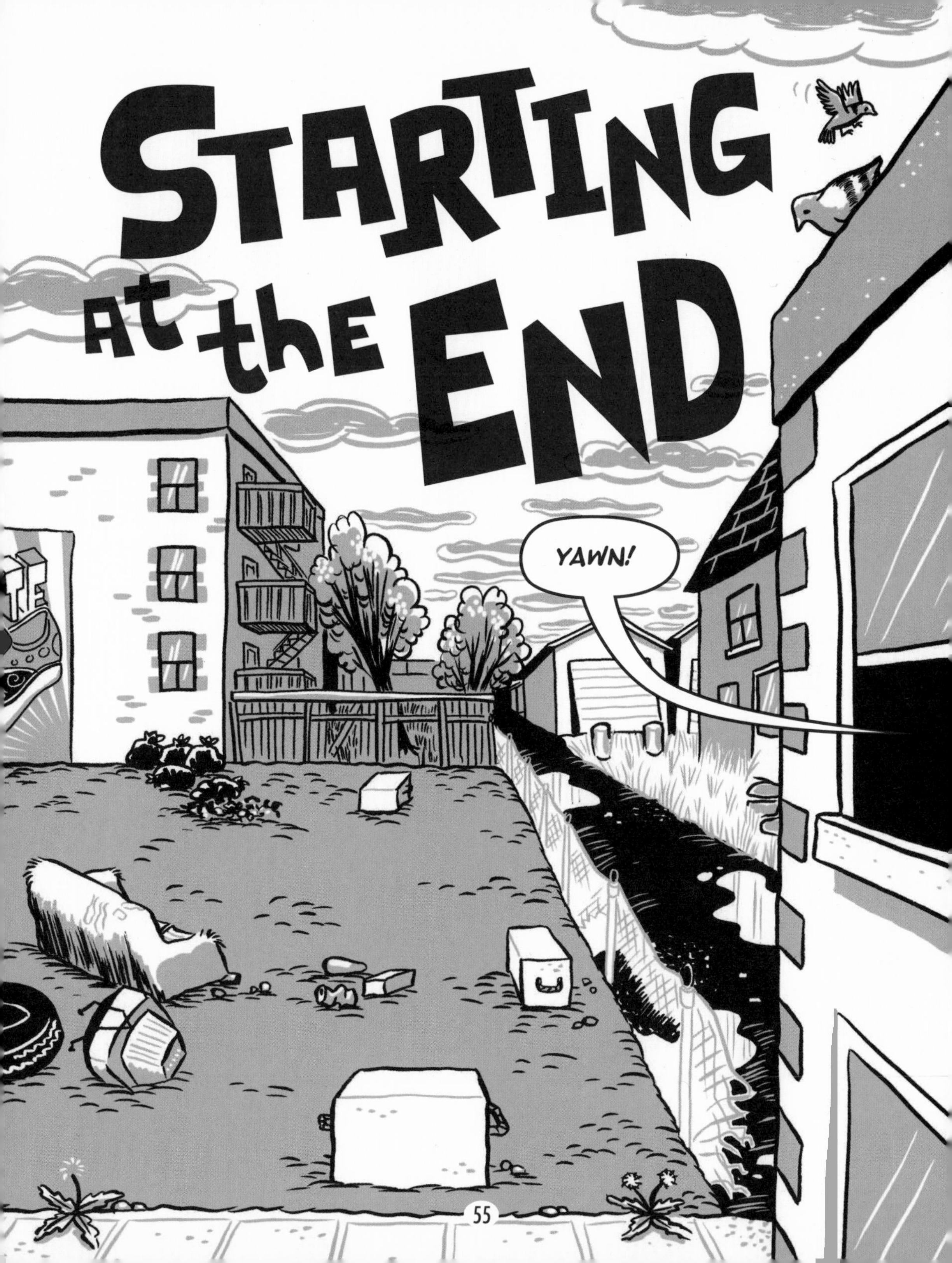
STARTING at the END
YAWN!

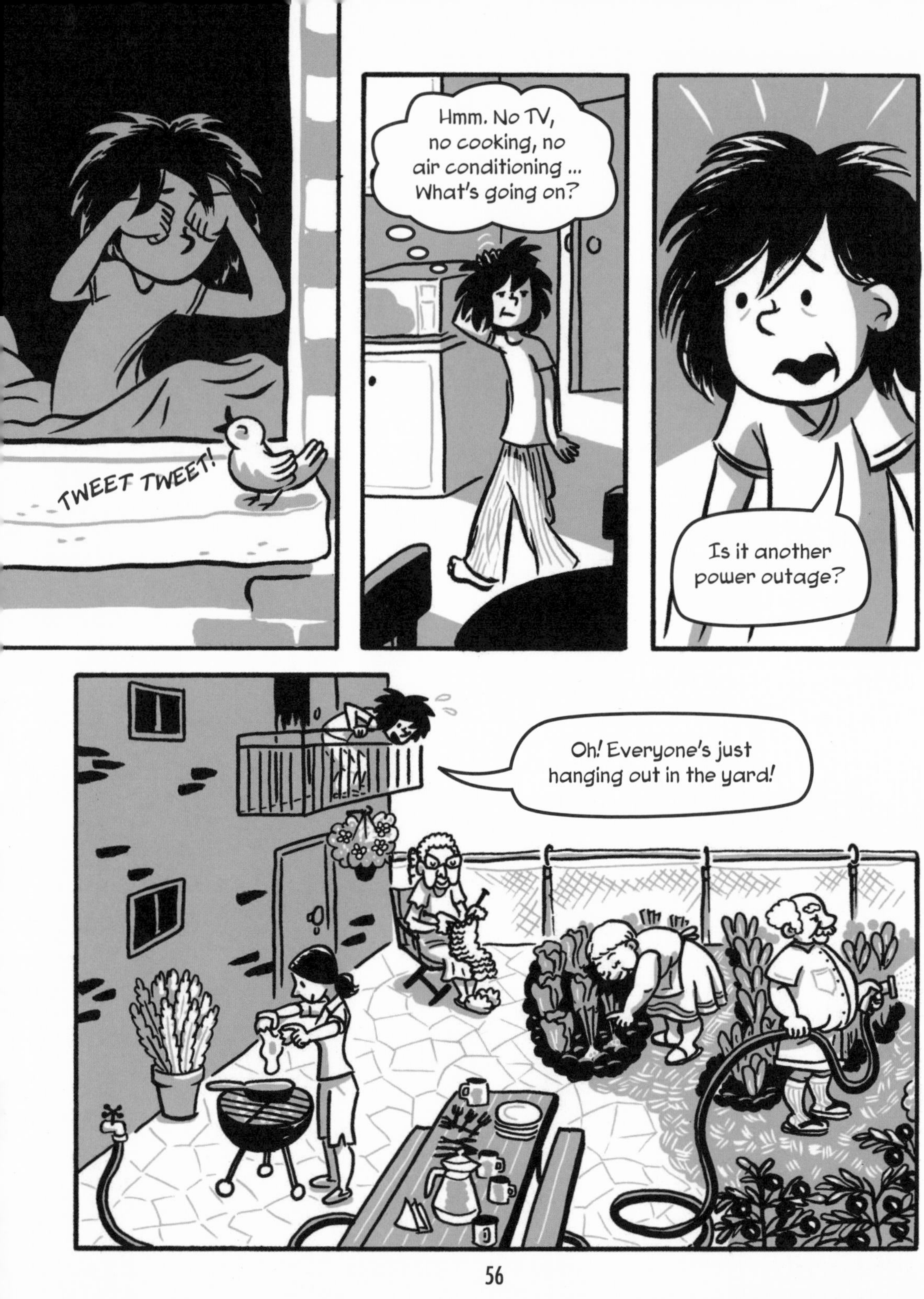
TWEET TWEET!
Hmm. No TV, no cooking, no air conditioning ... What's going on?
Is it another power outage?
Oh! Everyone's just hanging out in the yard!

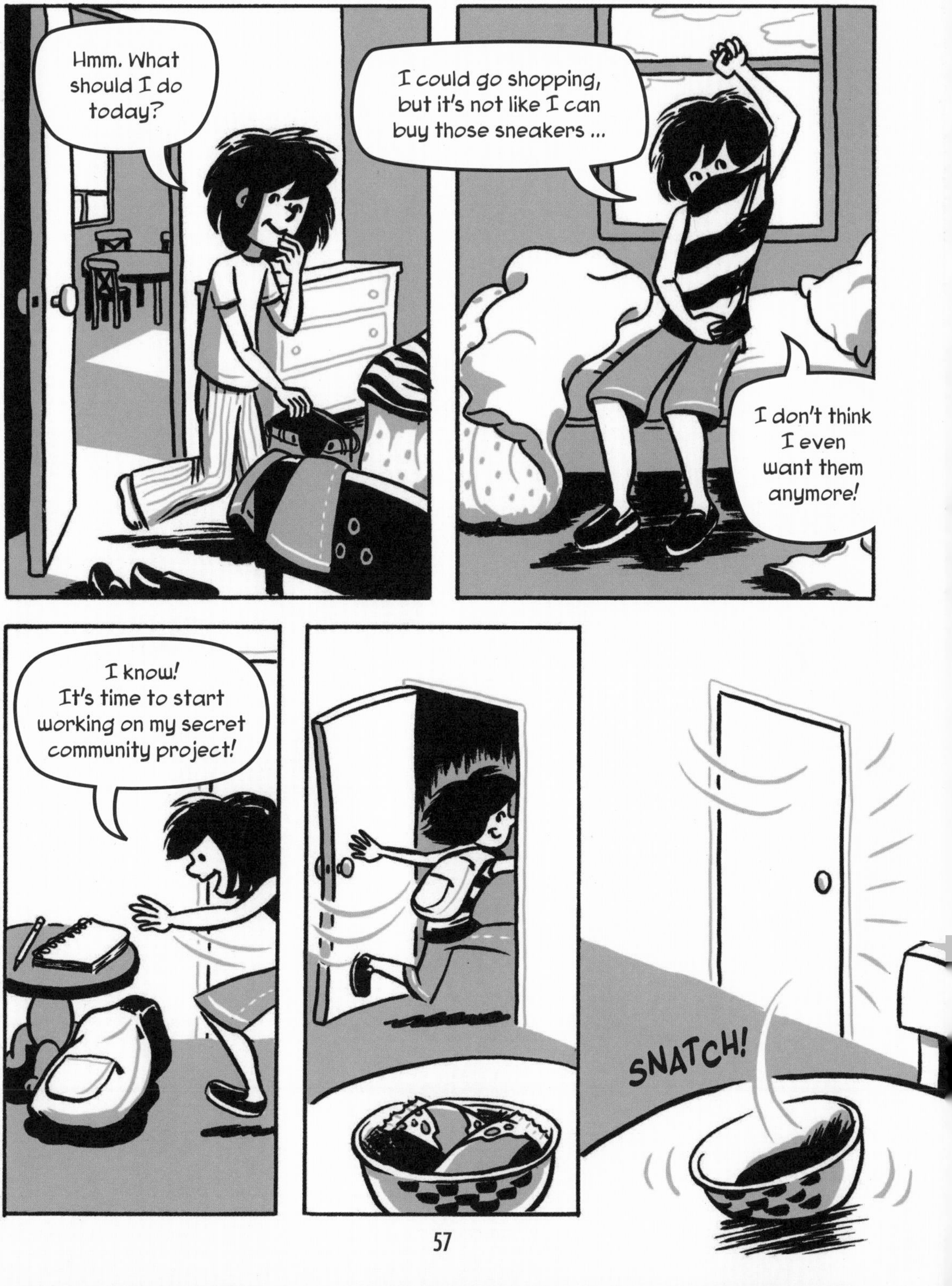
Hmm. What should I do today?
I could go shopping, but it's not like I can buy those sneakers ...
I don't think I even want them anymore!
I know! It's time to start working on my secret community project!
SNATCH!

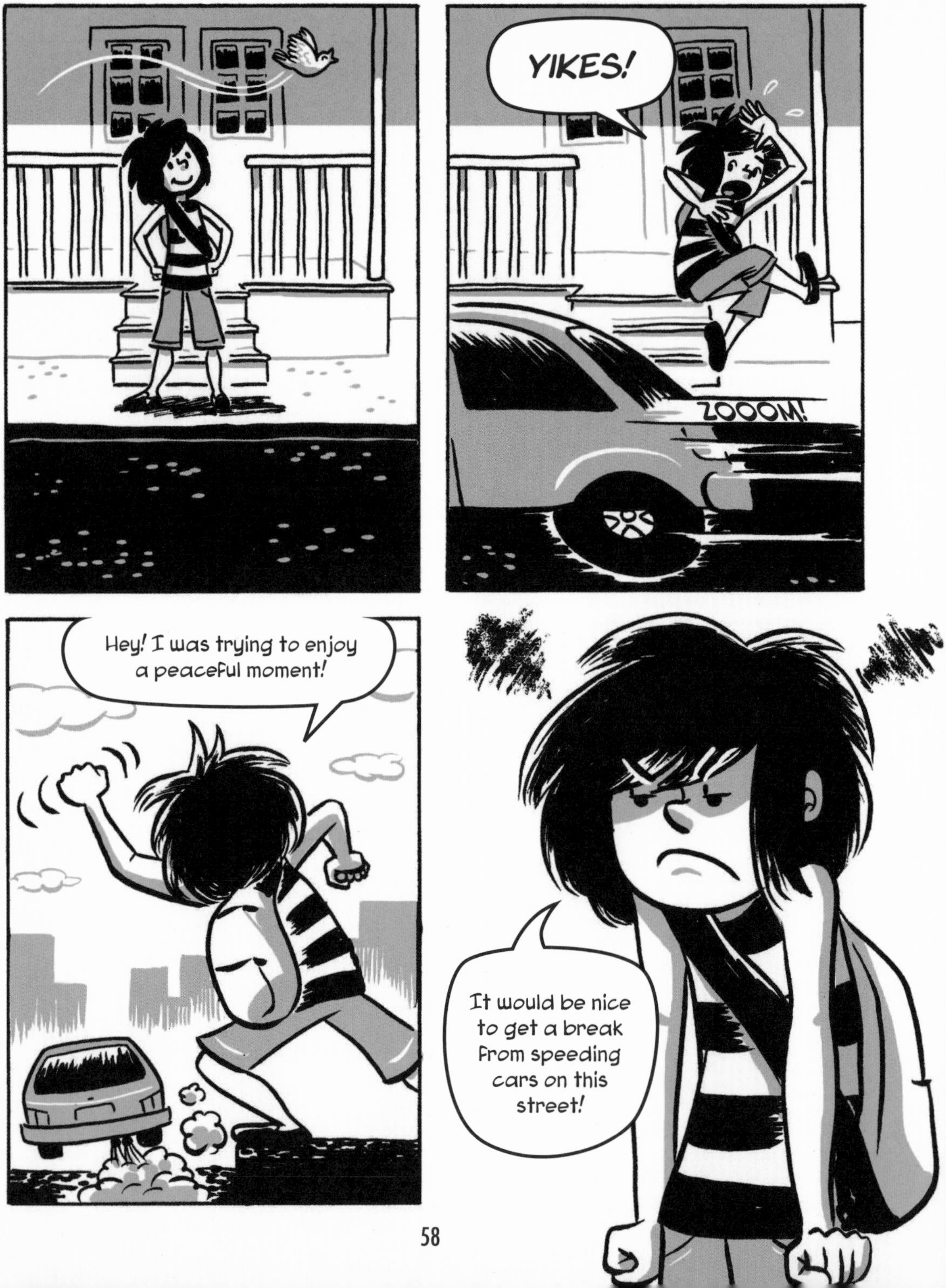
YIKES!
ZOOOM!
Hey! I was trying to enjoy a peaceful moment!
It would be nice to get a break from speeding cars on this street!

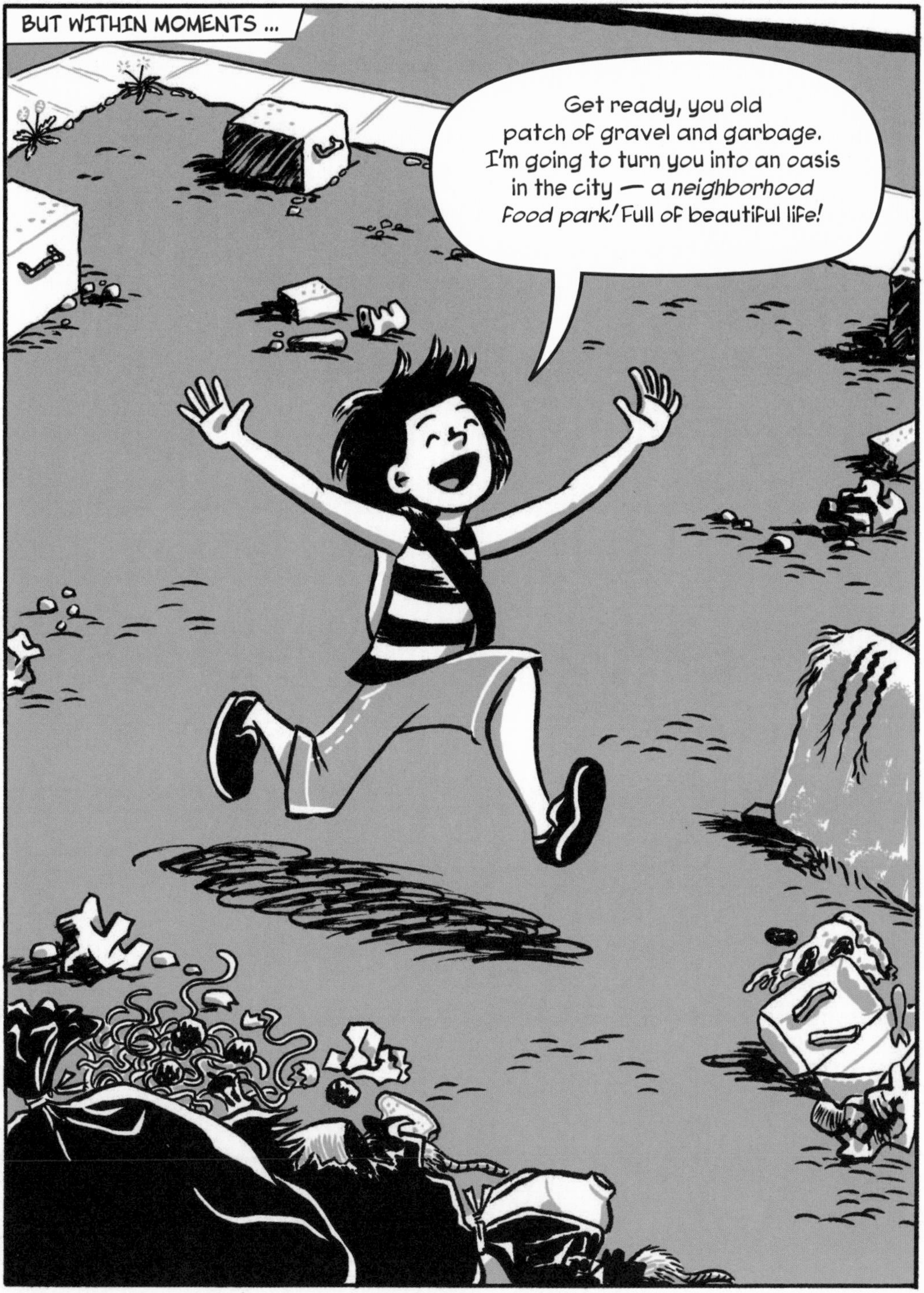
BUT WITHIN MOMENTS ...
Get ready, you old patch of gravel and garbage. I'm going to turn you into an oasis in the city — a *neighborhood food park!* Full of beautiful life!

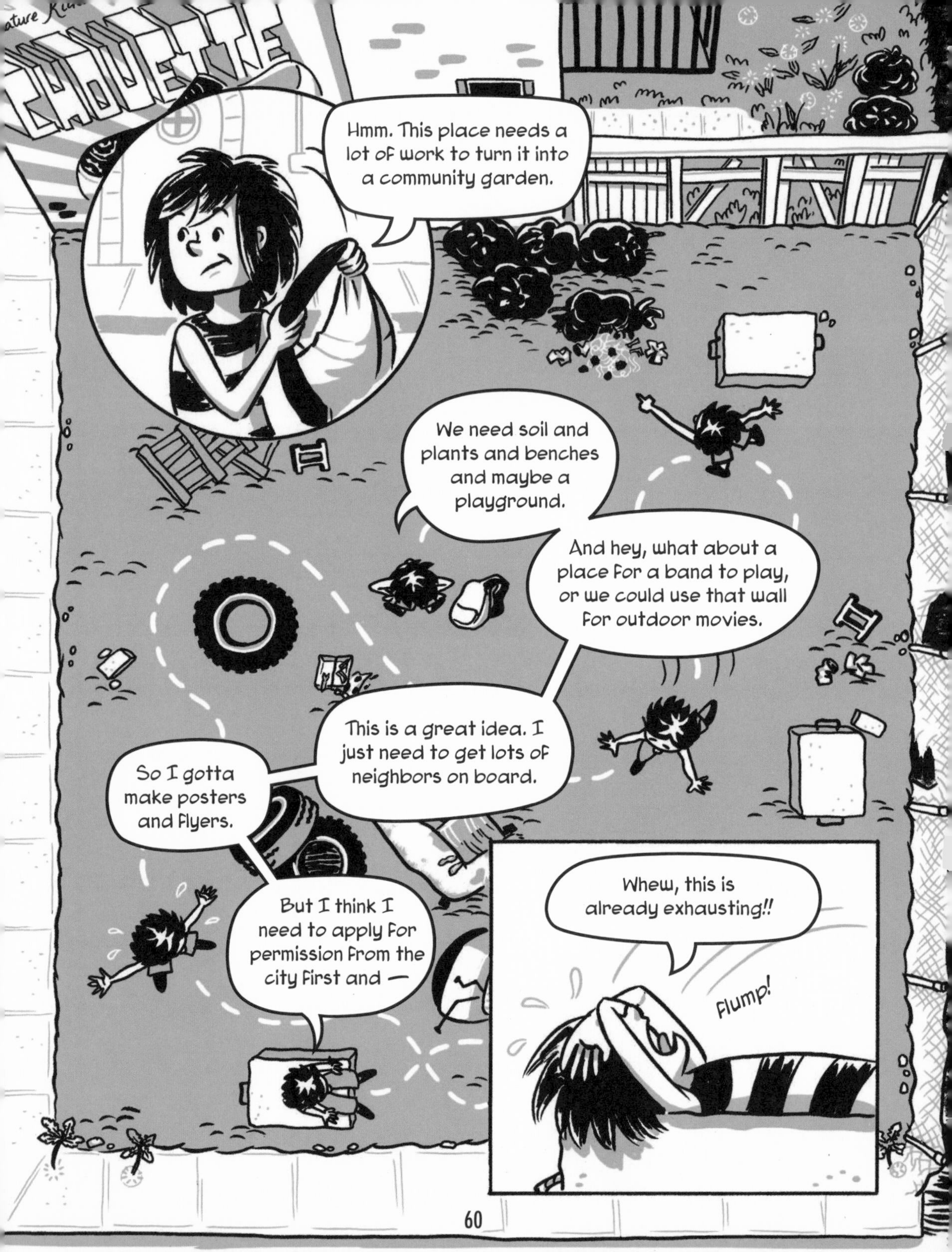
Hmm. This place needs a lot of work to turn it into a community garden.
We need soil and plants and benches and maybe a playground.
And hey, what about a place for a band to play, or we could use that wall for outdoor movies.
This is a great idea. I just need to get lots of neighbors on board.
So I gotta make posters and flyers.
But I think I need to apply for permission from the city first and —
Whew, this is already exhausting!!
Flump!

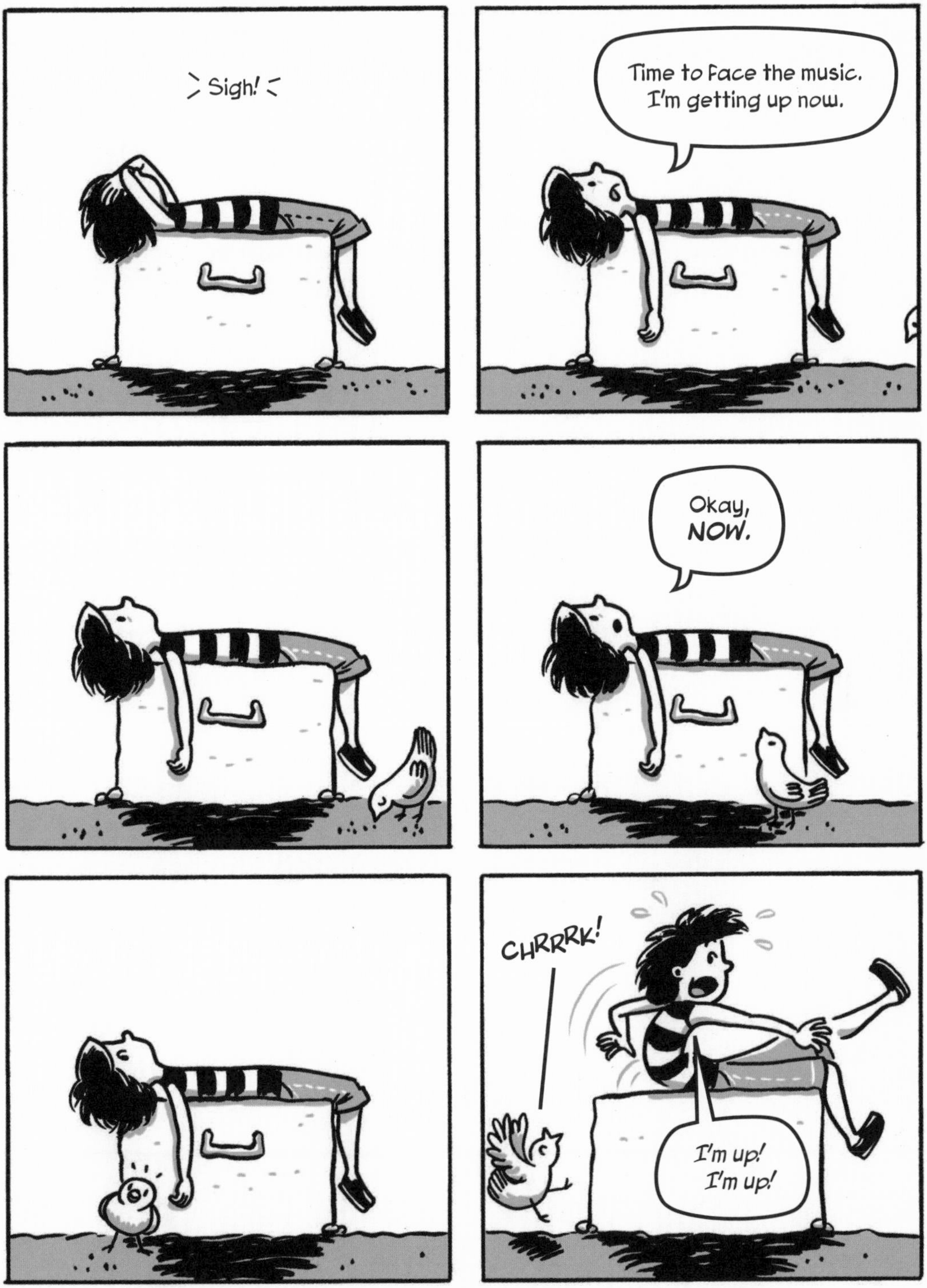
Sigh!
Time to face the music. I'm getting up now.
Okay, NOW.
CHRRRK!
I'm up! I'm up!

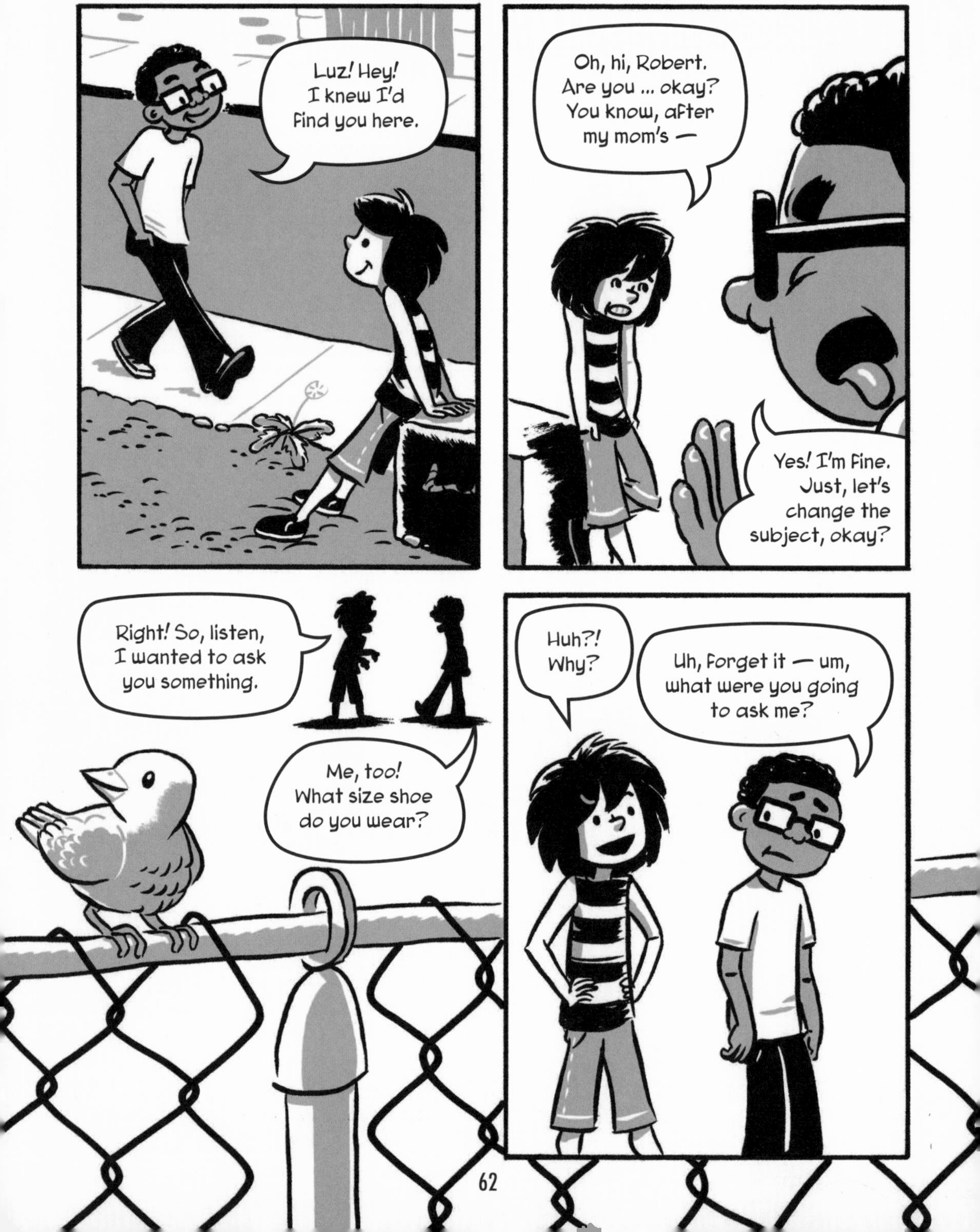
Luz! Hey! I knew I'd find you here.
Oh, hi, Robert. Are you ... okay? You know, after my mom's —
Yes! I'm fine. Just, let's change the subject, okay?
Right! So, listen, I wanted to ask you something.
Me, too! What size shoe do you wear?
Huh?! Why?
Uh, forget it — um, what were you going to ask me?

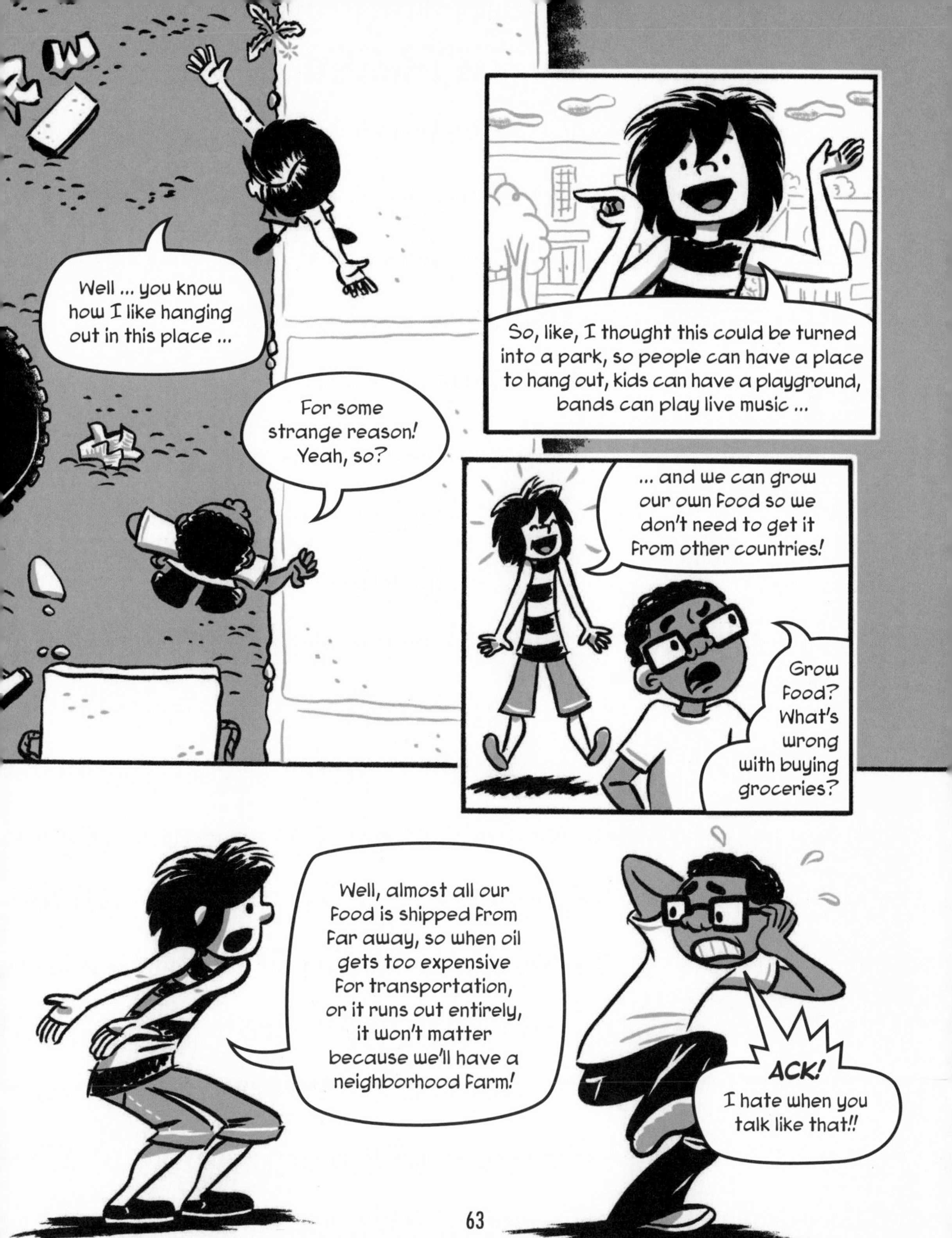

Well ... you know how I like hanging out in this place ...
For some strange reason! Yeah, so?
So, like, I thought this could be turned into a park, so people can have a place to hang out, kids can have a playground, bands can play live music ...
... and we can grow our own food so we don't need to get it from other countries!
Grow food? What's wrong with buying groceries?
Well, almost all our food is shipped from far away, so when oil gets too expensive for transportation, or it runs out entirely, it won't matter because we'll have a neighborhood farm!
ACK! I hate when you talk like that!!

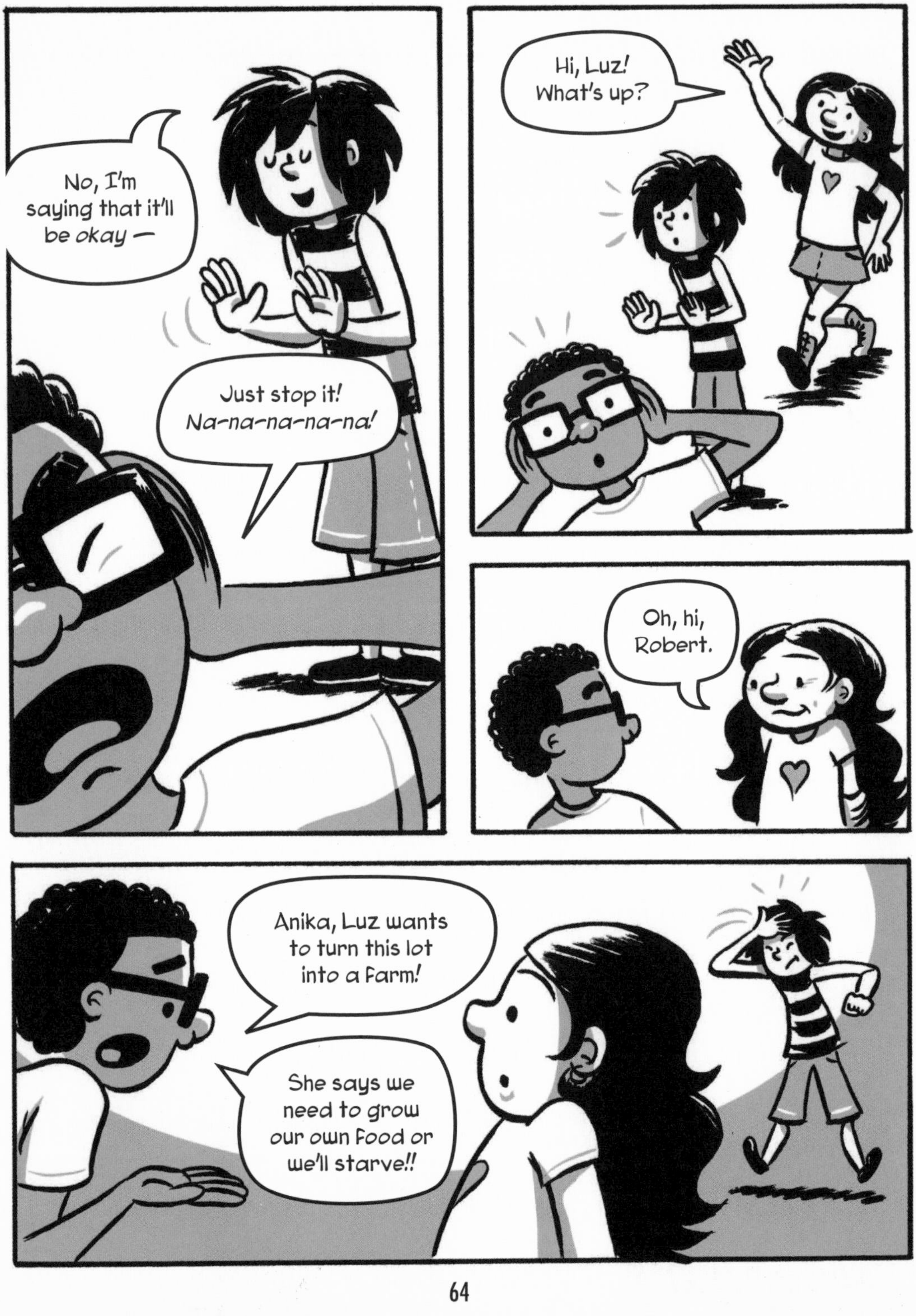
No, I'm saying that it'll be *okay* —
Just stop it! Na-na-na-na-na!
Hi, Luz! What's up?
Oh, hi, Robert.
Anika, Luz wants to turn this lot into a farm!
She says we need to grow our own food or we'll starve!!

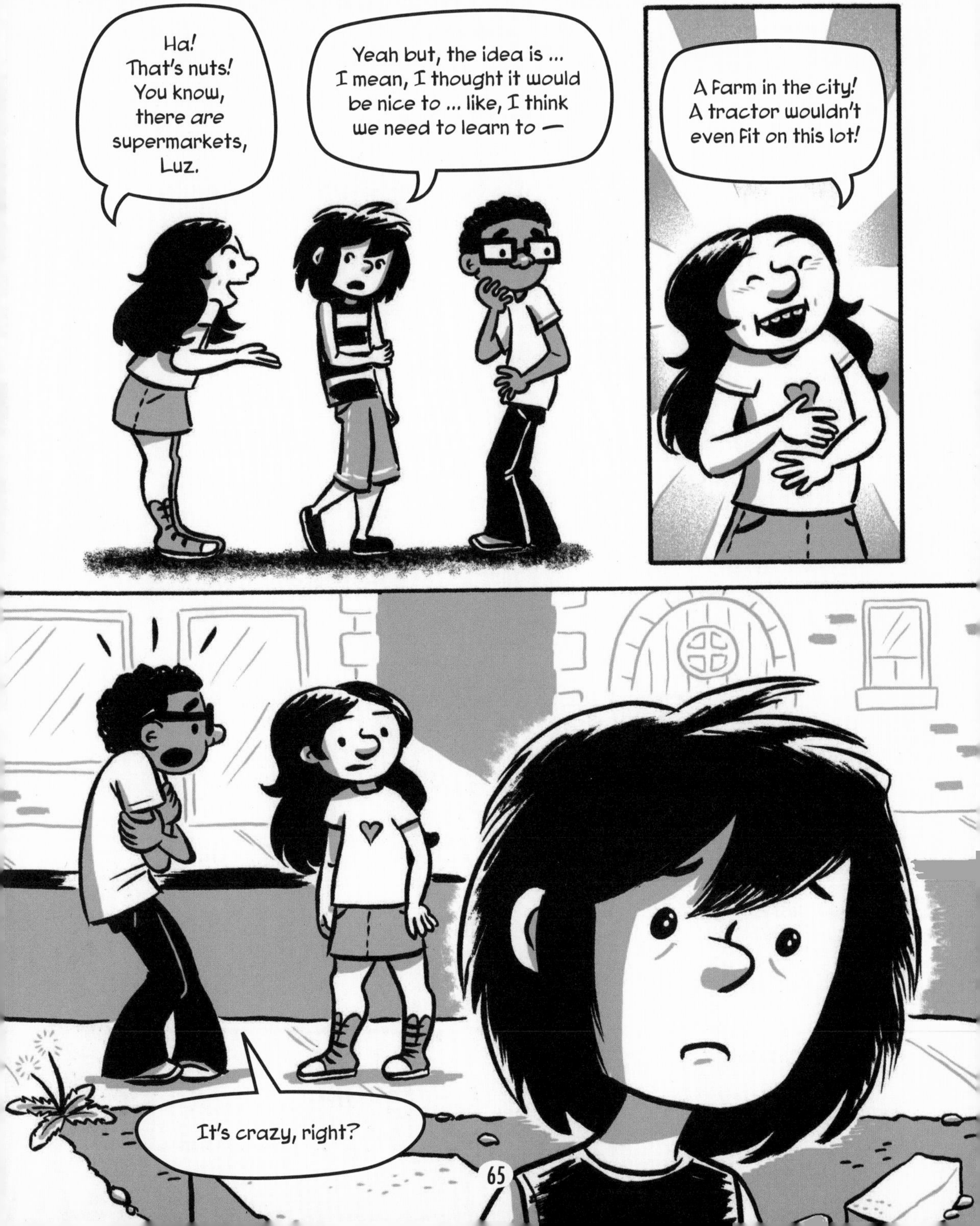
Ha! That's nuts! You know, there *are* supermarkets, Luz.
Yeah but, the idea is ... I mean, I thought it would be nice to ... like, I think we need to learn to —
A farm in the city! A tractor wouldn't even fit on this lot!
It's crazy, right?

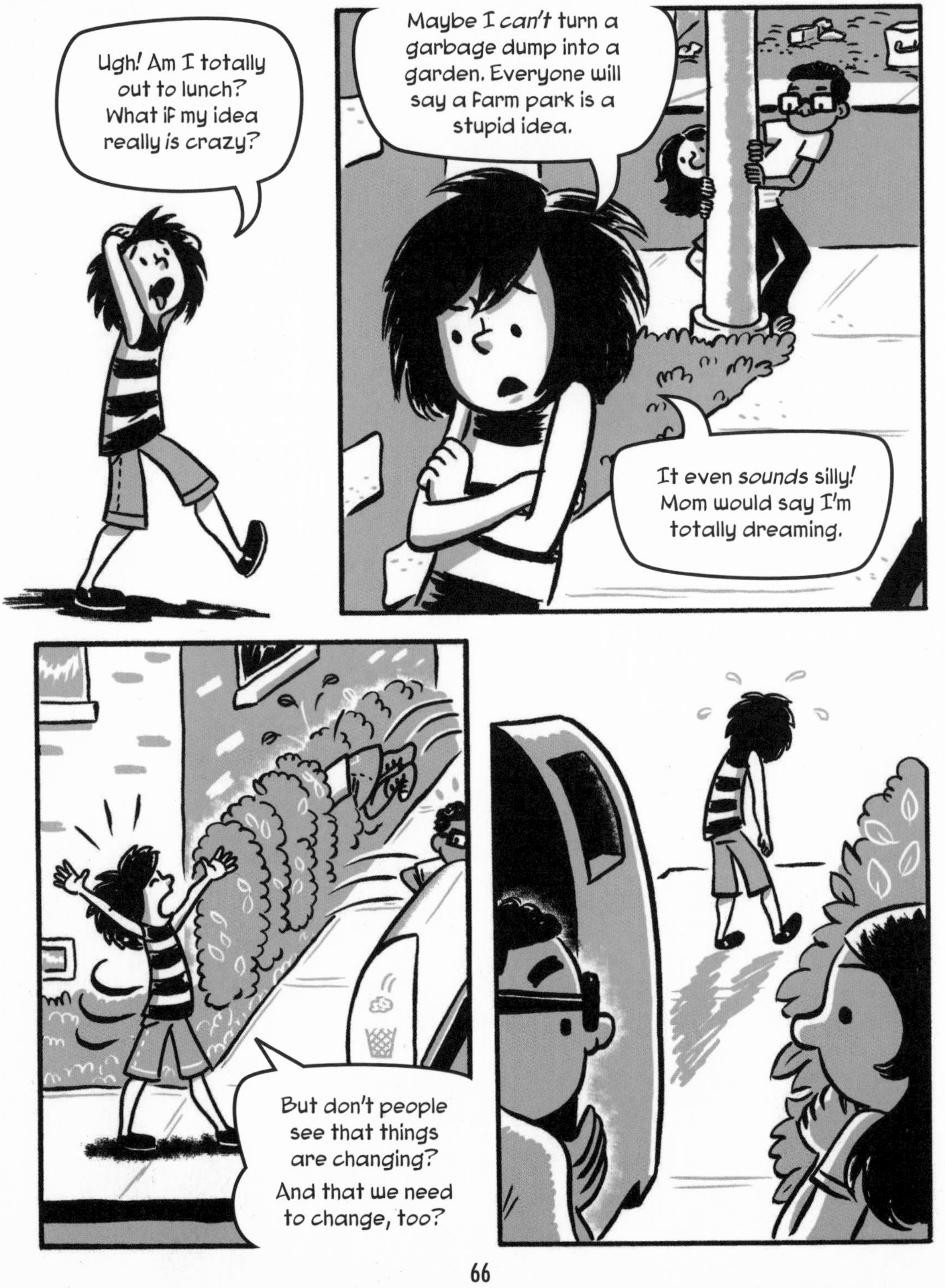
Ugh! Am I totally out to lunch? What if my idea really *is* crazy?
Maybe I *can't* turn a garbage dump into a garden. Everyone will say a farm park is a stupid idea.
It even *sounds* silly! Mom would say I'm totally dreaming.
But don't people see that things are changing?
And that we need to change, too?

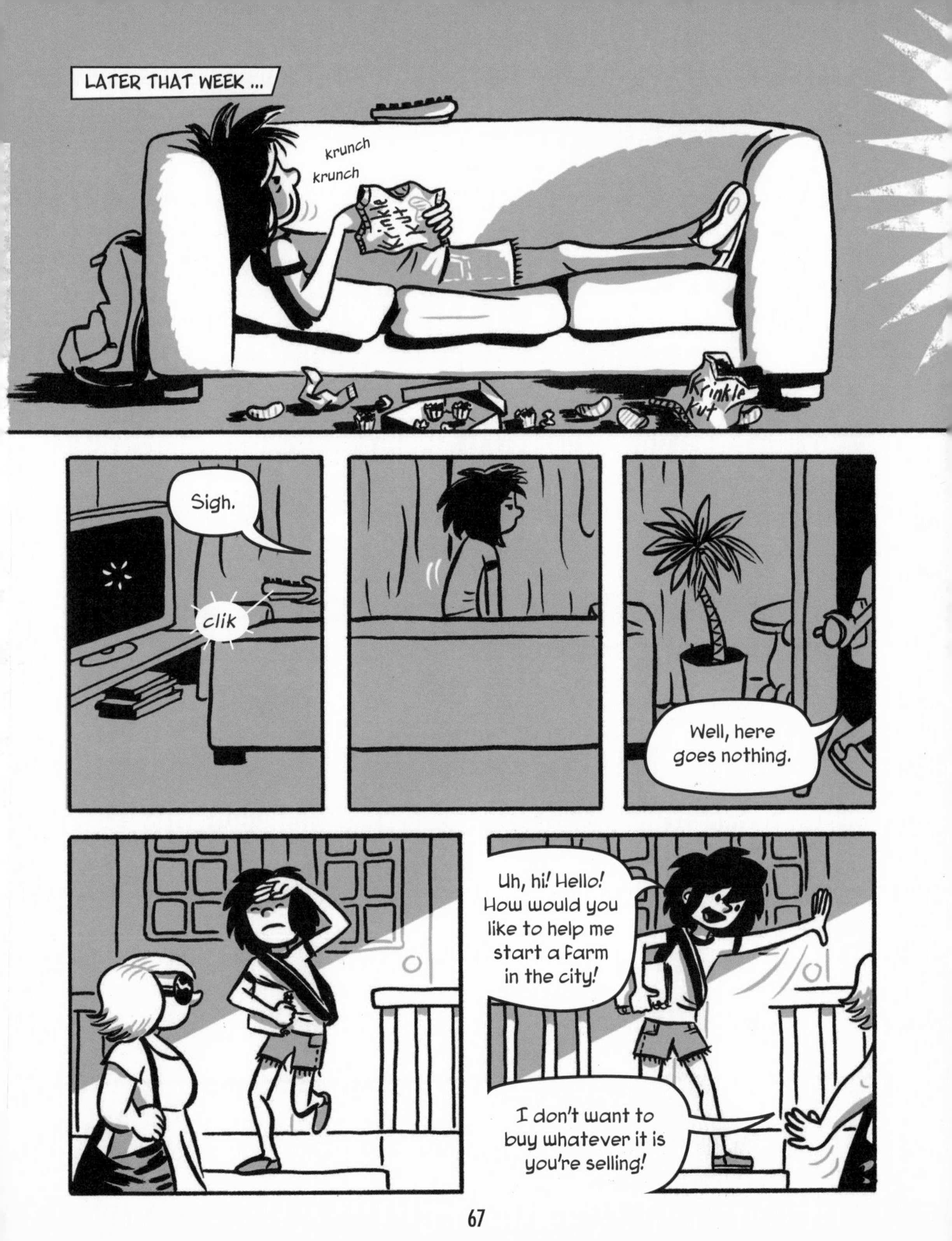
LATER THAT WEEK ...
krunch
krunch
Krinkle Kut
Krinkle Kut
Sigh.
clik
Well, here goes nothing.
Uh, hi! Hello! How would you like to help me start a farm in the city!
I don't want to buy whatever it is you're selling!

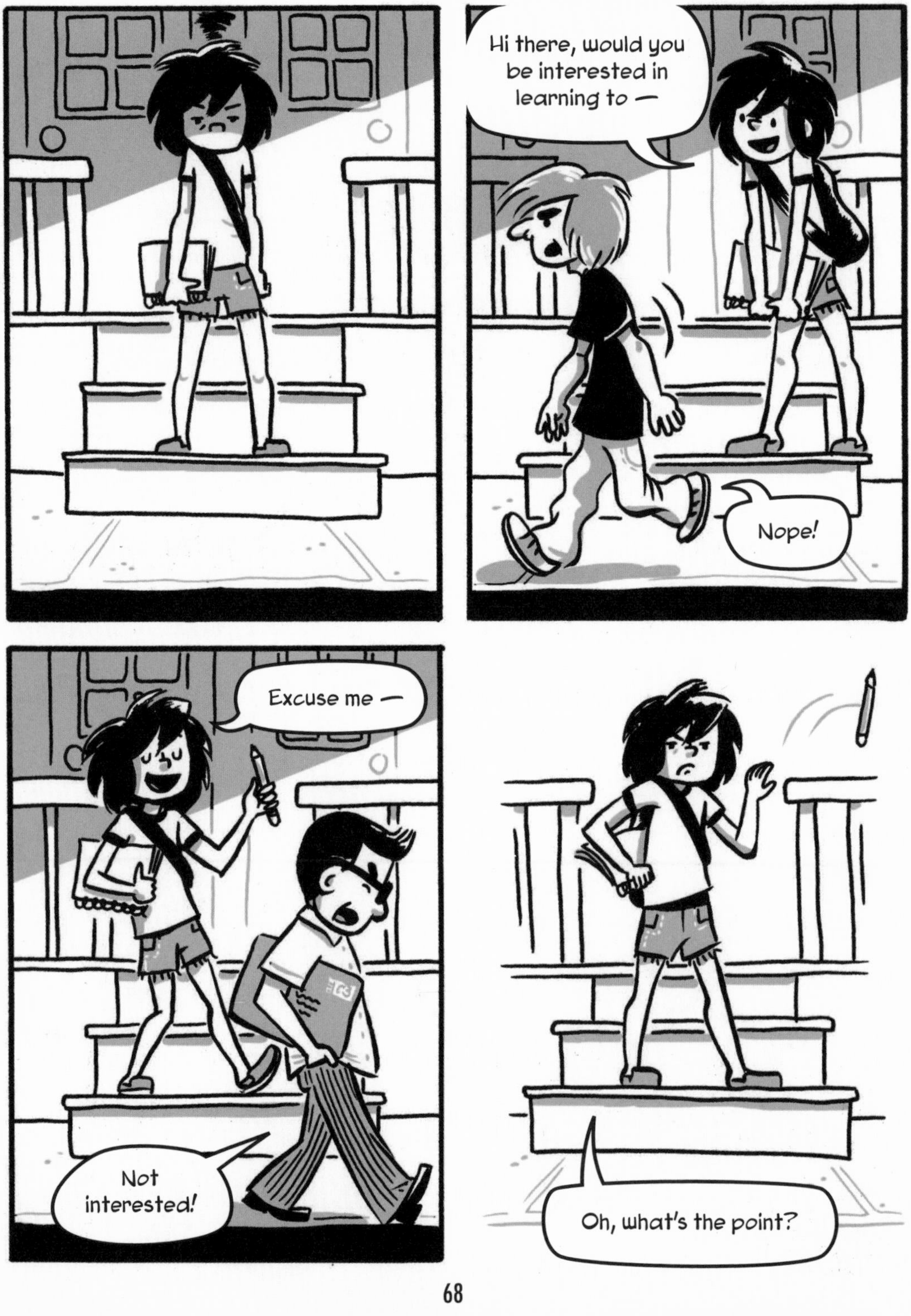
Hi there, would you be interested in learning to —
Nope!
Excuse me —
Not interested!
Oh, what's the point?

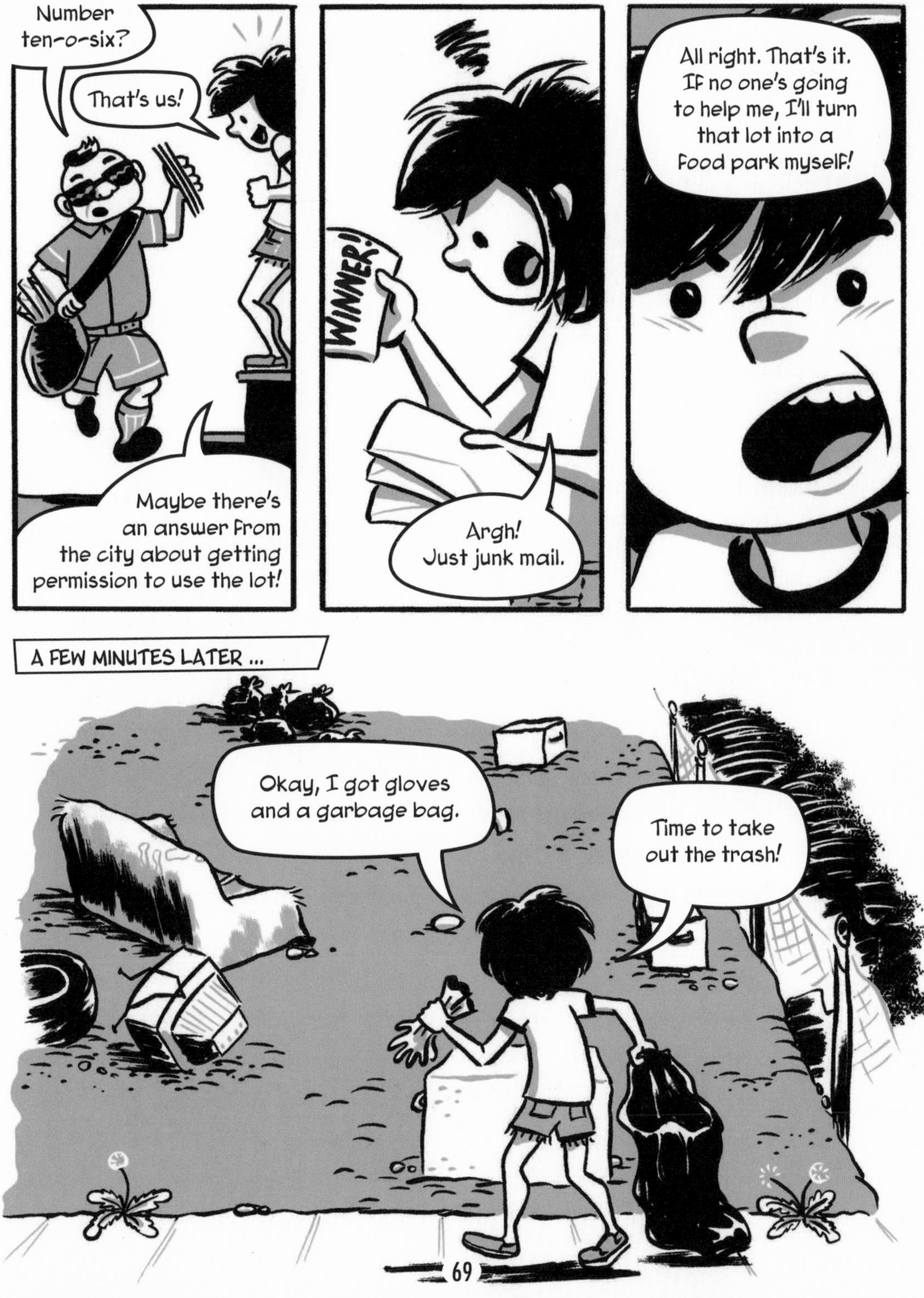
Number ten-o-six?
That's us!
Maybe there's an answer from the city about getting permission to use the lot!
WINNER!
Argh! Just junk mail.
All right. That's it. If no one's going to help me, I'll turn that lot into a food park myself!
A FEW MINUTES LATER ...
Okay, I got gloves and a garbage bag.
Time to take out the trash!

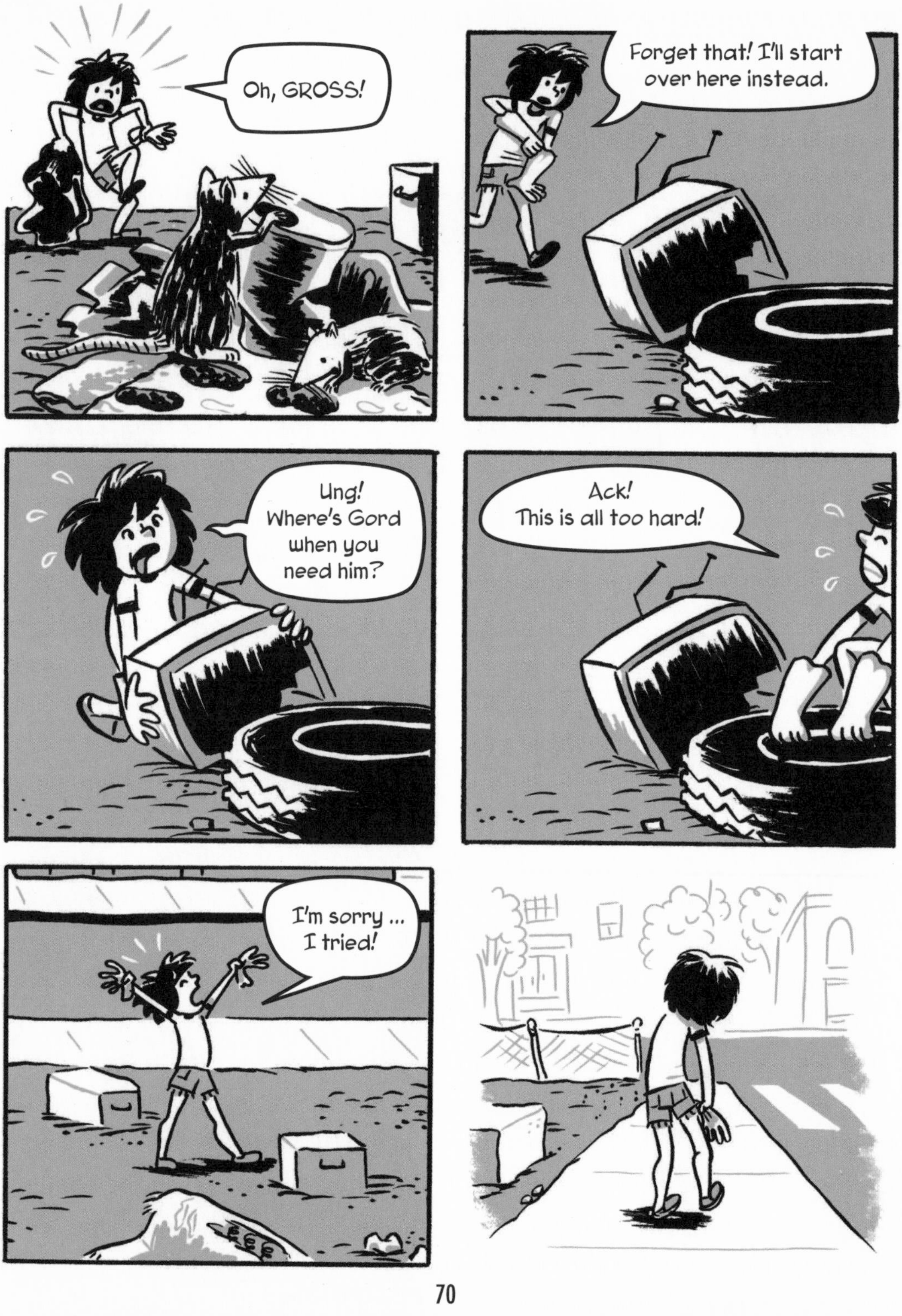
Oh, GROSS!
Forget that! I'll start over here instead.
Ung! Where's Gord when you need him?
Ack! This is all too hard!
I'm sorry ... I tried!

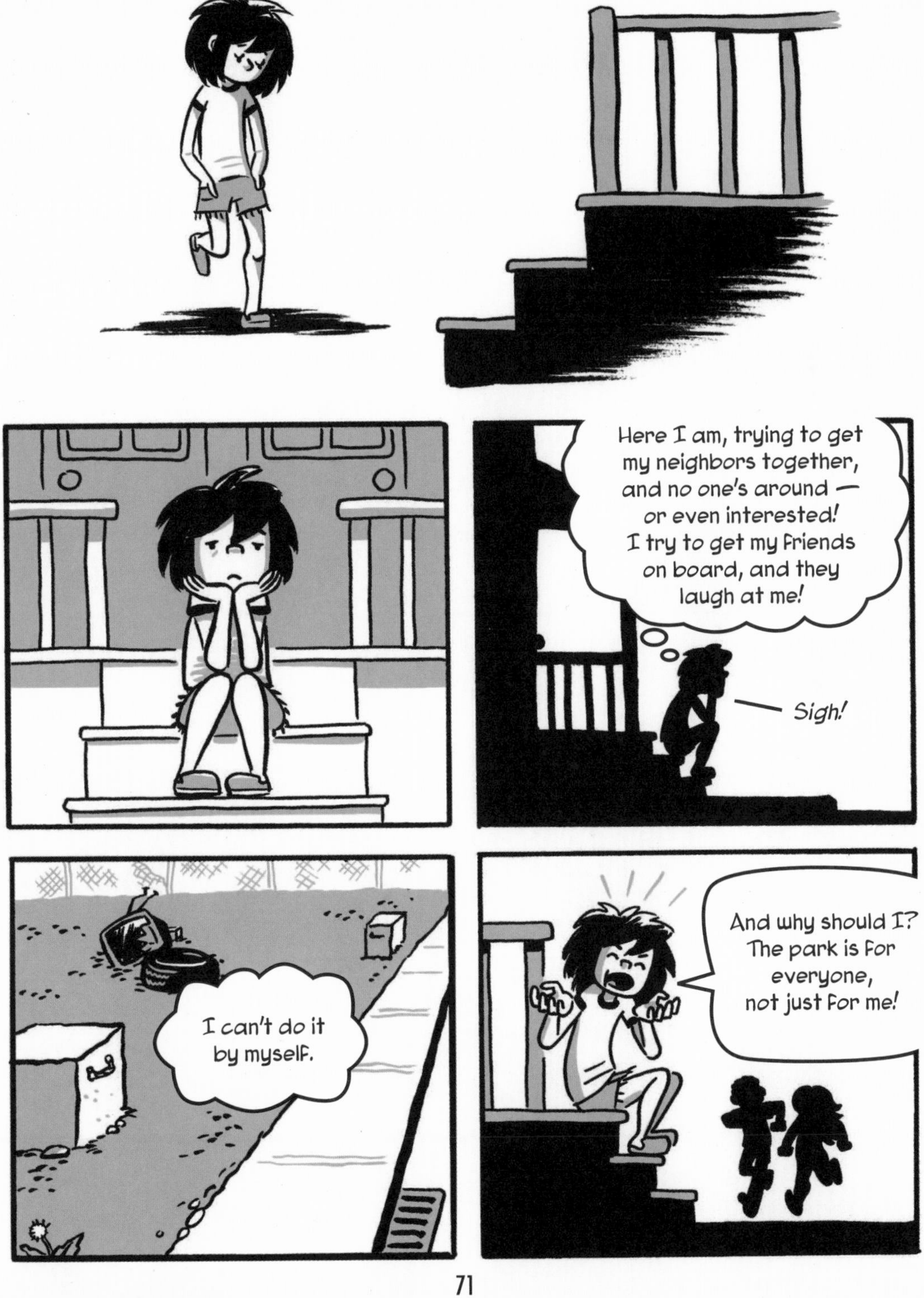
Here I am, trying to get my neighbors together, and no one's around — or even interested! I try to get my friends on board, and they laugh at me!
Sigh!
I can't do it by myself.
And why should I? The park is for everyone, not just for me!

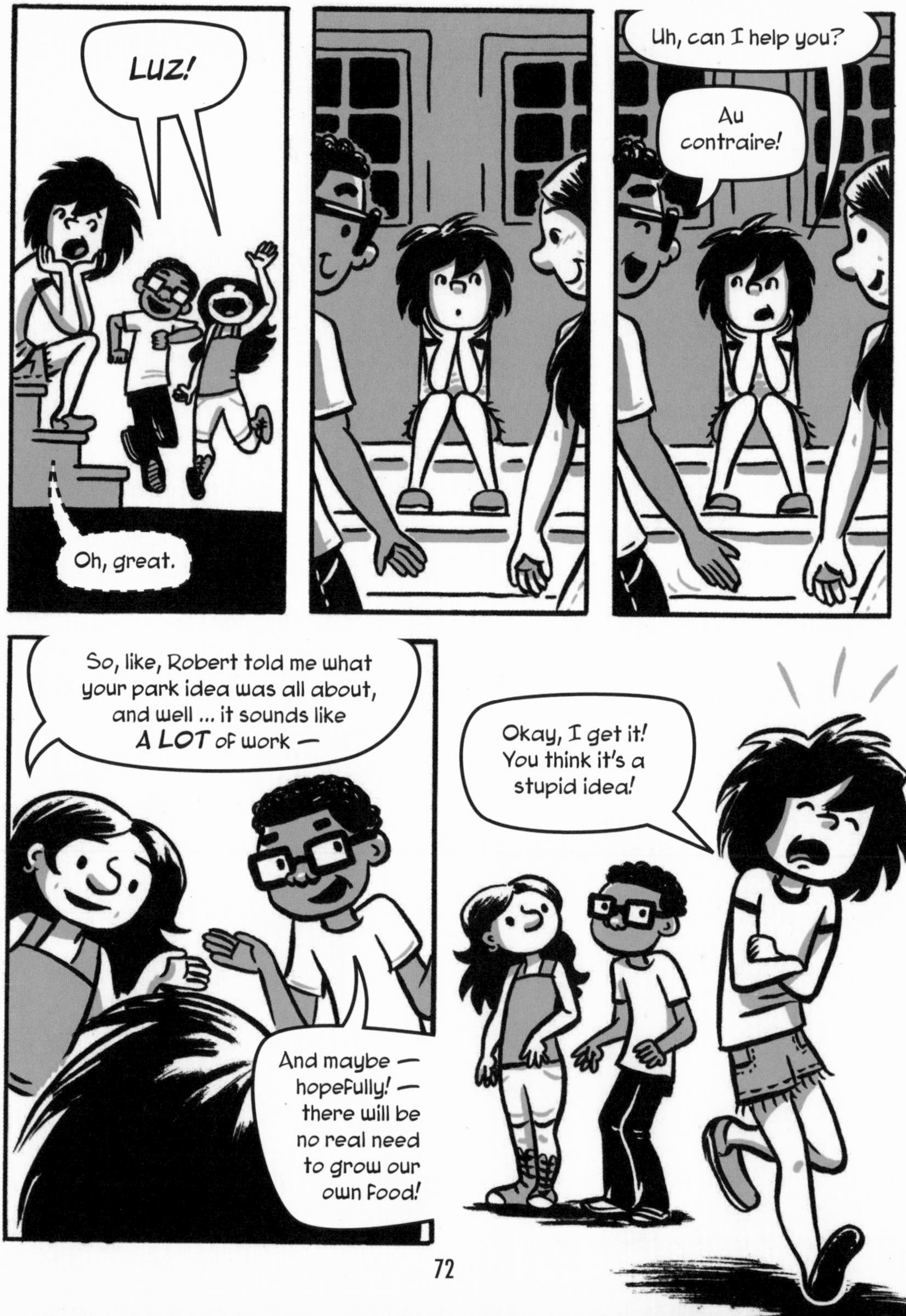
LUZ!
Oh, great.
Uh, can I help you?
Au contraire!
So, like, Robert told me what your park idea was all about, and well ... it sounds like A LOT of work —
And maybe — hopefully! — there will be no real need to grow our own food!
Okay, I get it! You think it's a stupid idea!

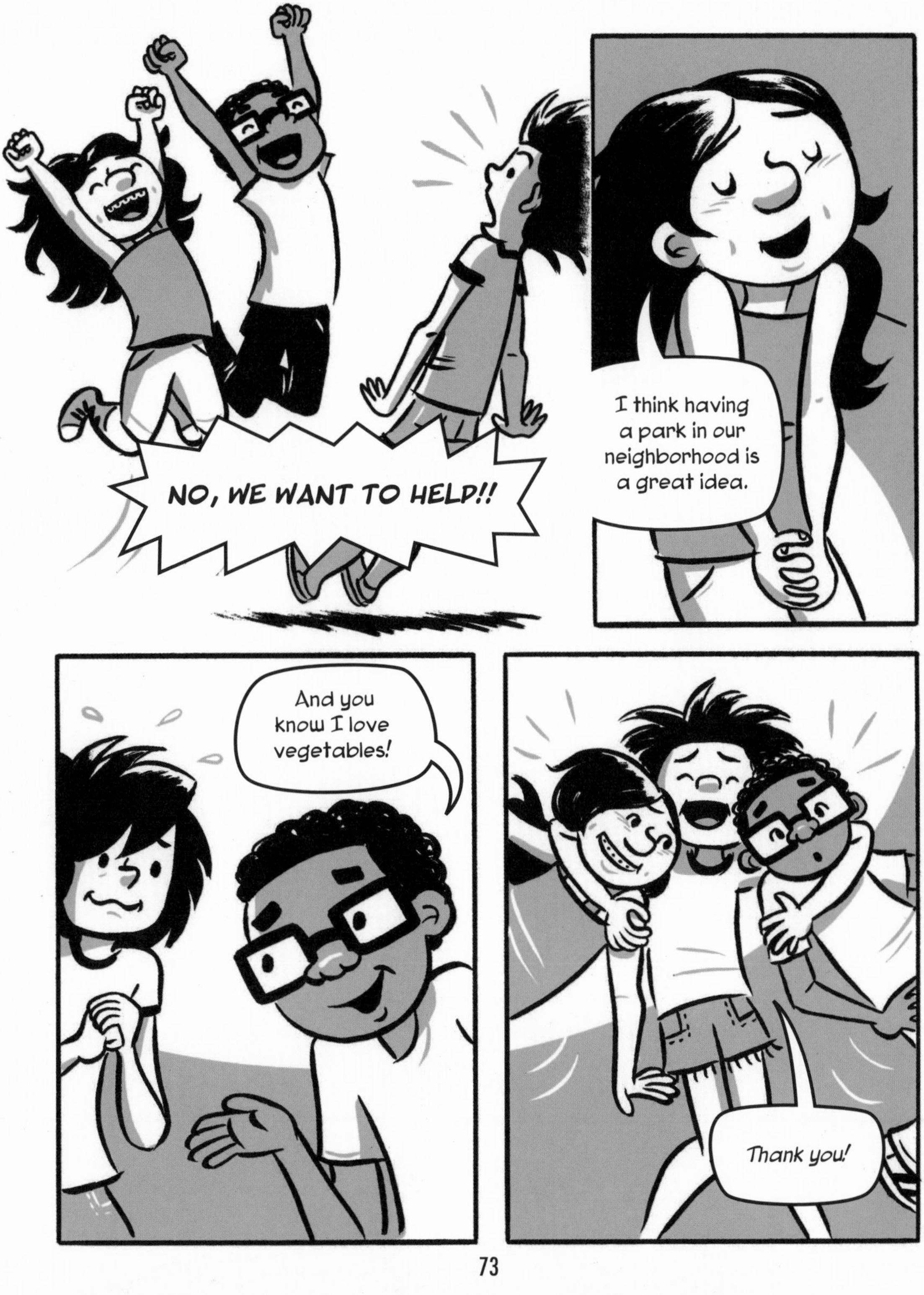
NO, WE WANT TO HELP!!
I think having a park in our neighborhood is a great idea.
And you know I love vegetables!
Thank you!

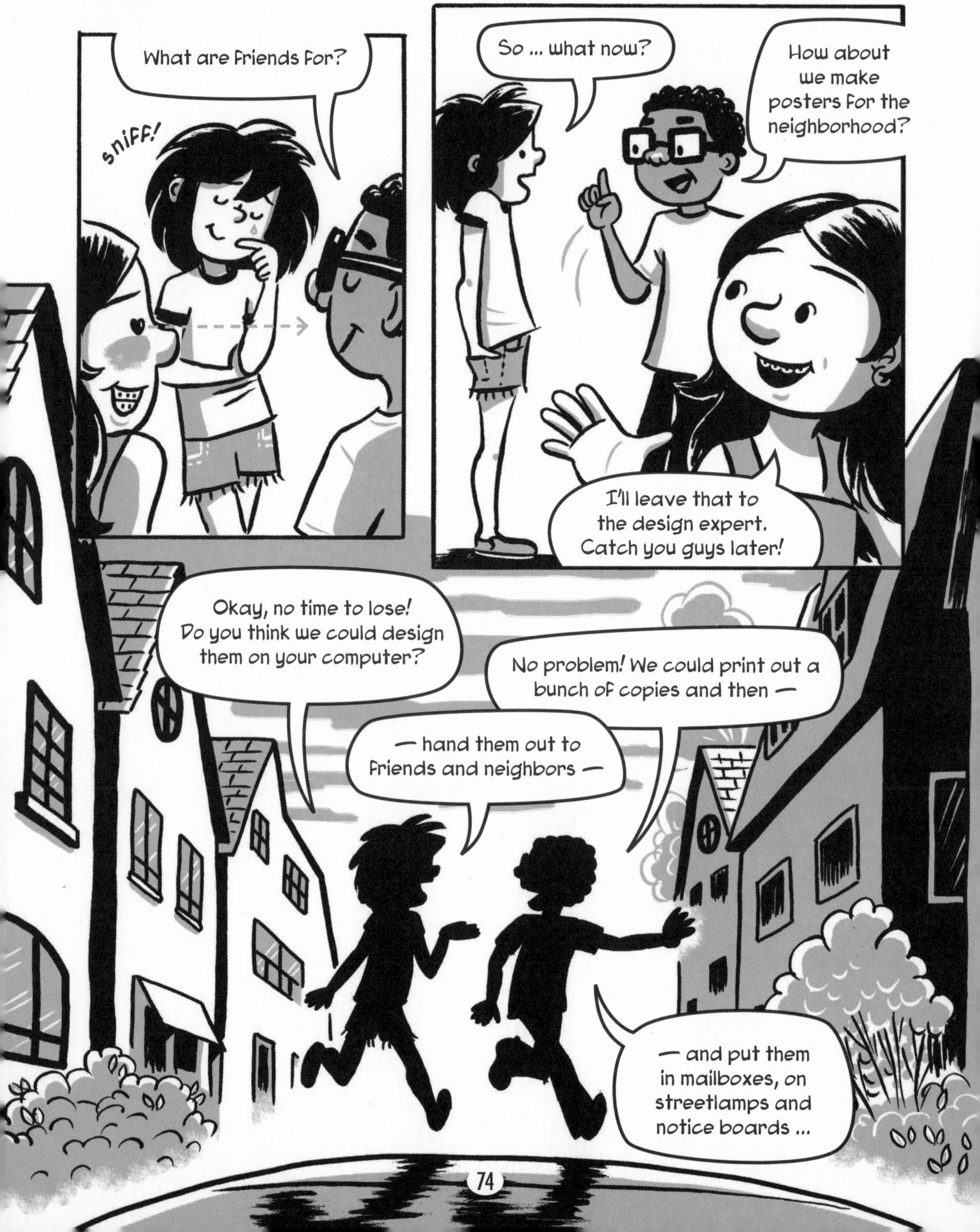
What are friends for?
SNIFF!
So ... what now?
How about we make posters for the neighborhood?
I'll leave that to the design expert. Catch you guys later!
Okay, no time to lose! Do you think we could design them on your computer?
No problem! We could print out a bunch of copies and then —
— hand them out to friends and neighbors —
— and put them in mailboxes, on streetlamps and notice boards ...

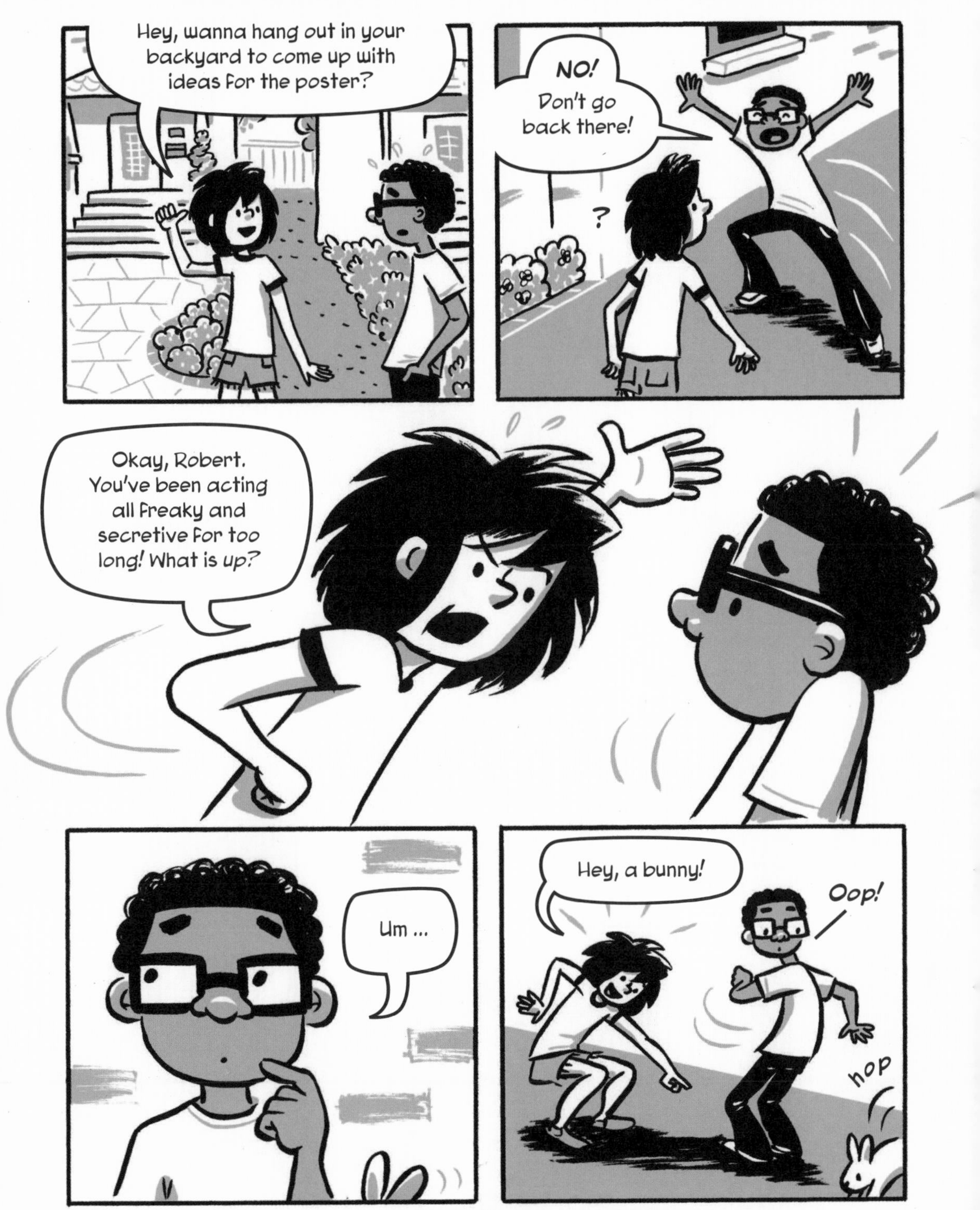
Hey, wanna hang out in your backyard to come up with ideas for the poster?
NO! Don't go back there!
?
Okay, Robert. You've been acting all freaky and secretive for too long! What is up?
Um ...
Hey, a bunny!
Oop!
hop

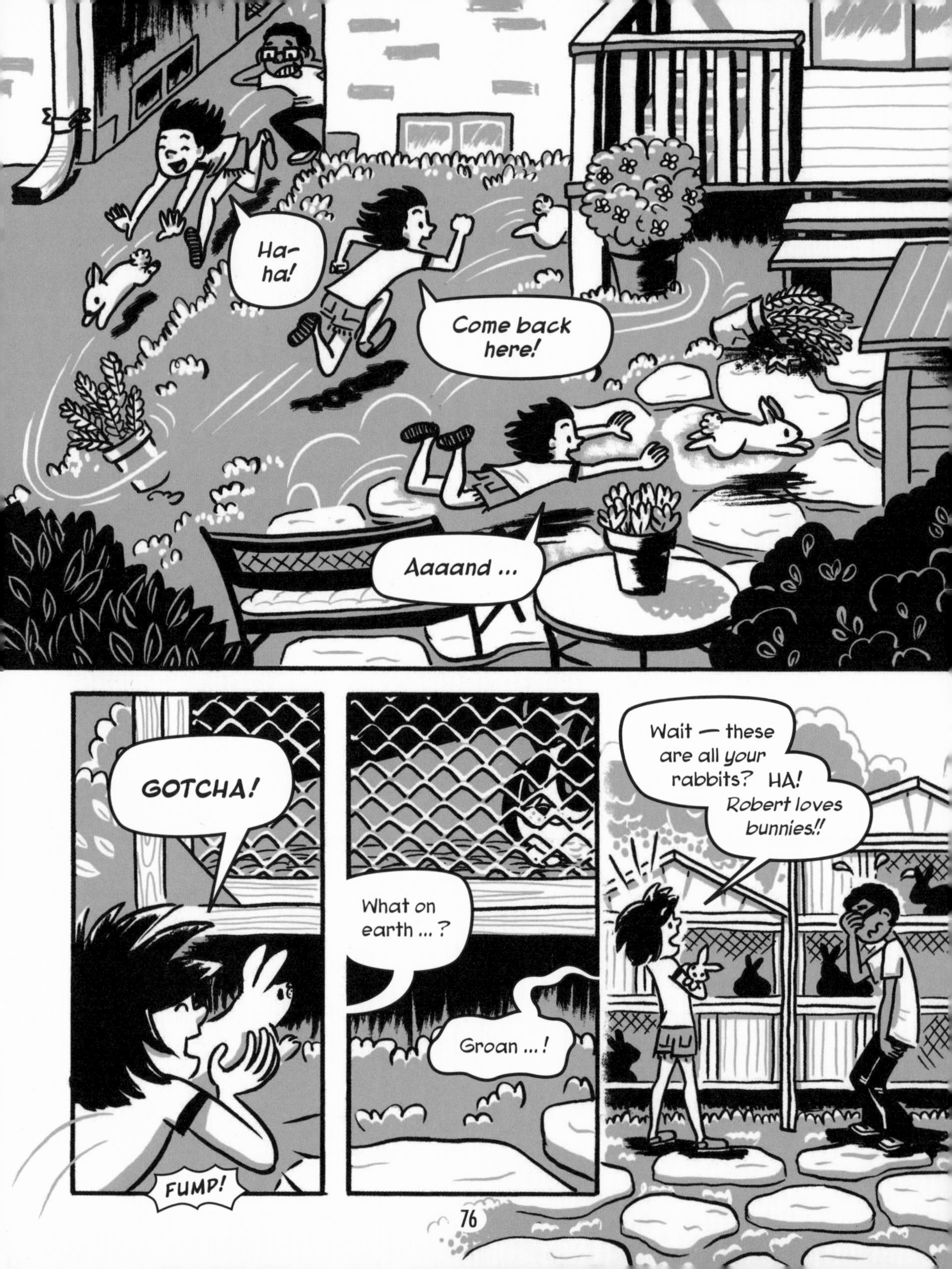
Ha-ha!
Come back here!
Aaaand ...
GOTCHA!
FUMP!
What on earth ... ?
Groan ...!
Wait — these are all *your* rabbits? HA!
*Robert loves bunnies!!*

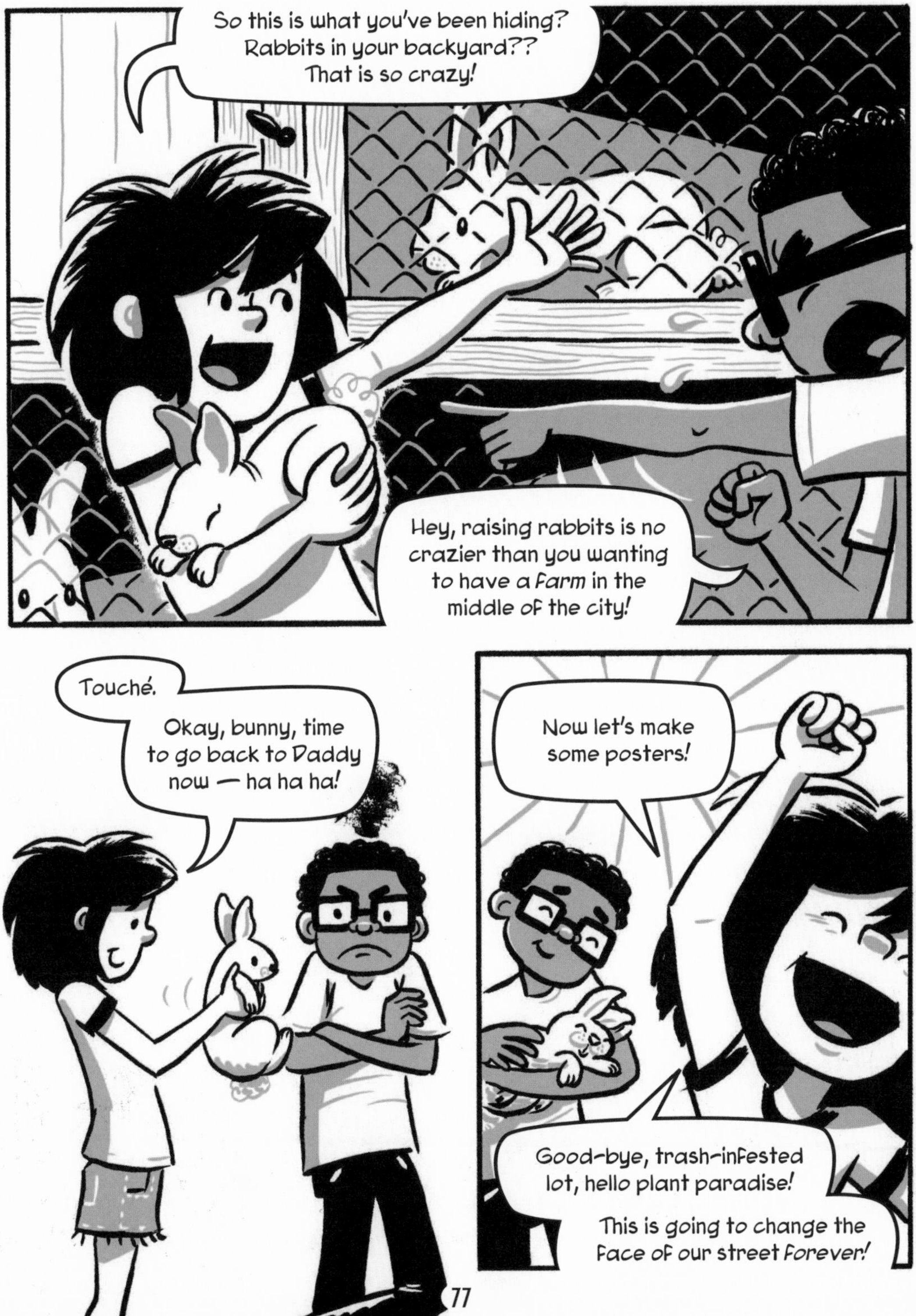
So this is what you've been hiding? Rabbits in your backyard?? That is so crazy!
Hey, raising rabbits is no crazier than you wanting to have a *farm* in the middle of the city!
Touché.
Okay, bunny, time to go back to Daddy now — ha ha ha!
Now let's make some posters!
Good-bye, trash-infested lot, hello plant paradise!
This is going to change the face of our street *forever!*

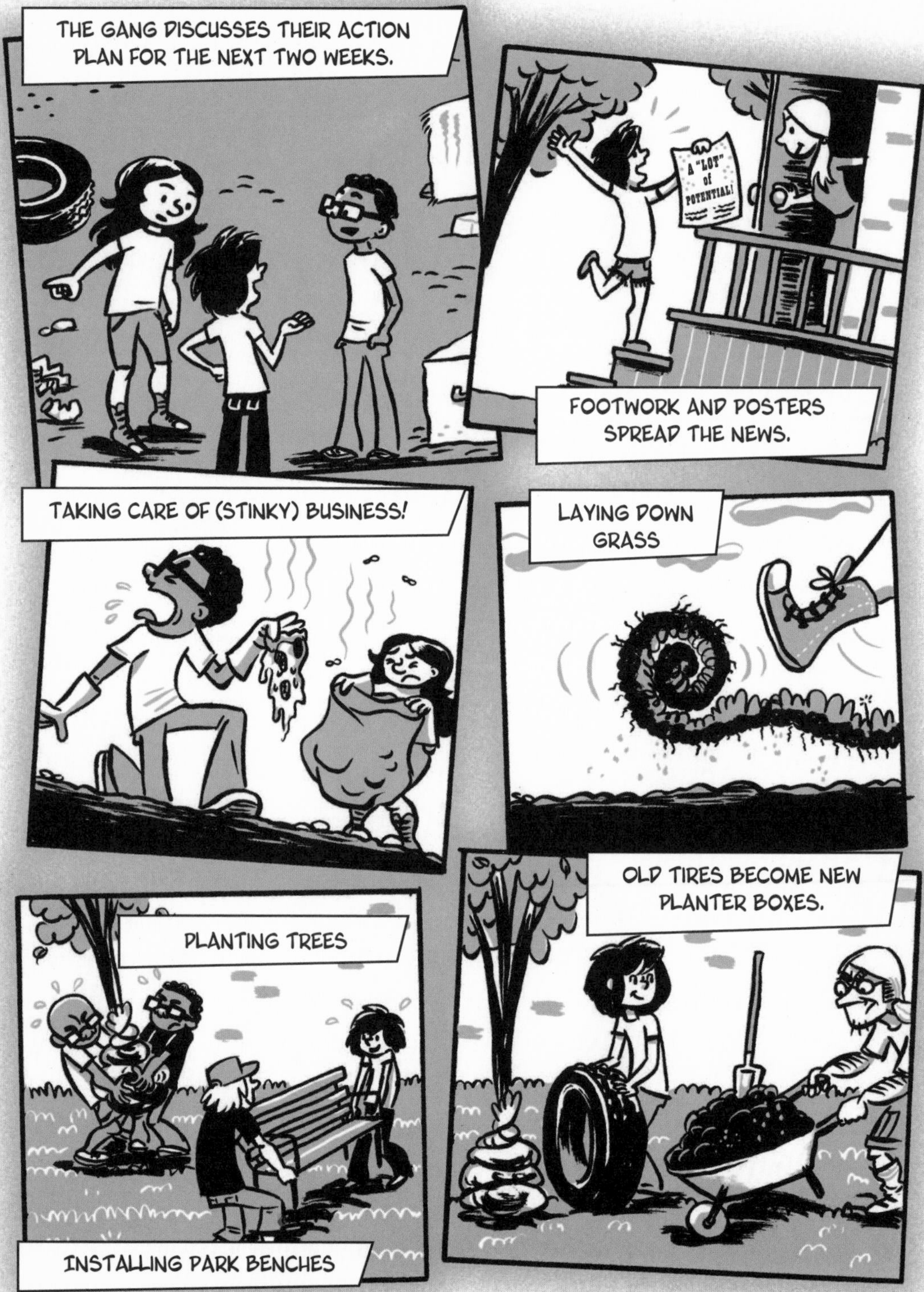
THE GANG DISCUSSES THEIR ACTION PLAN FOR THE NEXT TWO WEEKS.
A "LOT" of POTENTIAL!
FOOTWORK AND POSTERS SPREAD THE NEWS.
TAKING CARE OF (STINKY) BUSINESS!
LAYING DOWN GRASS
PLANTING TREES
INSTALLING PARK BENCHES
OLD TIRES BECOME NEW PLANTER BOXES.

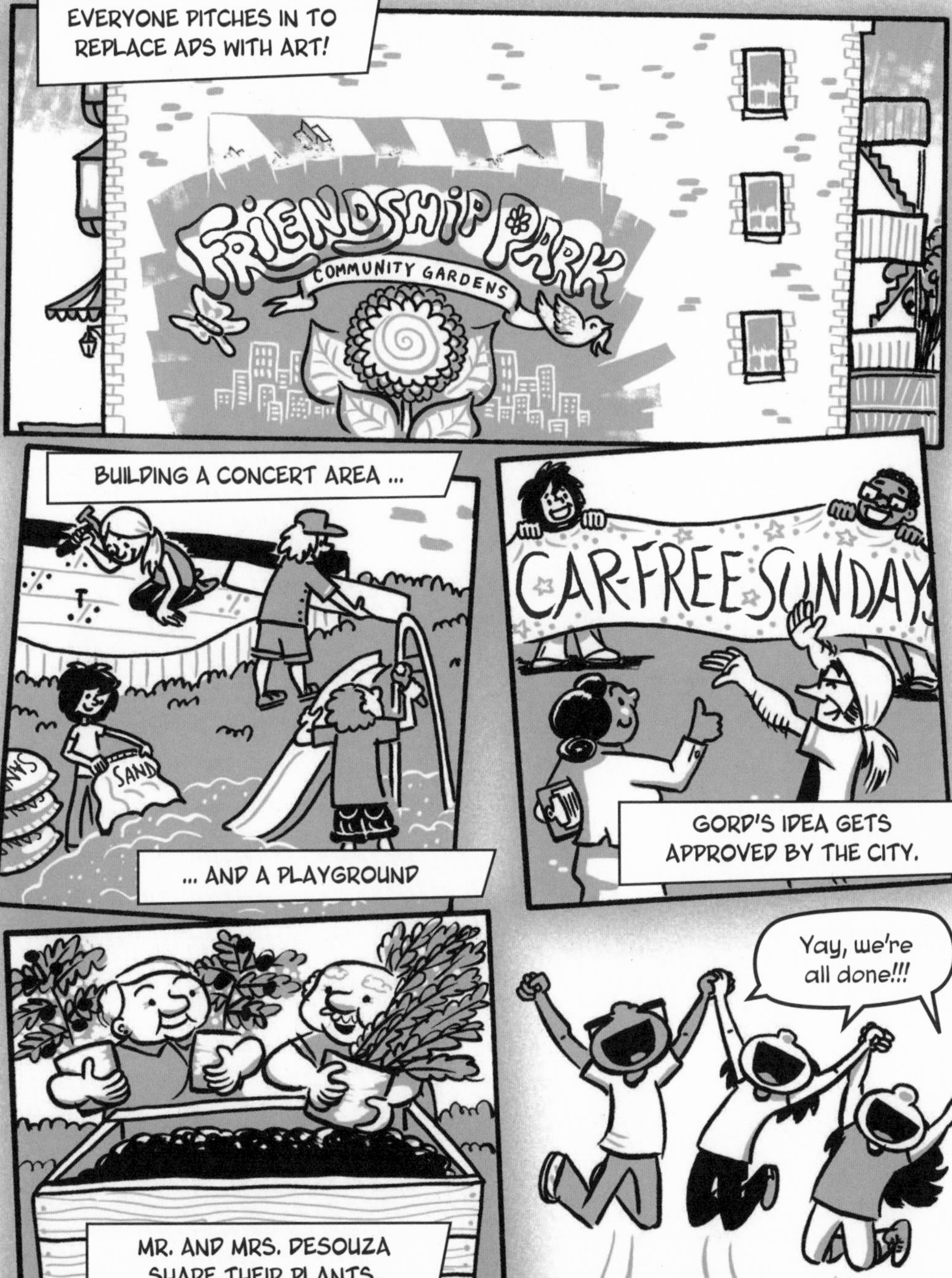
EVERYONE PITCHES IN TO REPLACE ADS WITH ART!
FRIENDSHIP PARK
COMMUNITY GARDENS
BUILDING A CONCERT AREA ...
SAND
... AND A PLAYGROUND
CAR-FREE SUNDAYS
GORD'S IDEA GETS APPROVED BY THE CITY.
MR. AND MRS. DESOUZA SHARE THEIR PLANTS.
Yay, we're all done!!!

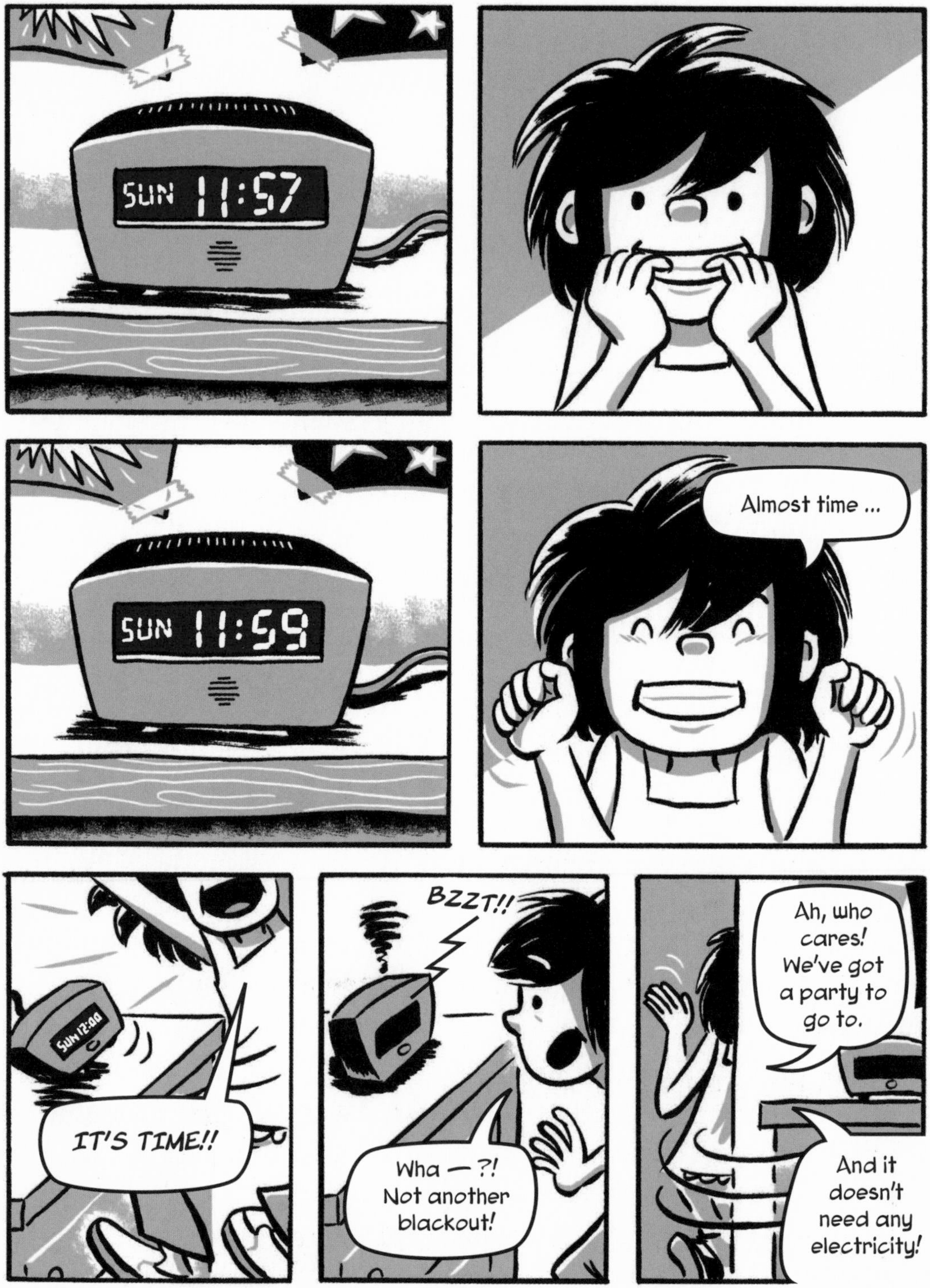
SUN 11:57
SUN 11:59
Almost time ...
SUN 12:00
IT'S TIME!!
BZZT!!
Wha — ?! Not another blackout!
Ah, who cares! We've got a party to go to.
And it doesn't need any electricity!

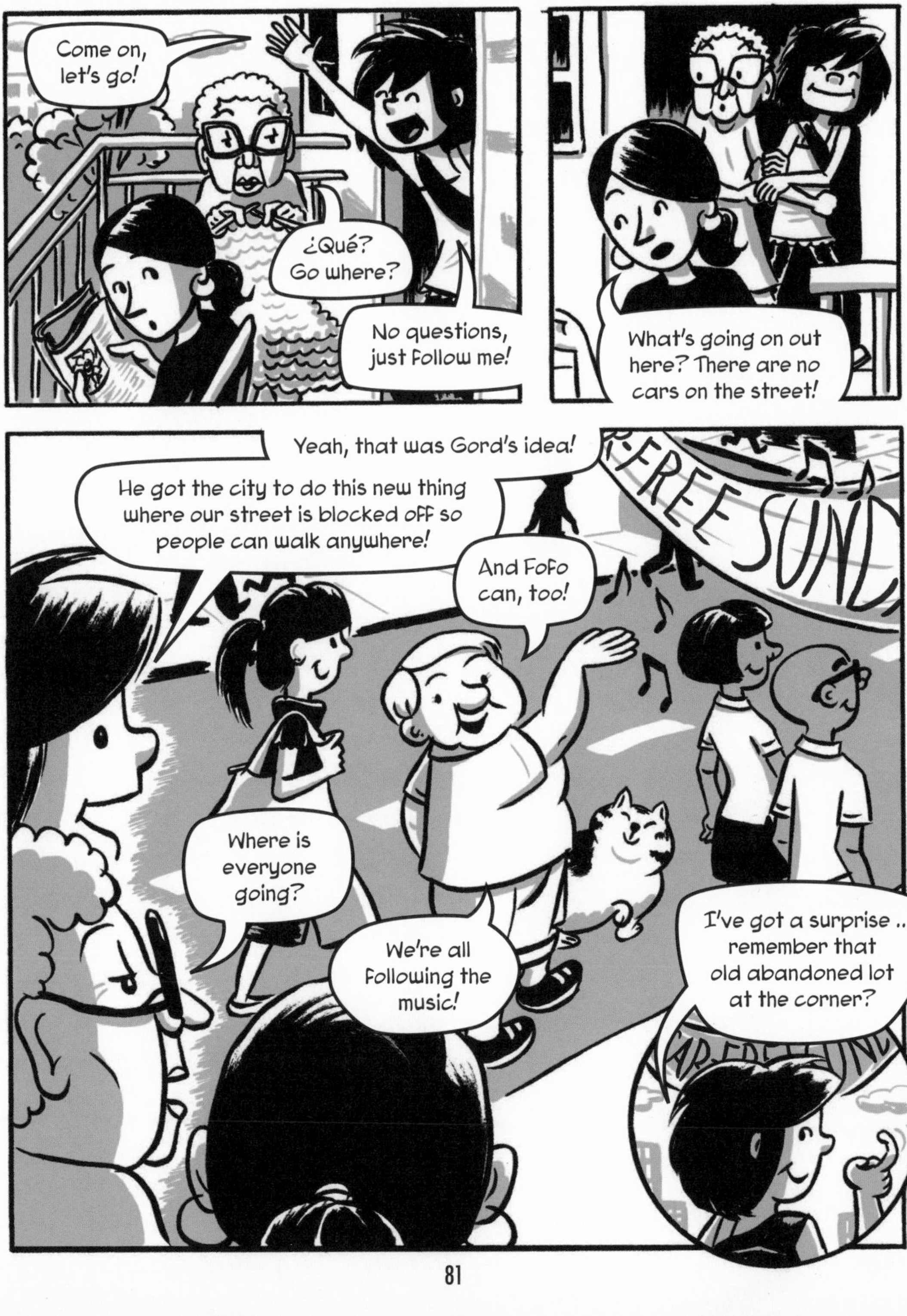
Come on, let's go!
¿Qué? Go where?
No questions, just follow me!
What's going on out here? There are no cars on the street!
Yeah, that was Gord's idea!
He got the city to do this new thing where our street is blocked off so people can walk anywhere!
And Fofo can, too!
-FREE SUND
Where is everyone going?
We're all following the music!
I've got a surprise ... remember that old abandoned lot at the corner?

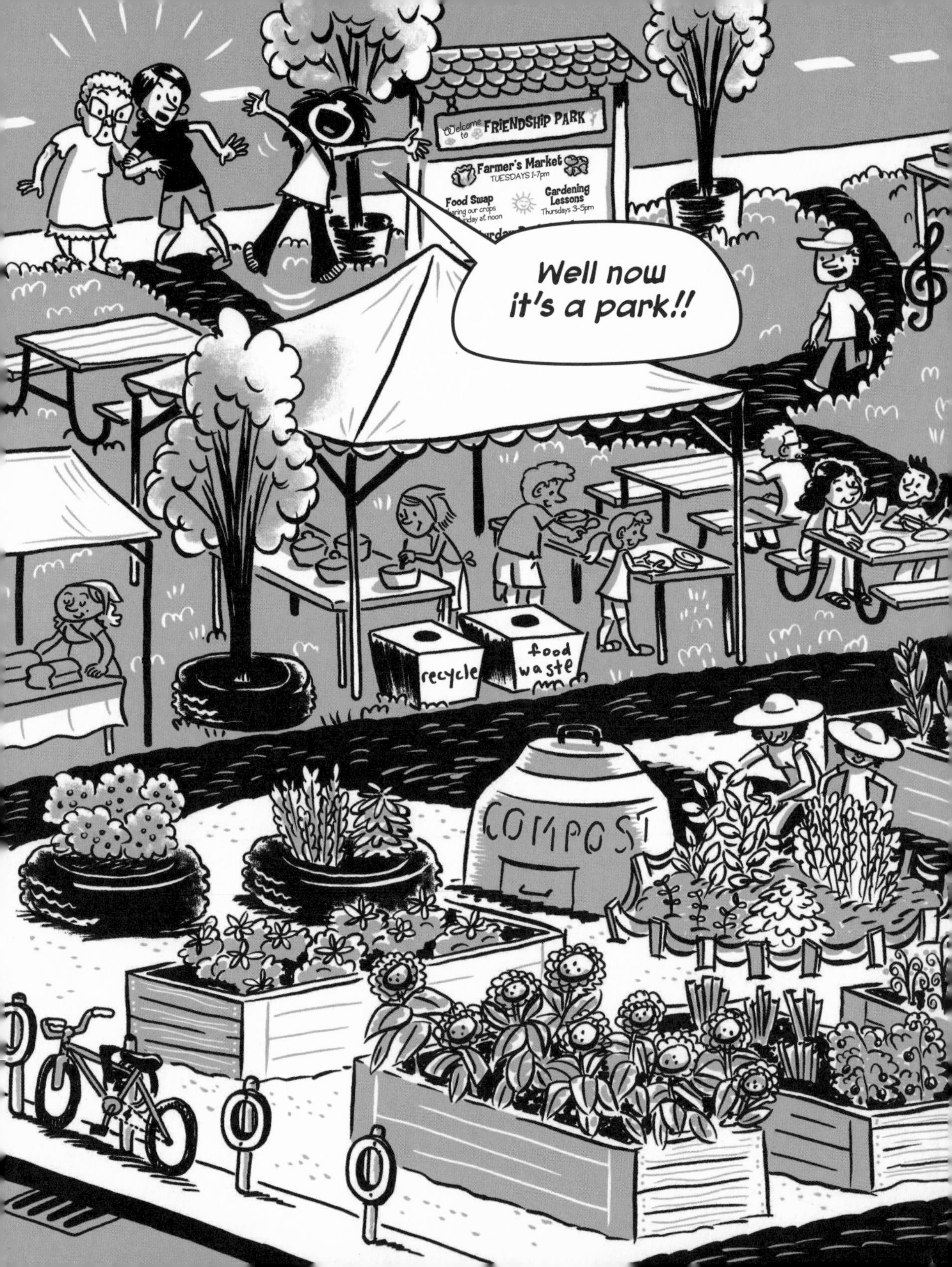

Welcome to FRIENDSHIP PARK
Farmer's Market
TUESDAYS 1-7pm
Food Swap
Gardening Lessons
Thursdays 3-5pm
Well now it's a park!!
recycle
food waste
COMPOST

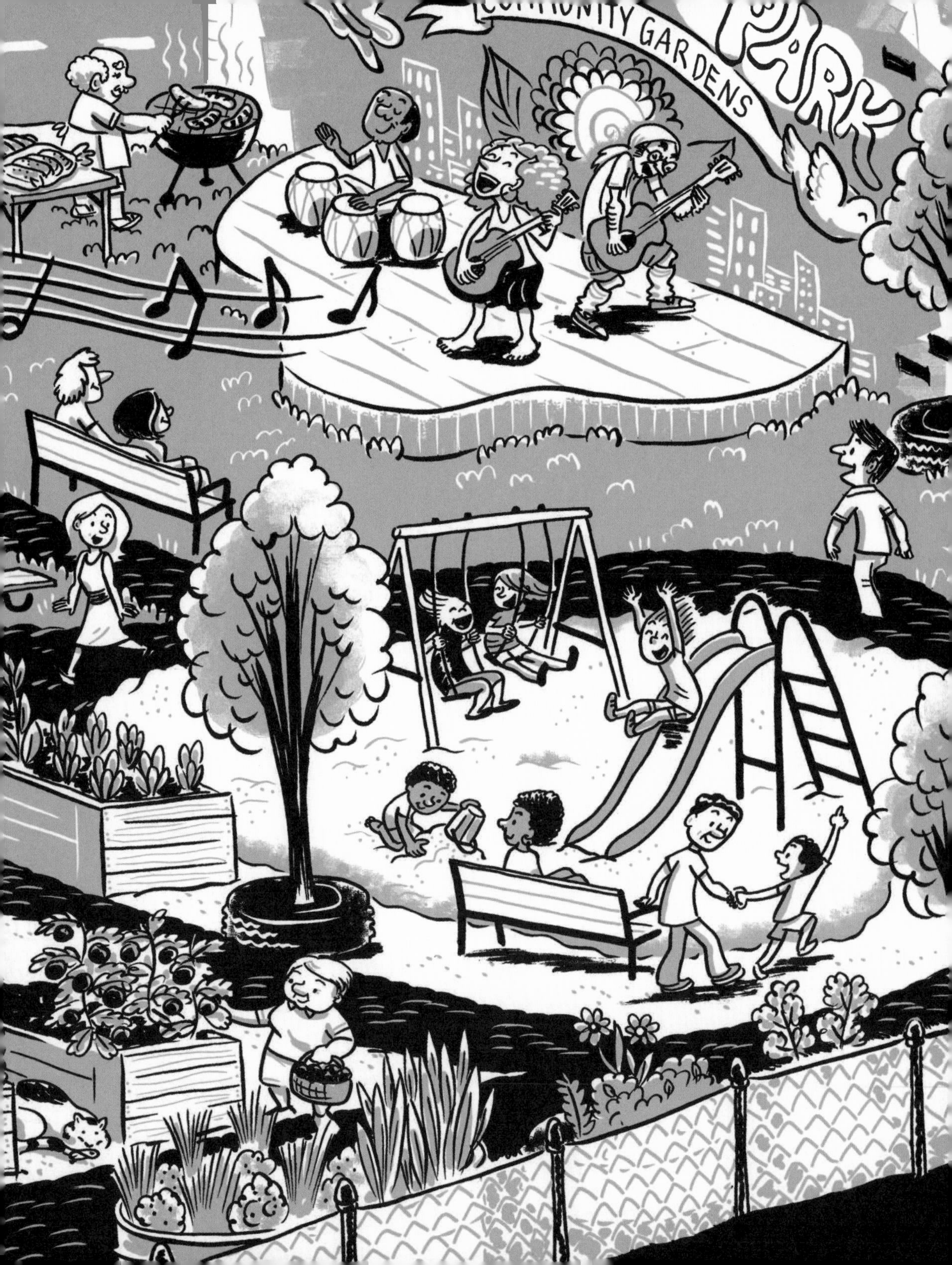
GARDENS
PARK

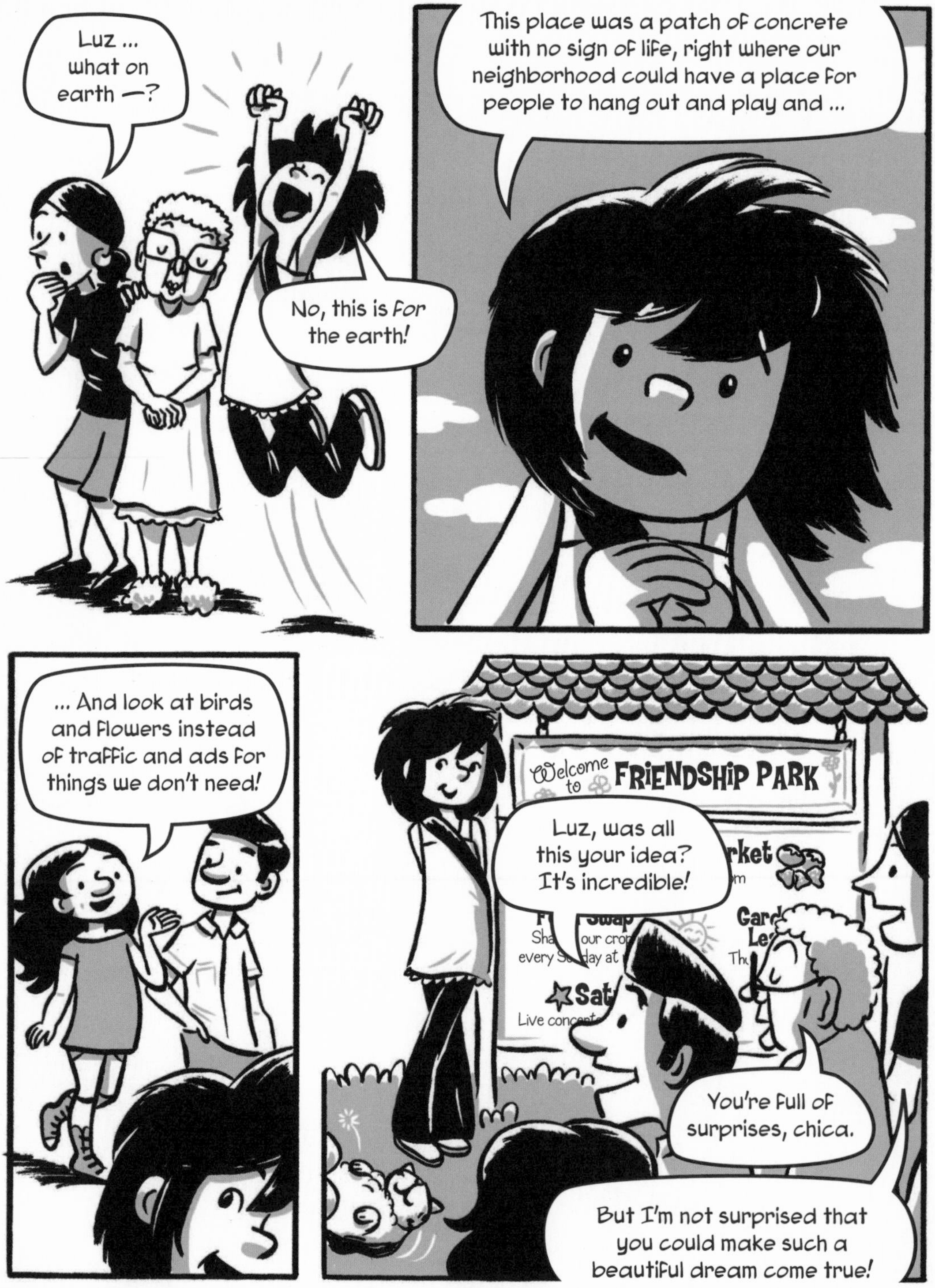
Luz ... what on earth —?
No, this is for the earth!
This place was a patch of concrete with no sign of life, right where our neighborhood could have a place for people to hang out and play and ...
... And look at birds and flowers instead of traffic and ads for things we don't need!
Welcome to FRIENDSHIP PARK
Luz, was all this your idea? It's incredible!
You're full of surprises, chica.
But I'm not surprised that you could make such a beautiful dream come true!

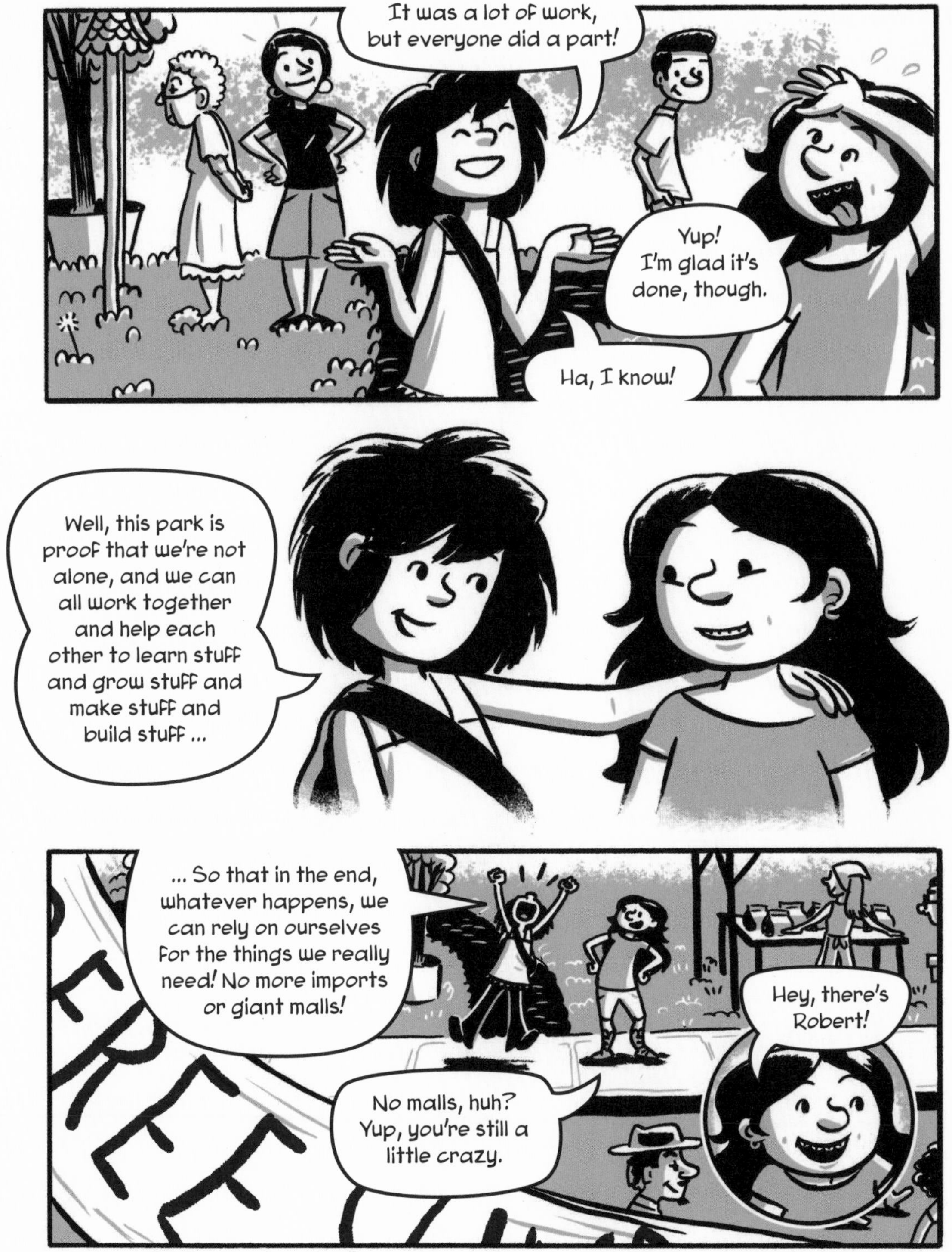
It was a lot of work, but everyone did a part!
Yup! I'm glad it's done, though.
Ha, I know!
Well, this park is proof that we're not alone, and we can all work together and help each other to learn stuff and grow stuff and make stuff and build stuff ...
... So that in the end, whatever happens, we can rely on ourselves for the things we really need! No more imports or giant malls!
No malls, huh? Yup, you're still a little crazy.
Hey, there's Robert!

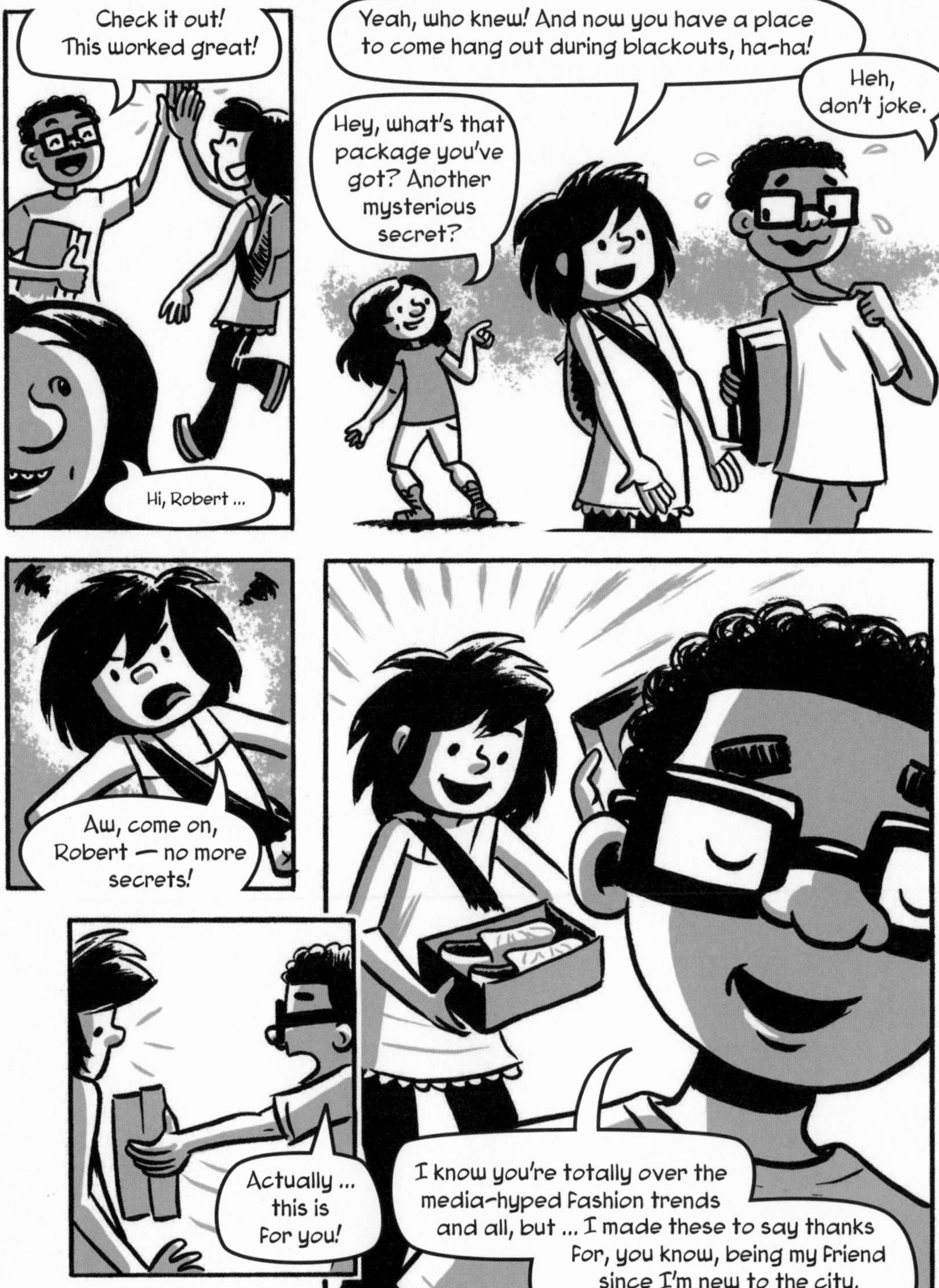
Check it out! This worked great!
Hi, Robert ...
Yeah, who knew! And now you have a place to come hang out during blackouts, ha-ha!
Heh, don't joke.
Hey, what's that package you've got? Another mysterious secret?
Aw, come on, Robert — no more secrets!
Actually ... this is for you!
I know you're totally over the media-hyped fashion trends and all, but ... I made these to say thanks for, you know, being my friend since I'm new to the city.

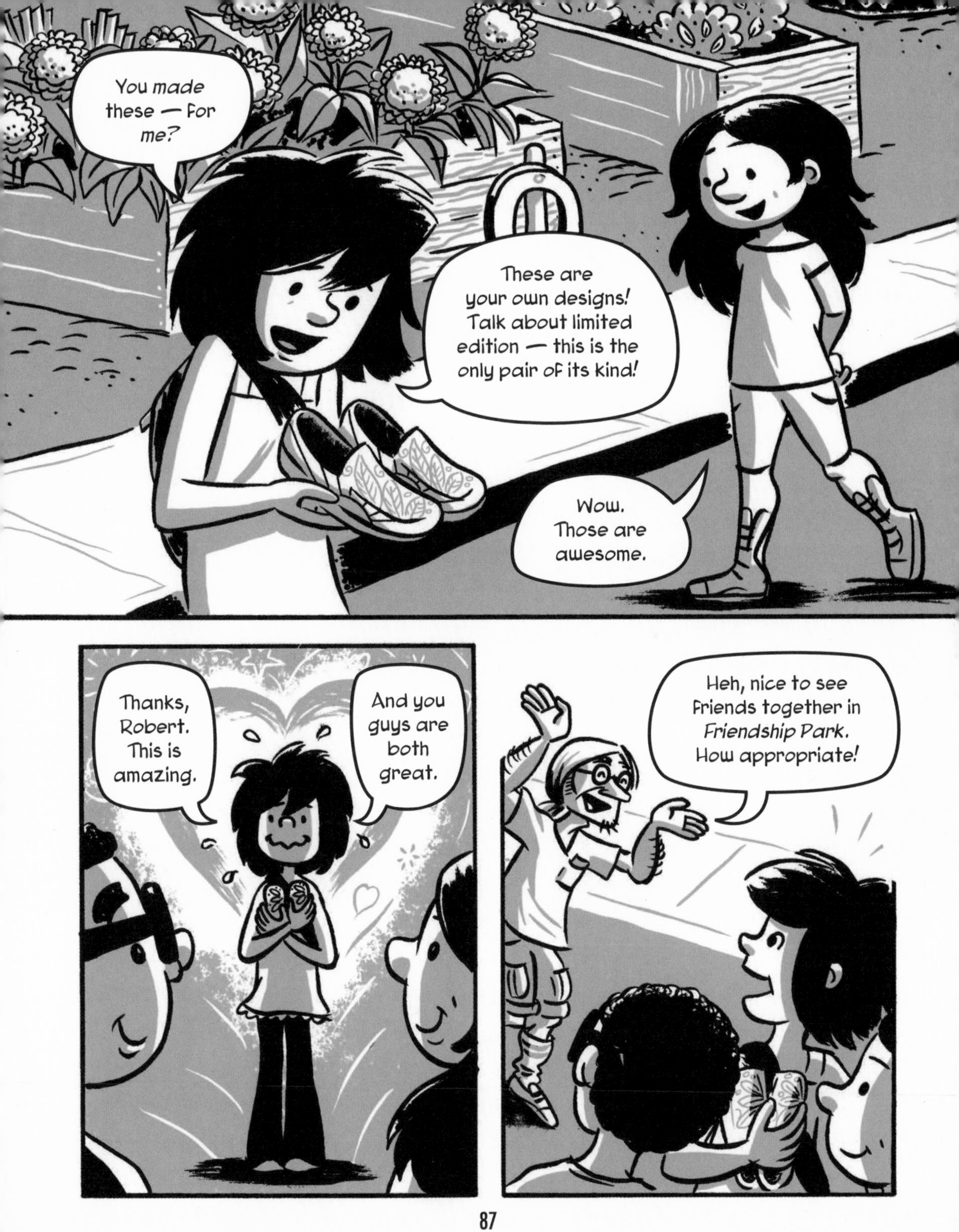
You made these — for me?
These are your own designs! Talk about limited edition — this is the only pair of its kind!
Wow. Those are awesome.
Thanks, Robert. This is amazing.
And you guys are both great.
Heh, nice to see friends together in *Friendship Park*. How appropriate!

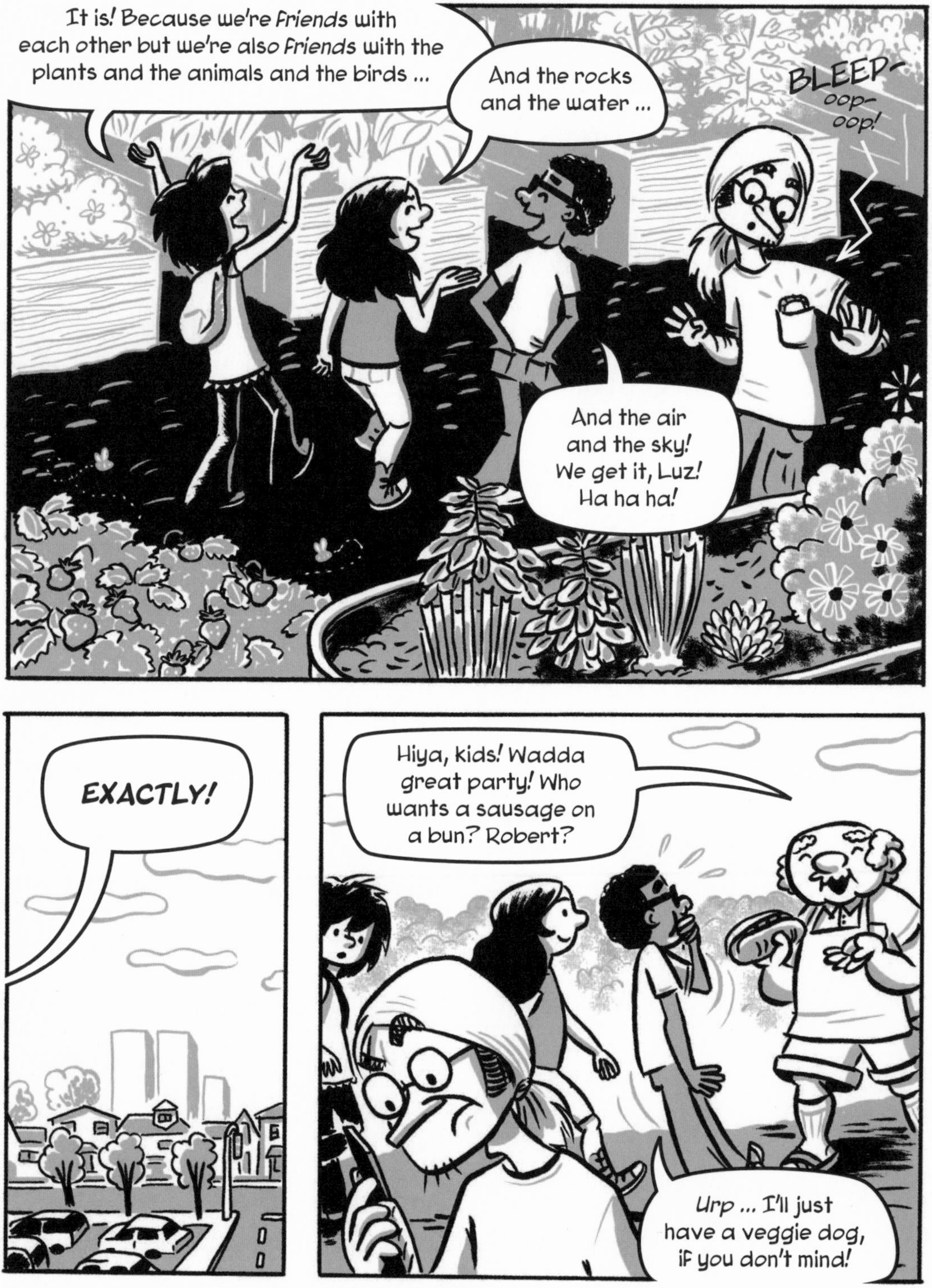
It is! Because we're friends with each other but we're also friends with the plants and the animals and the birds ...
And the rocks and the water ...
BLEEP-oop-oop!
And the air and the sky! We get it, Luz! Ha ha ha!
EXACTLY!
Hiya, kids! Wadda great party! Who wants a sausage on a bun? Robert?
Urp ... I'll just have a veggie dog, if you don't mind!

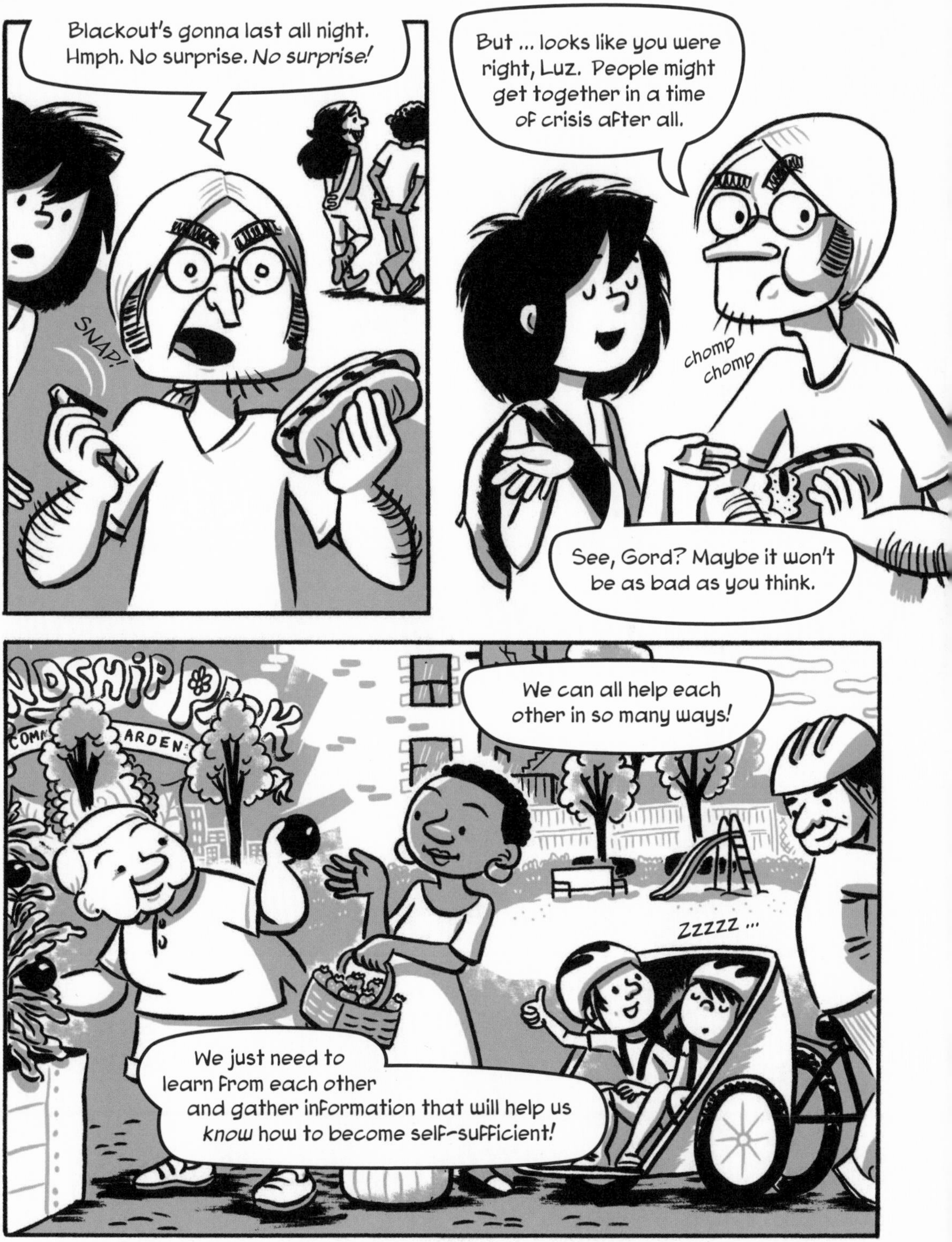
Blackout's gonna last all night. Hmph. No surprise. *No surprise!*
SNAP!
But ... looks like you were right, Luz. People might get together in a time of crisis after all.
chomp chomp
See, Gord? Maybe it won't be as bad as you think.
We can all help each other in so many ways!
Zzzzz ...
We just need to learn from each other and gather information that will help us *know* how to become self-sufficient!

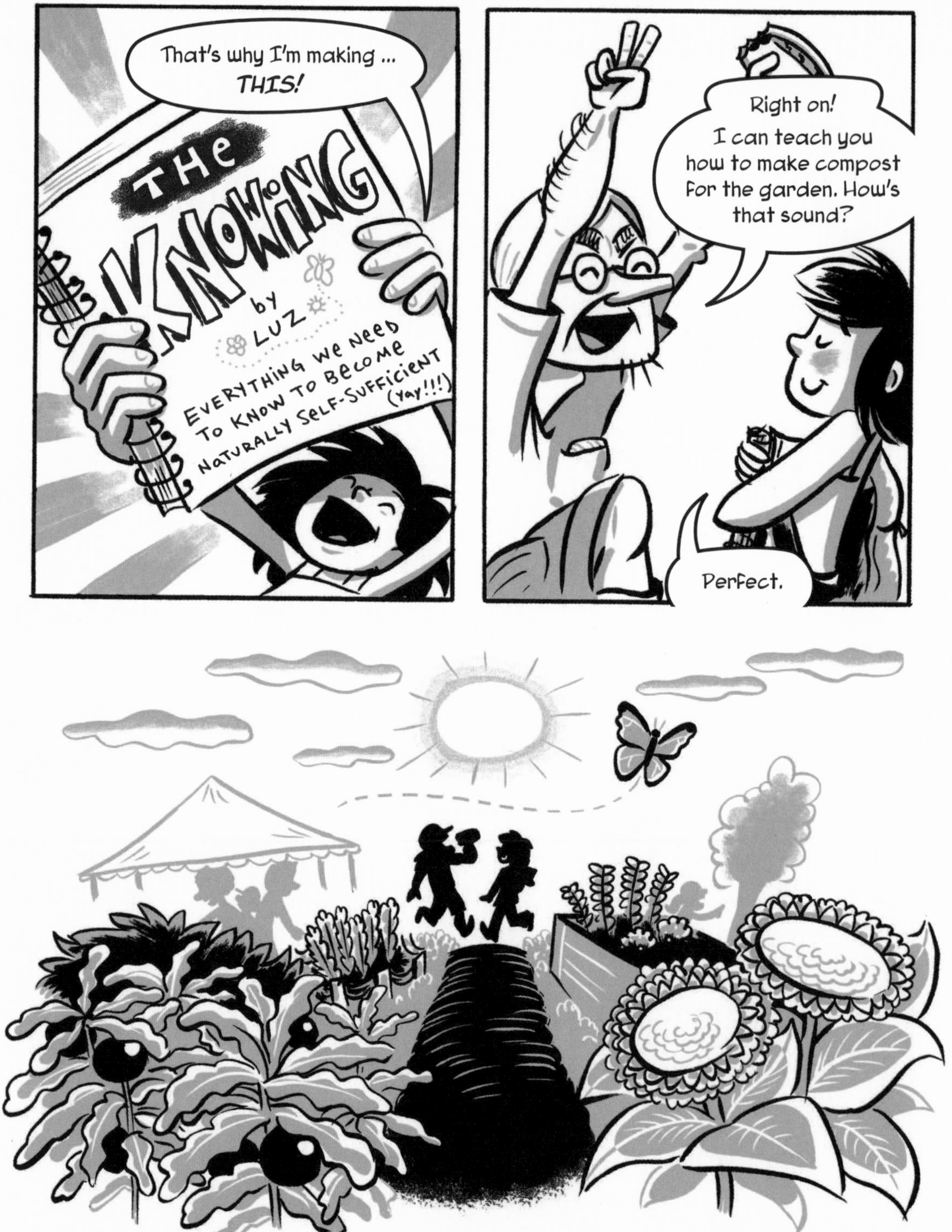
That's why I'm making ... THIS!
THE KNOWING by LUZ
EVERYTHING WE NEED TO KNOW TO BECOME NATURALLY SELF-SUFFICIENT (YAY!!!)
Right on! I can teach you how to make compost for the garden. How's that sound?
Perfect.

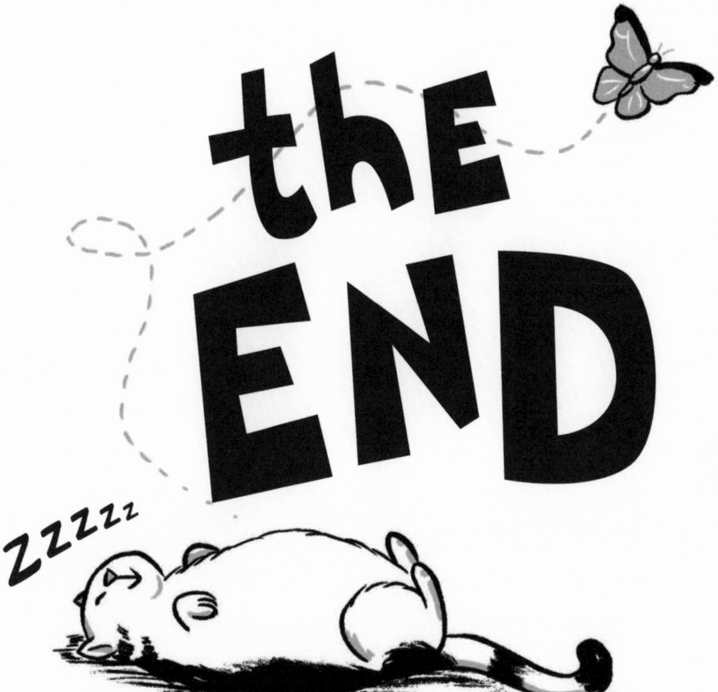
the
END
Zzzzz

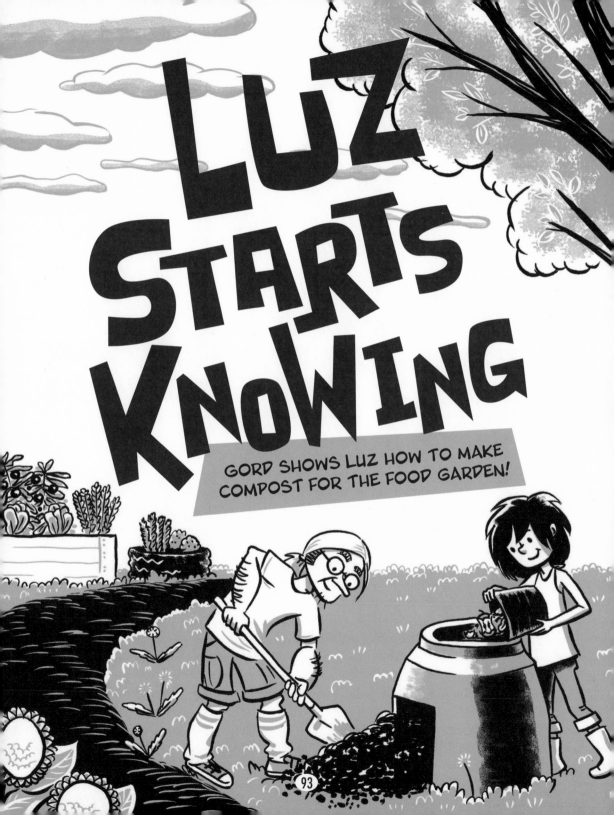

# LUZ STARTS KNOWING

GORD SHOWS LUZ HOW TO MAKE COMPOST FOR THE FOOD GARDEN!

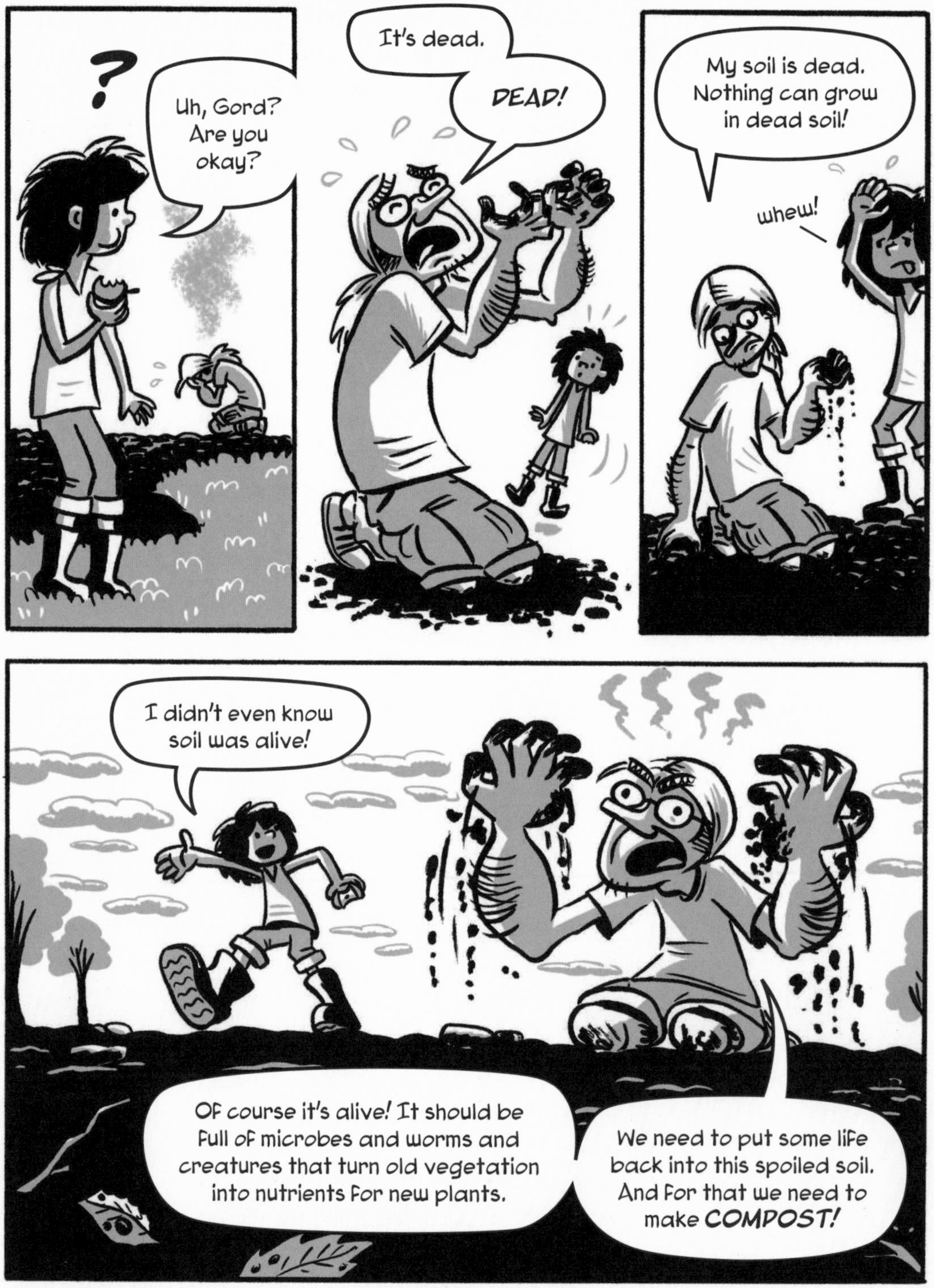
?
Uh, Gord? Are you okay?
It's dead.
DEAD!
My soil is dead. Nothing can grow in dead soil!
whew!
I didn't even know soil was alive!
Of course it's alive! It should be full of microbes and worms and creatures that turn old vegetation into nutrients for new plants.
We need to put some life back into this spoiled soil. And for that we need to make COMPOST!

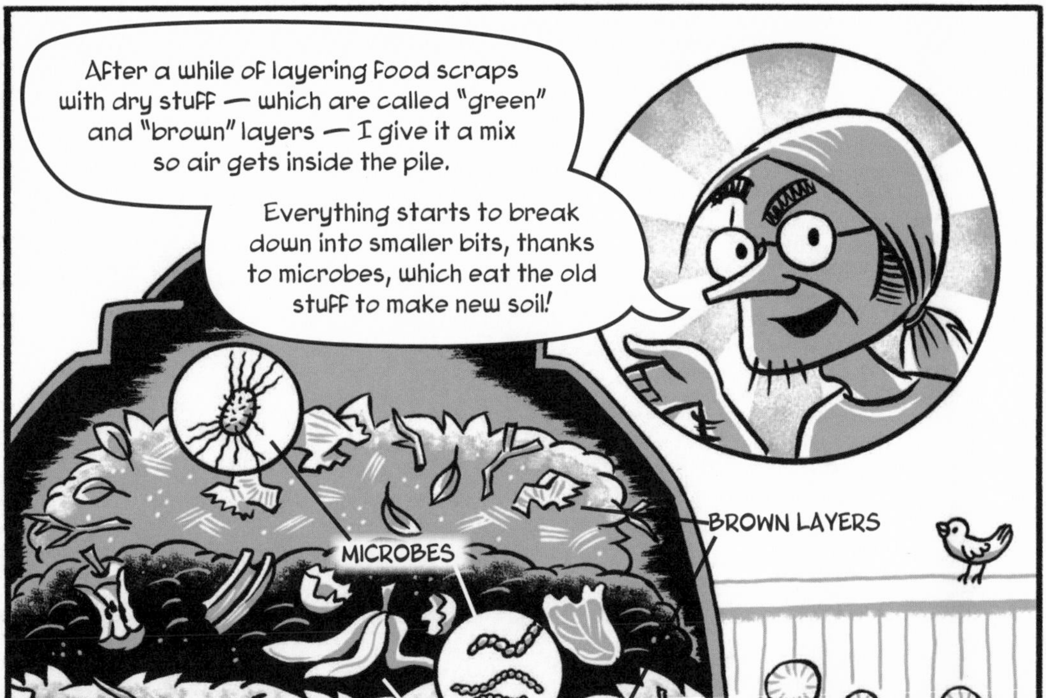
After a while of layering food scraps with dry stuff — which are called "green" and "brown" layers — I give it a mix so air gets inside the pile.
Everything starts to break down into smaller bits, thanks to microbes, which eat the old stuff to make new soil!
MICROBES
BROWN LAYERS
WORMS
GREEN LAYERS

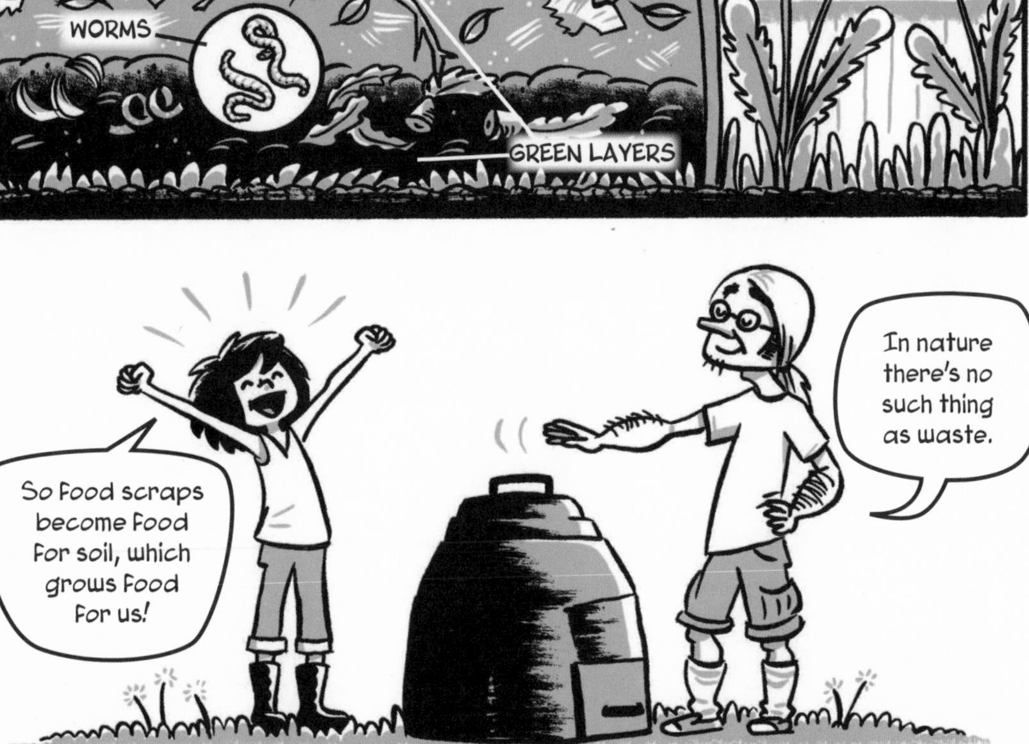
So food scraps become food for soil, which grows food for us!
In nature there's no such thing as waste.

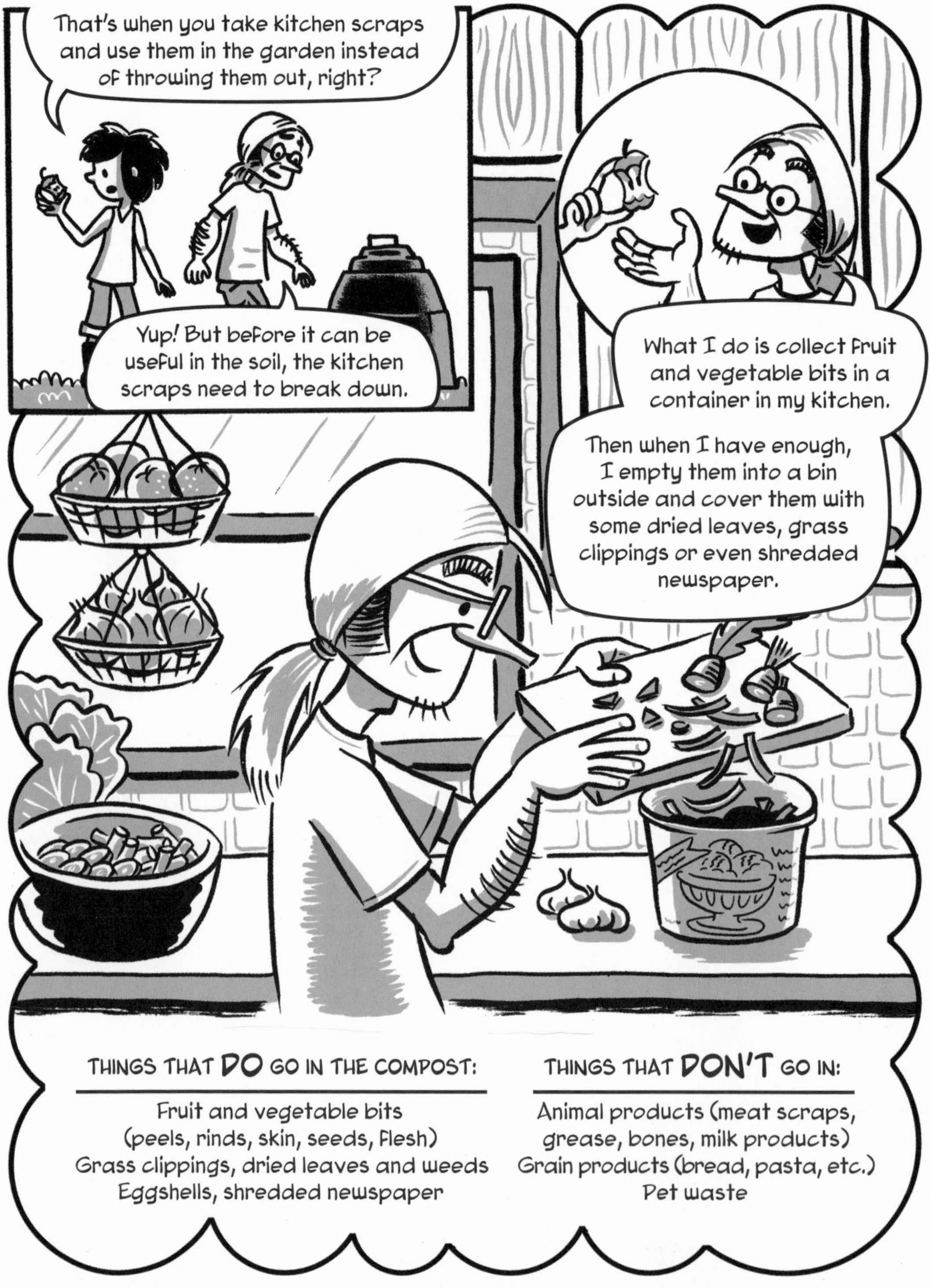

That's when you take kitchen scraps and use them in the garden instead of throwing them out, right?
Yup! But before it can be useful in the soil, the kitchen scraps need to break down.
What I do is collect fruit and vegetable bits in a container in my kitchen.
Then when I have enough, I empty them into a bin outside and cover them with some dried leaves, grass clippings or even shredded newspaper.
THINGS THAT DO GO IN THE COMPOST:
Fruit and vegetable bits (peels, rinds, skin, seeds, flesh)
Grass clippings, dried leaves and weeds
Eggshells, shredded newspaper
THINGS THAT DON'T GO IN:
Animal products (meat scraps, grease, bones, milk products)
Grain products (bread, pasta, etc.)
Pet waste